SEASON OF BLOOD

SEASON OF BLOOD

A Crispin Guest Medieval Noir

Jeri Westerson

This first world edition published 2017
in Great Britain and the USA by
SEVERN HOUSE PUBLISHERS LTD of
19 Cedar Road, Sutton, Surrey, England, SM2 5DA.
Trade paperback edition first published
in Great Britain and the USA 2018 by
SEVERN HOUSE PUBLISHERS LTD.

British Library Cataloguing in Publication Data
A CIP catalogue record for this title is available from the British Library.

ISBN-13: 978-0-7278-8747-4 (cased)
ISBN-13: 978-1-84751-862-0 (trade paper)
ISBN-13: 978-1-78010-925-1 (e-book)

All Severn House titles are printed on acid-free paper.

Severn House Publishers support the Forest Stewardship Council™ [FSC™],
the leading international forest certification organisation.
All our titles that are printed on FSC certified paper carry the FSC logo.

Typeset by Palimpsest Book Production Ltd.,
Falkirk, Stirlingshire, Scotland.
Printed and bound in Great Britain by
TJ International, Padstow, Cornwall.

*To Craig, who has spent many seasons supporting me
and this crazy vocation of mine.*

'By God's precious heart, by God's nails,
And by the Blood of Christ that's now at Hailes.'

Chaucer, 'The Pardoner's Tail'

GLOSSARY

Chevet	An addition to an apse, a small, chapel-like enclosure, usually for the purpose of housing a shrine or tomb.
Close	A narrow alley.
Cod	Archaic for male genitalia.
Corrodian	A pensioner who pays to live out their retirement within the precincts of a monastery.
Croft	Upper floor.
Garth	An enclosed garden or yard beside a house or building.
Girdle	In the medieval sense, it is a belt.
Monstrance	A usually circular, flat reliquary made of crystal or glass so the object of veneration can be seen from both sides.
Pintle	A term for penis.
Portcullis	Gate to a castle that can be raised or lowered.
Quarter days	The four days a year when rents were due, they fell on religious festivals between the equinoxes and solstices: 25 March, Lady Day (or Feast of the Annunciation); 24 June, Midsummer Day (the summer solstice or St John's day); 29 September, Michaelmas (Feast of the Archangels, Saints Michael, Gabriel, Uriel and Raphael); 25 December, Christmas.
Reliquary	A decorative container for a relic.
Sarding	Expletive, in the sense of carnal knowledge.

Scapular   A flap of fabric, like a poncho or tabard,
                        worn over a cassock. Often included
                        the hood.
Sennight   Seven nights, or a week.
'Slud   Contraction of God's Blood. An oath.
Unseelie Court   Fairy kingdom of the dangerous kind.
White Monks   Monks of the Cistercian order.
Wimple   Covering over the head and around the
                        face, for women.

ONE

London, 1390

The hollow steps echoed off the naked alley walls, pinging like moths against the dark timbers. No question about it. Crispin was definitely being followed.

A cold March night was no place to be alone with an unknown person on one's tail. Crispin looked back over his shoulder. February had retreated, leaving behind slush and mud, though icicles still dripped from eaves as a reminder that winter was not yet willing to release its talons. London was now a dragon's breath of mist, with its shadow shapes of men trudging the muddy lanes and its houses and shops disguised as louring canyons.

There was usually no one prowling about at this hour. Proper citizens were sitting at their suppers, telling tales of the day just as Crispin longed to do, but couldn't very well lead his pursuer home with him.

No, there were other options.

He continued, neither slowing nor hurrying. The echoes followed him down every winding alley, each narrow close. Did his pursuer know he was leading them in a tightening spiral?

He counted only one set of footfalls. Light. Someone young, perhaps. A cutpurse.

A feral smile curved his lips. *Let us see where this takes us.*

He itched to grasp the hilt of his dagger but kept his hand swinging lightly at his side. Slipping into a gloomy alley, he headed for its far end. When he reached the corner, he stepped to the side, hiding under a stair, waiting for his pursuer to emerge.

Quickened steps. Perhaps they feared they had lost him. A shadow flew past the opening and Crispin simultaneously reached out to grab a wrist and drew his dagger, slamming the hapless shadow against a wall. His knife reached a throat just as the hood fell away . . .

He choked on the curse on the tip of his tongue.

The woman stared up at him with wild, wide eyes, blue as woad.

He stumbled back and let the knife fall to his hip. Her wrist was still encaged in his fist and, when she looked down at it, he released the pale skin as if it were a hot iron.

-He was in deep trouble.

'Forgive me, my lady. I . . . I . . .' But what was he to say? I thought you were a thief, a murderer? Still with head bowed, he waited for her escorts to cut him down.

He waited and waited some more.

Squinting upward, he saw she was quite alone.

That was not good either.

She rubbed her wrist and her gaze dropped to her feet. Her long-toed slippers were covered in mud. She must have been following him a long way.

'Demoiselle,' he tried, peering behind for any other persons along the deserted alley. 'I do apologize. I did not realize . . . Well. I beg your mercy most humbly.'

'Good sir. Kind sir. God grant that you are the man I seek. Please, I beg of you. Tell me.'

'Whom do you seek?'

'Crispin Guest, a man whom they say was once a knight.'

Stunned, Crispin stood immobile for far longer than was polite. He cleared his throat and nodded once. 'Demoiselle, you have found me. I *am* Crispin Guest.'

Her eyes fluttered closed in gratitude. 'Not here,' she said quietly, opening them. 'Is there a safe place we can talk undisturbed?' She pulled the fur collar of her cloak against her cold-reddened cheek.

'Most certainly.' He bowed again and motioned for her to follow, regretting that her poor slippers would never be the same. Stepping quickly down Paternoster Row up to Cheap, he took a left at the Shambles. When he looked back to check on her progress, her face was pale and her eyes darted ceaselessly.

A distant dog barking and the occasional loud snore from behind a closed shutter were the only sounds on the quiet street. They reached the shop that used to be a poulterer's and indeed still sported the crumbling remnants of a pullet-shaped sign. He stepped up to the door, unlocked and opened it.

One glance at the small parlor told him his servant and

apprentice, Jack Tucker, was not there. But the hearth ashes were carefully banked over the coals and the place was clean, proving the boy's occasional habitation.

It was a modest hall, some ten by ten feet with a low ceiling. The stairs behind him lying in shadow led up to two small bedchambers.

A recent acquisition of some months, Crispin was still becoming used to such grand surroundings – grand for this portion of his life at any rate.

A table in the center of the room had three chairs, each of disreputable origin. But they were comfortable. A sideboard and a coffer where the only accoutrements in the barren room, but they were enough.

He pulled a chair from the table and offered it to her. A window shutter overlooking the back courtyard banged against the sill and he stepped quickly to pull it closed.

Crossing to the hearth, he hid his anxiety by poking roughly at the fire. It wasn't his fault she did not make herself known. Anyone could have accosted her. Foolish woman.

Licking his lips and wiping the hot damp from his palms on his cote-hardie, he returned to the table. He lit the candles in the bent candelabra that Jack had discovered in a coffer and slowly eased down onto one of the chairs opposite her, watching the candles' meager flames glow in her large eyes.

'And so we are safe,' he said firmly. 'What may I do for you?'

She seemed restless, her movements jerky. She glanced behind her though the door was closed.

A sword in a scabbard hung by a peg beside it. A gorse broom leaned against the sword in casual repose.

After another long pause, she spoke. 'I have heard of your unusual vocation. That you discover puzzles. Do . . . all manner of services. All for a fee.'

He cleared his dry throat. 'Er . . . yes, demoiselle. I . . . yes. What is it you need solving?'

'Solving? No. There is a man. My niece—' She dropped her disarming gaze and clasped her hands on the table, fingers churning over knuckles. 'I should start at the beginning.' Her teeth dug into her lip. 'My niece, a very young and impression-able girl, is being pursued by an unsuitable man. She has been in my care for some time. Her parents were relying on me to be her tutor in all things proper. Alas. I have failed her. She has disappeared. I fear she has run off with this man and I have pursued them to London. She was always a pious child and so my hope is that she has taken herself to a nunnery rather than soil herself with this man.'

'I see. Have you no kinsmen to do such work?'

He studied her gown. Even though the candle's light was scant, he discerned that the fabric had frayed. There were shiny spots on the elbows. The fur was old and tattered. If merchant or courtier, she was not among the wealthy. 'No,' she said. 'I do not wish to involve them. This is a private matter and must be kept secret. At all cost. I sought you for your . . . discretion.'

'Just so. Well, then. Is this man a London citizen?'

'Oh, yes. He is a London citizen.' She rose and made her way to one of the front windows. Her finger rested on the uneven wood of the shutter. The candle glow softened the edge of her shoulders with gold. Her veil fluttered down her back.

She turned, seemed to consider his scant furnishings, eyes restless over the coffer shoved against the wall beside the smoky hearth, the small pile of sticks in the other corner.

Glittering eyes suddenly squared on Crispin's. 'So many tales are told about you,' she said.

'All good, I hope.'

Her smile was gentle. 'Of course.' She waited, seeming to expect something.

He mentally smacked his forehead. 'May I offer you some wine?' But even as he asked, he wasn't certain if the jug had any in it.

'That would be . . . very pleasant.'

Of course it would be, if he actually had any. He approached the sideboard and opened the cabinet. There was cheese wrapped in cloth on a wooden plate, a wizening apple, a small basket of eggs, two wooden bowls, two wooden goblets and a cracked horn-beaker. The jug still had a good amount of wine left in it and he poured a scant amount into both goblets. It was to her credit that she didn't wince when she tasted it. She seemed the type used to better fare despite her gown's deficiency. Courtier? Possibly, though why she was unescorted so late at night troubled him.

She sipped and glanced up at him through her lashes. He felt a definite warming in his belly. 'And so. This man . . .'

'Yes.' She glanced over the hall again but the view held nothing except shadow and poverty. 'I fear . . .' her voice dropped low, '. . . I fear he knows of my quest. I might have been followed.'

Rising, Crispin went to one of the front windows. He pushed the shutter gently and peered out to the street. He had memorized each stall, each window, every shadow, and saw nothing out of place. Just the same, he pulled it closed. Easing away from the window, he returned to his seat. 'I saw no one.'

Her shoulders sagged in relief. 'God be praised.' She shook her head. 'I don't know what to do. I fear the wrath of this man. He is dangerous, though my poor niece would hear nothing against him. Oh, if only her father were still alive!'

Crispin teased his goblet with his fingertips. He waited for more.

'They say you are much like a private sheriff. That is why I sought you. Though my method was unorthodox, I admit.' She took up her goblet again and sipped delicately, her lips tracing the rim. 'If I tell you what I know . . . you will keep it secret?'

'I give you my word, demoiselle. If these are secret things you need to tell me, then I will be silent about them. Your fee can buy you much.'

'Fee? Oh, yes.' She stood and scrambled at the scrip tied to her girdle, but Crispin magnanimously waved her off.

'There is no need for that just yet. Perhaps you should tell me . . .'

She nodded, fluttering her veil. Standing above the table, she seemed at odds with sitting or remaining standing. Sitting won out. 'You see, the man – that horrible man who has seduced my dear niece – is married.'

Crispin suspected as much. What a cur to use a maiden so! He couldn't wait to get his hands on the man.

'And worse still,' she continued, 'I understand he used to be the Lord Sheriff. Of London.'

His hot blood froze. 'What?'

'Simon Wynchecombe is his name,' she said. 'I am certain he has taken her.'

Shock kept Crispin's world suspended for a moment. And when he opened his mouth to speak, nothing came out.

Simon Wynchecombe? A common seducer? It almost seemed too good to be true. Six years ago, Wynchecombe had made his life miserable with his belligerence and bullying. The man would sooner clout Crispin than talk with him. With one side of his mouth he'd insult Crispin's heritage and on the other would hire him to do Wynchecombe's dirty work without so much as a by-your-leave.

'Surely you must be mistaken. I have been acquainted with Master Wynchecombe and I do not think he would . . . would be the cause of such mischief.'

She pushed her goblet aside and leaned on the table. Crispin, unable to stop himself, mirrored her actions. 'What if I were to tell you that I have proof of it? Are you man enough to accuse the former sheriff?'

Was he? Wynchecombe was no longer the sheriff, true, but that didn't mean he couldn't be again. Or even become the Lord Mayor. Wynchecombe was an alderman, a highly regarded citizen. If Crispin accused him and Wynchecombe were found innocent, where would that leave Crispin?

On the other hand, if he were guilty he could not be allowed to steal this niece's virtue.

His frown was grim. 'I will do what I must.'

Her eyes seemed satisfied. 'I believe you will. Very well. I will tell you what I know. And so.' Delicately, she opened her scrip and pulled out a small, embroidered pouch. She reached in and placed six small silver coins on the table. 'Sixpence a day, is it not?'

He nodded.

They both stared at the coins for some time before Crispin slid them toward him and dropped them into his hand off the edge of the table. He clutched them tightly in his fist before slipping them into the pouch on his belt. They fell over one another with a hollow clink. He opened his mouth to ask for her proof when a deep *thump, thump* nearing his door stayed him.

He glanced at the closed door, cocking his head toward the footsteps clearly making their slow march toward his lodgings. Too heavy to be Jack Tucker's. He flicked his gaze at her. 'Your escort?'

She shook her head, her eyes confused. 'I came without an escort.' She sprang to her feet, knocking over the chair. He drew his dagger and pushed her behind him, staring at the door as the heavy footfalls drew closer. When they reached the threshold, the steps stopped and then silence. They waited, looking at one another.

Both jumped at the sudden pounding on the wood.

Crispin took a breath, tightened his grip on the hilt and pulled it open.

A monk in a dirty white habit and long black cloak shouldered the doorway. His black cowl was drawn low over his forehead and he was looking down at his feet. From what Crispin could see of it, his face was ashen with dark circles under his eyes. His lips were gray and the fringe of dark hair around his head was plastered flat with sweat.

'C-Crispin . . . Guest?' he panted.

The man staggered forward. Crispin stepped back just in time for the monk to tumble to the floor. It was then he noticed the sticky crimson patch between the wool-covered shoulder blades . . . and the knife still embedded there.

The woman screamed.

Something rolled out of the monk's tight fist. A crystal, flat on one side and rounded on the other that looked suspiciously like something Crispin would rather avoid. But he tossed the thought aside and fell to his knees by the monk's stilled body. He touched his neck, confirming his fears.

'God have mercy. I'm afraid . . . he is dead.'

His eyes slid toward the dagger and his gut did a little flip. Even with its smear of blood, Crispin easily recognized the jeweled pommel, the worn leather of the hilt. He had had close acquaintance with it too many times to count. There was no mistaking this dagger. It belonged to Simon Wynchecombe.

He opened his mouth to tell the woman . . . to tell her . . . God's blood! He knew not what to tell her. With a curse on his lips, he turned to say something, anything of comfort.

But his door lay wide open, and the woman, along with the strange, circular crystal, was gone.

TWO

C rispin stared at the open doorway in disbelief. What had just happened? Had that woman – that *unknown* woman, he realized, having not yet gotten her name – *stolen* that artifact from the monk? The very dead monk now bleeding copiously all over his floor?

'God's blood!' How a beguiling face could confound him! He vowed solemnly to never let such a thing happen again . . . but with another curse on his lips, he knew full well that it would.

He rose from his crouching position and glared at the dead man as if it were his fault he had a knife in his back. For all Crispin knew, that might be so.

A scuffle of steps outside told him he was not alone. With dagger in hand he peered out, expecting the killer but hoping at the very least that the woman had returned. Instead he saw his neighbor, the butcher Roger Lymon. He was slowly approaching Crispin's door, scrutinizing with his candle held low the suspicious dark drops along the mud. His white fleshy face frowned, from the slender brows down to his round chin, grayed with a day-old beard.

Standing at the threshold, Roger raised his eyes and caught Crispin's gaze. 'Crispin?' he said. 'What's amiss? I heard a scream and then a woman flew by and . . . well. Me wife bid me investigate.'

'I fear, Roger, that you will regret your decision.' He gestured down with his knife just as the butcher reached the doorway.

'Blessed Virgin! Crispin!' He crossed himself and then clutched Crispin's arm. 'What have you done?'

'I have done nothing but open my door. Trouble seems to find me.'

'Is he . . . is he . . . dead?'

'Very,' said Crispin. He knelt again and studied the knife hilt. Yes, there was no doubt. He'd seen that dagger many a time. Mostly after Wynchecombe had cuffed Crispin so hard he had fallen to his knees, just at the perfect height to stare at the dagger hilt.

'The sheriffs,' Roger sputtered. 'We shall have to call in the sheriffs. I hate the sheriffs.'

Crispin agreed wholeheartedly. *God's blood, but this was shaping up to be a wretched evening!*

'If you could, Roger, go to Newgate and inform the sheriffs' men. I would be much obliged.'

'Me? Oh, no. I . . . I should probably stay here. Maybe *you* should go.' He stared down at the bloody mess the monk had made. At least the blood did not bother the man.

'I *could* go. However, the murderer may return to make certain of his handiwork. And where would that leave you?'

Roger might be a big man hefting carcasses all the working day and slicing and chopping into them in a bloody display, but he was as timid as a mouse. He pressed his stubby fingers to his lips in thought. 'I'll go. You stay.' The man trotted out of the door, the candle sputtering in his hand.

Crispin watched him go with a mixture of dread and amusement before he turned back to his unwelcome guest. 'First of all,' he said, sliding to his knees again, avoiding the crimson puddle, 'do I know you?'

Gently, he grasped the chin and turned the man's face. The mouth was slack and the chin was scratchy from an uneven shave. Pale blue eyes stared distantly. His brows were dark and thick. Crispin turned the face a bit more but did not recognize the man. Yet he had spoken his name, found his lodgings. He obviously knew of Crispin.

By the color of the monk's cassock, he recognized that he was a monk of the Cistercian order, the White Monks. He would have to suggest to the sheriffs' men that the monk came from the Abbey of St Mary Graces. The Smithfield monastery was the only Cistercian house in London.

He lifted the man's hands and examined them, pushing up the sleeves to look at his arms. No, not a fight. The monk was plainly attacked from behind. Why would Wynchecombe do that? There had to be a reasonable explanation. The man was cruel and base but it was difficult to believe that Wynchecombe would go about haphazardly slaying monks.

The sound of running feet made him cautiously peer around the jamb a second time.

Jack Tucker's ginger hair was a bird's nest of curls and his pale, freckled face was flushed with exertion with matching pink spots on both cheeks. His beard was cropped close to his face, just as red as his hair. He lifted amber eyes to Crispin and smiled broadly. 'Master! You're home. Sorry I'm late. I lingered too long with Isabel Langton . . . until Gilbert chucked me out.'

Crispin said nothing while sheathing his knife. He merely stepped aside for the boy but when Jack slipped through the doorway he jerked to a halt with a startled yip. 'God blind me!' he gasped. Falling back against the door, his eyes took in the knife, blood, and finally Crispin. 'Master Crispin! You shouldn't have done it.'

He cuffed the boy with a huff of impatience. 'I did no such thing, you knave. He came to me with that ornament in his back and had the poor judgment to die on my floor.'

''Slud.' Jack straightened his coat and wiped his nose across his knuckles. 'He came to you with a knife in his back?'

'Yes,' said Crispin thoughtfully. Now that the initial shock had worn off he began to feel guilty. The man was a monk, perhaps a priest, and he had been killed most foully. 'It . . . it is a wretched thing, Jack. A horrendous murder.'

'Did he tell you who?'

'No. He spoke only my name. And he had with him a strange object. It looked like . . . it appeared to be some sort of reliquary.'

Jack stared at Crispin. 'Blind me. People do like to involve you with them relics, don't they?'

'Yes, they do,' he muttered. A dark sensation hovered over him each time he contemplated the numerous times he had been involved so. It never led to anything good.

'Then . . . where is it?'

He sighed and leaned against the door beside the boy. 'Stolen.'

'What? Just now?'

'Yes. There is more to the tale. And I had rather tell you before the sheriffs arrive.'

'Why, sir?'

'I'll explain.' But how? He felt like a fool. Letting the girl go. Not even getting her name! 'There was a woman—'

'There's always a woman,' Jack muttered.

He felt like cuffing the boy again but refrained. 'She came to me. Wanted to hire me to find her niece. She insisted that . . . er . . . a man was following her. Perhaps to do her harm.'

Jack said nothing. His brows arched wide and he stole wincing glances at the corpse on the floor.

'She . . . uh . . . claimed the man was . . . was Simon Wynchecombe.'

''Slud,' Jack murmured again.

'And then this wretched monk appeared, carrying the reliquary which he let drop. And the next thing I knew, she was gone, as was the relic.'

'So you let a woman steal from you.'

Crispin grunted. 'I did not *let* her. I had other worries on my mind at the moment,' he said with a gesture toward the corpse. But the damnable thing of it was Jack was right. He had let the woman get the better of him. And that was never good. 'Though, she did at least pay me for my trouble first,' he grumbled.

'That will go well when you're carted off to Newgate, I reckon.'

No, it wasn't Crispin's imagination. The boy was decidedly sharp-tongued of late. It would not do. Just because he was betrothed, the boy felt he was somehow superior to Crispin. 'I believe I've had enough of that mouth of yours, Tucker, and if you know what is good for you—'

'Aye, master. I beg your mercy. It's just . . .' He waved his hand toward the monk. 'There's a dead man on our floor,' he whispered. 'Again!'

Crispin sighed. 'And that is not the worst of it.' He knelt and lightly touched the deeply imbedded blade. 'This – I am certain – belonged to Wynchecombe.'

Jack scrutinized the weapon for a long time before he let out a low whistle. 'God's teeth and bones, master, but I think you are right. What will the sheriffs do, do you think?'

Crispin clenched his jaw. He grasped the hilt and yanked it out. A spurt of blood followed, sprinkling down upon the already bloody cassock and scapular. Jack squealed and fell back on his bum.

Crispin thrust the dagger toward the boy. 'Jack, wrap this in something and conceal it in yon coffer.'

Jack stilled, staring at the bloody dagger and Crispin's crimson hand. 'But . . . that's evidence!'

'Against a former Lord Sheriff? I doubt that John Walcote and his equally fawning compeer John Loveney have the bollocks to bring in Wynchecombe. Even with evidence such as this. Take it, Jack. Make haste. I hear horses without.'

Jack reached out with a reluctant hand and, taking a rag from the pantry shelf, did his best to wrap the dagger tight. He opened the coffer, dropped it in and slammed the lid shut. Looking down at his sticky red hands, he nearly tripped over himself getting to the bucket in the corner to scour his skin.

The sound of spurred boots clanged up to his threshold and Crispin braced himself. He wiped his blood-sticky hand on the monk's black cloak and stood just as Sheriff Walcote stepped over the threshold followed by his associate, Sheriff Loveney. Their eyes widened on beholding the dead monk. Roger slid through the door after them with a twisted mouth.

'By God's Holy Name,' gasped Walcote. 'Master Guest, what is here?'

'A dead monk, my Lord Sheriff.'

Walcote raised his thin brows. 'I can well see that for myself. But *why* is he here in your lodgings?'

'Yes,' Loveney interjected. The slight, dark-bearded sheriff stood further back than the clean-shaven Walcote who hovered curiously over the body.

'Master Guest, this habit of yours, encountering dead men . . . well! Something must be done.'

Crispin nodded. 'Yes, Lord Sheriff, but what?'

Loveney moved closer and peered from behind Walcote's shoulder. 'What do you make of it, Master Guest?'

'A murder, my lords.'

Both sheriffs clucked their tongues.

Loveney tended to defer to Walcote as Walcote had a temper. Crispin kept himself alert around him. The man was not above using the same tactics as Wynchecombe and Crispin bore the bruises to prove it.

'So what is he doing *here*?' murmured Walcote. He shook his russet-haired head and continued to study the corpse. 'There is blood on his cloak.'

Loveney remained slightly behind his companion and swallowed hard. He looked pale. 'Indeed. What mayhem occurred?'

'Stabbed in the back,' said Crispin.

Loveney whirled on him. 'And how do you know that, Master Guest?'

Crispin pressed his hands behind his back and turned from the body. He looked at Jack, who wore a terrified expression. 'I am familiar with such wounds from many a battle, my lords. From the look of the tear in the cloak and the blood spattered about it, I must assume the blade landed just above the shoulder blades.'

Walcote studied the monk's back. 'I suppose an examination will tell us for certain.' He turned away from the corpse, gesturing toward Roger. 'This man claimed that he heard a woman scream. Where is she?'

'That was no woman,' said Crispin, making his silent apologies to Jack. 'That was my servant.'

Out of the corner of his eye he saw Jack lurch forward in protest but the boy had the sense to keep silent. 'Er . . . aye. That was me.'

Walcote trained a calculated glare on Roger. 'You said it was a woman.'

Roger looked from Crispin to Jack. 'Well . . . I . . . what I heard was . . .' Crispin caught his eye and Roger screwed his face in concentration. 'I suppose . . . it could have been young Jack here. My shop is two houses down, after all.'

Walcote appeared to know he was being lied to but what could he say? His gloved hand massaged his smooth chin. 'And so, a White Monk is dead on your floor. Can you offer any explanation, Guest?'

'None whatsoever, my lord. The man sought me out, spoke my name as surely he has heard of me, but that was as far as it went.'

'The coroner will arrive anon,' said Loveney. He inclined his head toward Walcote and they both made for the door.

'My lords,' said Crispin. They stopped and glanced back at him. 'Er . . . is that all? You will leave this now for the coroner?'

'There is little left for us, Master Guest. Wait for him and do *not* move the body.'

As if he needed reminding. Crispin bowed stiffly. 'As you wish.'

Walcote withdrew with a flourish of his cloak and Loveney sidled after him.

Crispin waited until he heard them mount and ride away before heading for the door himself.

'Wait!' cried Roger.

He paused.

The butcher stared at the body nervously. 'Where are you going?'

Jack joined Crispin on the threshold; a look of relief brightened his face when Crispin made no move to object.

'I'm going to investigate this murder, Master Lymon.'

'But . . . the sheriffs told you—'

'I'm certain you can give adequate testimony to the coroner when he arrives, Roger. At any rate, the coroner knows where he can find me should he need me.'

'But that isn't fair, Master Guest. I'm just a neighbor. I don't know nothing about any of this.'

He waved and left Roger still sputtering behind him as he and Jack set out along the Shambles. 'Where are we going, master?' asked Jack once they had left their friend behind.

'Smithfield,' he answered.

Jack said nothing as he followed Crispin through the silent streets. At least the boy had learned to keep quiet near curfew. But Jack couldn't seem to stand their hushed progress any longer. 'Master Crispin!' he hissed. 'What's in Smithfield?'

'A Cistercian monastery. It must be the place our dead monk came from.'

They headed the long way to London's northern wall, to Postern gate, and managed to bribe the guard to allow them through. They cut across the dark, grassy expanse of Tower Hill, skirting the ghostly apparitions of sleepy sheep. The moonrise brightened the dim field and lit their treacherous path to Hog Lane. St Mary Graces stood humbly between Hog Lane and East Smithfield.

'Master,' whispered Jack when they'd reached the gate and the bell rope. 'Isn't it too late to call out them monks – I mean *those* monks? It's after Compline.'

'I realize that, Jack,' he replied quietly. 'But there is always a porter at the gate. Their abbot will not wish to speak with me now. He will be under the Great Silence, but we have little choice.'

'Can't it wait till morning?' Jack asked hopefully.

'Very well. Shall we return and catch some sleep while that monk rots on our floor?'

Jack shivered. 'I'll pull the rope, shall I?'

Jack pulled more vigorously than was necessary and the bell seemed to peal far louder in the still of the evening.

A nearby dog howled his displeasure.

Crispin knew it would take a while and his dark thoughts took him back to the woman. Who was she? What part had she to play in this? And how the devil was he to find her! A hot flush crept up his neck, thinking of how she had stolen from him. Why had she done it? For protection? Simon Wynchecombe's dagger was no illusion. It was very real and very perplexing. Why would Simon kill a monk? Surely he had a good reason. But a stab in the back? Even Wynchecombe had more honor than that! Yes, it was inevitable. Once he discovered what he needed to about this cleric, he would have to track down Wynchecombe.

Even with the moonrise, the shadows deepened. With a sigh, he knew his questioning of the former sheriff would have to wait till morning.

After what seemed like hours, a scuffling step echoed from the passage. A young monk appeared. His white cassock was covered by a black scapular. His black cowl framed his gaunt face and large eyes. He gave the appearance of a disgruntled magpie.

'It is late,' he whispered impatiently.

'But it is urgent,' Crispin replied. 'I must speak with your abbot.'

'He is abed. All are abed. And I have broken my vow by speaking to you.'

'God will forgive you, brother. But the matter, as I said, is urgent.'

The monk shook his head. He murmured a blessing in the air and turned away, retreating. Realizing he was to be left at the porch without entrance, Crispin raised his voice. 'There is a dead Cistercian monk upon my floor.'

The monk turned sharply. 'What?'

'Take me to your abbot, and I will explain.'

THREE

A bbot William de Warden was white-haired with cheeks as pale as marble. The soft folds of his wrinkled face could not hide the fact that at one time he must have been a fine-looking man. His blue eyes were heavy with sleep and heavier with sadness as Crispin related what had occurred.

'*Jesu* mercy,' said the old monk, easing down into his chair by the fire. Crispin stood above him with Jack slightly behind. 'How can such a thing be?'

'I do not know, my Lord Abbot. Please accept my condolences for this unhappy event.'

The blue eyes tracked upward until they rested on Crispin's face. 'What did you say your name was?'

'Crispin Guest, my lord. They call me the Tracker. I investigate crimes.'

'Oh!' The white brows rose. 'Is it your cause, then, to discover who did this terrible thing?'

'Since it has come to my very doorstep, I find it impossible to ignore.'

'Brother Michael,' said the abbot to the porter. 'Go to the dormitory at once and see who might be missing. Make haste!'

'Yes, my Lord Abbot.' He ran.

'I will pay your fee, sir. The vile murderer must be brought to justice!'

Crispin bowed.

'You must do your godly work with all haste. These men,' he gazed fondly at the door through which the young cleric had disappeared, 'they are like my sons. To lose any one of them is like losing a portion of my heart.'

Crispin shuffled uncomfortably. It was by far the worst part of his task. 'Were any of your monks acquainted with any young ladies?'

Abbot William raised his face. 'Eh? Ladies? Oh, no. Such a thing is not to be. Who would any of our brothers know? We are cloistered here, Master Guest. Seldom do we leave the abbey's precincts.'

'And yet your brother was found outside these walls.'

The abbot sat back and sighed. 'Yes. I cannot explain it.'

'Were any acquainted with Simon Wynchecombe, the former sheriff of London?'

'Simon Wynchecombe? I do not know. Is it likely? What has the former sheriff to do with this misdeed?'

'I'm . . . not certain,' said Crispin.

'When can we retrieve our dear brother?'

'When the coroner is done with him. I imagine he will be released tonight to you. Perhaps your porter will await the cart?'

There was little left to say. They waited in silence for the young porter to return. The wood in the fire sparked and crackled.

Crispin wanted to pace but it seemed inappropriate. The old abbot mumbled prayers into his fingers and Jack wore a somber expression under his own hood while staring at the closed door.

At last, the door flung open and an out-of-breath Brother Michael braced himself in the doorway.

The abbot looked up. 'Well, brother? Who is it?'

Brother Michael shook his head. 'My Lord Abbot. I awoke all my brothers in the dormitory. Even searched in the privies. But my lord, there is no one missing. We are all accounted for.'

The abbot turned to Crispin. 'Master Guest. Are you absolutely certain your monk was a Cistercian?'

'I assure you, Father Abbot, it is not a mistake I am likely to make.'

'But we do not appear to be missing any brothers.' His eyes tensed, first with relief and then again with agitation. 'I cannot dispute what you believe to be true, but as you have heard . . .'

'Yes, so I *have* heard.' His gaze sought a puzzled Jack.

'I . . . I grieve for this brother monk,' said the abbot. His lips trembled but his eyes darted away. Not one of his own but still his problem. 'Of course, we shall accept this brother until his house can be found.' He made a vague sign of the cross before he seemed to remember he'd promised Crispin a fee. Fumbling at his belt for a key, he motioned to Brother Michael. 'Go to the strongbox, brother. Master Guest should receive his portion for his trouble.'

Crispin raised his chin. The man was not of their monastery. But a fee was a fee.

The brother made much of opening the strongbox, carefully counting out the coins and finally handing them to Crispin, who dispatched them quickly to his pouch.

He bowed to both monks and the porter was quick to show him the way out.

'What now, master?'

Crispin sighed into the night. 'That was puzzling. This is the only Cistercian house for miles.'

'Do you think he was lying?'

'No.' He eyed Jack curiously in the bright moonlight. 'Do you?'

Jack scratched his head. 'Naw. But it is curious. And people have lied to you before.'

'Yes, they have. But there seems little reason for lying. If the dead man were not a monk . . .' He had seen the tonsure for himself, which meant the man was either a monk or a clerk. But why go about dressed as a monk if not one? 'Well, there is little left to do at this late hour but to return to our lodgings and tell the coroner . . . ah. Tell him what? We know not who the man is or where he now belongs.'

'The coroner won't like that.' The boy peeked warily out from under his hood. 'Are we to keep the dagger?'

'Yes.'

'But why, sir? If that bastard Wynchecombe is guilty, are we not well rid of him?'

'These are very suspicious circumstances, Jack. I am not ready to believe that Master Wynchecombe is guilty of these crimes. Anyone can steal a dagger and use it for wicked purposes. Simon Wynchecombe never struck me as a careless man, and only a careless man loses track of his dagger.'

'Especially in the back of the man he killed, you mean.'

'Precisely. *All that we do is done with an eye to something else.*'

'Meaning he left it in the monk on purpose?'

'Or someone did. Mark me. There is some purpose to it.'

They trudged back down the winding streets until their noses told them they were back on the Shambles. Milling about near their front door, two servants stood holding the tethers of two horses. The men looked up as Crispin neared. A hand cart was positioned beside them outside the poulterer's shop and Crispin spied Roger Lymon's wife peeking at the commotion past her shutter.

Ignoring her, he drew closer and was stopped at his own doorstep by the coroner's clerk. 'Hold, sir. The coroner is at his duty and you are not permitted here.'

'This is my home,' he said. 'I am Crispin Guest.'

'Guest!' boomed the voice of the coroner from within. 'Get in here!'

Crispin smirked, shouldering the officious clerk out of the way. But he stopped abruptly when he saw the woman from earlier standing beside John Charneye, the coroner.

'What in God's name!' Charneye admonished. 'You have absented yourself, Guest, and left this poor fellow in your place.' He gestured toward Roger, who looked as if he had been wrung dry.

'My apologies, Lord Coroner . . . and to you, Master Lymon.' He paid them little heed. He wanted nothing more than to clasp his hands around the woman's throat, the woman who stood by so innocently. He bowed to her instead, body tight as a bowstring. 'But I had to find out from whence this poor monk came.'

'As if I could not have discovered that for myself from his cassock,' said the coroner. 'St Mary Graces, of course.'

'And so, too, did I think. But apparently, that is not so.'

'Eh? What nonsense is this?'

Crispin shook his head. 'There are no brothers missing from St Mary Graces, my lord. Or so I have been told.'

'Well . . . bless my soul. Where *did* he come from, then? And what was he doing so far from his abbey?'

'That I have yet to determine. But he knew of me and where I lived.'

'So this man has told me.'

Roger cringed behind the door. 'Yes. Are you done with me, Lord Coroner?'

The coroner glanced at his clerk who had been busily writing on his parchment. He nodded perfunctorily and Charneye seemed satisfied. He waved off Roger. 'Yes, you can go.'

Crispin had never seen the man move with such speed.

The coroner turned to the woman. 'This lady says she has been looking for you. I told her it was unfit her being alone but she insisted it was urgent. I do not know what England is coming to when young women find it fitting to travel alone . . . and after curfew.'

'I do not know either,' said Crispin between clenched teeth. He hoped his glare conveyed all the vinegar on his mind, but her perplexed and frightened expression dislodged his righteous anger.

Charneye gazed at him steadily. 'What more do you know about this business, Crispin?'

'More, my lord?' He was drawn away at last from her glistening eyes.

The coroner ticked his head and told the clerk to put away his writing things. 'We have no more to report. I have no doubt Master Crispin will work it out.' He ordered his clerk to bring the servants up to carry the body to the waiting cart.

Crispin and Jack stepped aside to let the coroner's men do their work. The limp body was carried slowly across the mud but a wide pool of blood was left behind, swathed across his floor by the monk's dragging clothes and many feet. Crispin stared at it in disgust and Jack with horror.

In the doorway, the coroner said, 'I leave you to it, Master Crispin.' He looked at the bloody floor. 'Best clean this with all haste before it starts to reek.'

With that, he was gone. Jack needed no prompting to rush to the bucket, and poured a good portion of its water on the floor. He took a rag and began to scrub, wincing all the while. The little splashes made the woman step back.

Crispin heard the coroner and his clerk ride toward Newgate. The cart turned the other way toward Smithfield.

Crispin faced the woman. 'You are a thief.'

She raised a hand to her throat while a tear trembled on her lash. 'A thief? What are you talking about? On what can you possibly base your rude assumption?'

He strode toward her, backing her against the wall. Jack scrambled to get out of the way. 'On the fact that you stole that object the dead monk brought to me, and then ran.'

'I ran in fear of my life! A man was murdered at your doorstep. Was I expected to remain?'

'Nevertheless. You have stolen that valuable object and I want it back. Now.'

'I have stolen nothing,' she whispered. She seemed to sink into her cloak and furs. Her face was even paler in the scant light of the hearth. 'You are very much mistaken.'

'I am *not* mistaken!'

'Master.'

'Not now, Jack.'

'But master . . .'

'God's blood, Jack! I'm busy!'

'But master.' He pointed under the coffer. 'There is something there.'

Crispin stopped and leaned down. Far in the corner under the rented coffer sat the crystal object that had been in the monk's hand. Without his asking, Jack scuttled and reached under with his long arm to retrieve it, then handed it to Crispin.

Crispin rose. His face flushed with embarrassment. He turned the odd object in his hand, not daring to look at the woman. 'It appears, demoiselle, that . . . well, that I . . . *was* mistaken. I apologize most humbly.'

'Perhaps I was very much mistaken about *you*, Master Guest. If this is the way you approach your tasks, then I am afraid I cannot in good conscience hire you. I shall have to take my chances with some local henchman.' She turned toward the door but Crispin stopped her by reaching for her cloak-covered sleeve.

'Wait. Demoiselle, I beg you to reconsider. I . . . I was in error. But I do my job well with few complaints. You cannot hope to do better with some other hireling. I will waive a day's wage to prove it to you.'

Jack gasped at that but Crispin ignored him.

Crispin released her arm. Jack crouched on the floor, wet rag in his hand, his eyes dancing from one to the other. The woman stood beside the door, seeming ready to flee. 'I will return your silver to you, then,' said Crispin with a sigh, 'and you may be on your way.'

She lowered her head and slowly moved toward the table, sinking wearily into the chair opposite him. 'No, keep the silver. If you only—' She trembled. 'I don't know what else to do.' Her face dropped into her open palms and he watched as she breathed, or was she weeping?

He did not know what ailed him. Why had he been so quick to accuse her? Was he losing his edge?

Finally, she raised her head and her eyes slowly focused on the object Crispin rolled in his hands. 'And what is this object that you would so readily accuse me of stealing?'

A circular monstrance, no bigger than a hand, made of beryl, perhaps. It was thick like a bowl on one side and flat and thin like glass on the other, and stoppered on the top end with a cross. The sides were sealed with ornamental silver.

'It looks to be a reliquary.' Inside was a rusty liquid moving slowly from one side of the crystal to the other. 'I suspect it is blood. Some martyr.'

'Mother Mary,' she said, crossing herself.

Crispin knew it could easily be goose blood or oil and wax. Relics were valuable as the grisly remnants of holy saints, but they were also valuable to the religious houses that kept and displayed them. Fees were collected from the countless pilgrims who came to venerate the objects. They were indeed valuable. Valuable enough to steal. He set it on its end on the table between them.

'Why did you think I took it?'

He felt his cheeks redden again. He'd been told how impetuous he was. He had thought that with maturity he would have grown out of it. 'It was missing and so were you.'

'One and one equals four?' She smiled weakly.

His accusation seemed to have been forgiven. He offered a tentative smile in return. 'Yes. Well.'

'It rolled under the coffer,' offered Jack. 'How was he to know?'

'My apprentice, Jack Tucker . . . who should be silent when I am with a client.'

Jack bowed, ignoring the last part, though he made himself scarce by tending to the fire.

'It occurs to me that I have not introduced myself, Master Guest. I am Katherine Woodleigh.'

'Demoiselle.' He nodded. 'Hmm. I seem to recall one of the barons, Sir Thomas Woodleigh, when I was . . . when I used to be at court.'

He glanced at her hand, which bore a ring. It had some arms on it but the design was too small for him to discern from that distance.

'He was my father. He died two years ago.'

'I am sorry.'

'So am I,' she said with a sigh.

'How do you know Simon Wynchecombe?'

'He has been a family friend since I was a child.'

'But you say you saw him with your niece.'

'Yes. And she confessed it. Said she would be his only.'

'I . . . Master Wynchecombe is married.'

'Yes, I know. That makes it all the more deplorable. I saw them together at my family home near Hailes. The door to the solar was open and I peered in. The fire in the hearth was low and in truth there were only silhouettes, but Master Wynchecombe is tall. It had to be him.'

'I see. Did he see you?'

She shivered. 'Yes. I saw him turn toward me and I fled. I needed a servant to help me confront him but by the time I returned with our steward he was gone.'

'When was this?'

'A sennight ago.'

'Where are you staying now?'

'The Unicorn Inn on Watling Street.'

'Forgive me, but why are you not staying at court?'

'My father left the estates in reduced circumstances. There was a scandal. I am not welcomed at court.'

Crispin could certainly empathize with that. He rose. 'I assume that is where you have your lady's maid. I need not tell you how unwise it is traipsing about London without an escort, whether day or night.'

She sucked in her bottom lip as she stared at the table.

'Well, it is late, demoiselle. I shall return you there now.'

'But—'

He raised a brow at her. 'It is late.'

She seemed reluctant to succumb to his insistence. But after a moment, she tilted her head and rose as well. 'You are correct, of course, Master Guest. It has been a trying evening.'

Crispin glanced back over his shoulder at Jack standing by the hearth before closing the door behind him. He motioned for her to stay on the step while he checked to see that the street was empty. Assessing the shadows, he was convinced and motioned again for her to come. In silence, they walked the quiet streets, with nothing but the soft song of crickets and the night air cold on his face.

They took the Shambles down to Watling Street where the inn sat, pressed between the cordwainer's hall and an alehouse. He stood at the door and bowed. 'Here I leave you. Shall I call upon you in the morning, or . . .?' In truth, he wasn't certain if she should be seen coming to his lodgings in the daylight unescorted. 'I shall come here,' he decided. Under her hood, her eyes shone hopefully. Before she could utter another sound, he spun on his heel and turned back toward the Shambles.

Women. She was beautiful, to be sure. No doubt, so was Eve, and perhaps just as dangerous. Secrets she had, for he wasn't entirely certain she had told him all. Where had she gone when she fled and why had she returned? For his expertise? But she was distressed and very beautiful and, curse him, but he was not immune to it.

Damnable secrets. Annoying enough without a murder joined to it. He preferred not to go on the assumption that Wynchecombe was a murderer. It would be difficult to prove and, 'Dammit!' As much as he disliked him, he didn't want to believe it of the man. No, there was something else afoot. Secrets, stolen daggers, a dead monk—

Crispin stopped. The street was quiet, like a tomb after the stone has been laid in place. Crickets, yes, but it was not a cricket he heard. Carefully, he eased himself back into the shadow of an alley. His whole body listened, sensing the vibrations from the lane. Was that the swish of a cloak? A step? And then silence. Was someone following him? Again?

He waited a long time, listening to his own shallow breaths

ease in and out. Nothing. He ventured forth and listened with all the skill he had taught himself while he made his way back to the Shambles, uneasy.

FOUR

Crispin awoke early. He was anxious to get to the inn and obtain more answers from the woman. He told himself it was because of the puzzle, not her features or the curve of her figure. Though, in truth, it had been too long without a woman's comfort.

Steady, Crispin. She's a lady. He could no longer play the coy games of courtly love. His current status told him that.

Jack entered his bedchamber and rattled his clay pots over the fire. Crispin examined the crystal monstrance again, turning it in his calloused fingers as he sat upon his bed. The liquid eased from side to side along the transparent surface. He ran a finger over the line of liquid and felt a tingle in his hand. Hastily he put it down, rubbing his fingers till the tingle subsided. He found himself looking up at Jack, who had stopped what he was doing to stare at Crispin.

'What's wrong?' the boy asked.

'Nothing. Is that water ready yet?'

Jack pressed his chapped lips together and silently poured the hot water into a chipped basin. Bare-chested, Crispin walked to the brass mirror leaning against the wall on the mantel where he kept his meager soap cake and razor. While he carefully shaved, Jack stood behind him, his reflection distorted in the polished metal.

'I know there is something about that relic,' said Jack and, even though his voice was soft, Crispin nicked himself and cursed. 'There always is. It means trouble, sir. Get rid of it. Now, before it's too late.'

Crispin continued passing the steel blade over the contours of his face, wincing when he nicked himself again. 'It's nothing. It is only some sort of blood. But as always, it is worth much. To someone. Keep it hidden while I'm gone.'

'Where are you going? Aren't I going with you?'

Crispin cupped his hands and rinsed his face, feeling the stings of the cuts in the warm water. 'I am going to meet Demoiselle Woodleigh. And you are staying here.'

'Why is it every time we encounter a beautiful client *I* have to stay here?'

'Tucker, is it your age or your temperament that makes you so insolent?'

He crossed his arms over his chest. 'Both, I suspect.'

Crispin hid his smile in the linen rag he used as a towel. Jack, at eighteen, was becoming ever more of a handful. 'Nevertheless, you are not going with me. May I suggest you use the time to practice your letters? Your Greek has never been as good as your Latin.'

'Letters,' he muttered and moved toward the fire. 'I'm always learning me letters. I thought it would be more fun learning how to read. I didn't know it would be so much tedious work.'

'*We cannot learn without pain.*'

'Sarding Aristotle,' he grumbled.

'Who has more to teach you. But only when you learn your letters.'

'Why would a tavern keeper need Greek?'

Crispin had just finished pulling up clean braies and tying fresh stockings to them. He stood, chilled without his chemise but staring at Jack. 'I know your plans for Gilbert's niece draw on apace, but . . . have you abandoned your quest to be a Tracker after me?' He blurted it out. He hadn't meant to. Jack's future was his own affair and he had been gladdened that it was better than Crispin's. But there was a pang of . . . something . . . in his heart when he realized Jack might move on without him.

Jack took down the warmed chemise from its place before the fire and held it up for Crispin. 'Who said I was abandoning becoming a Tracker?'

Ducking his head into the chemise to hide his reddening cheeks, Crispin turned away from his apprentice. 'Well . . . when you inherit the Boar's Tusk you will not have time for such . . . trivialities. Such danger. You will have a family to see to . . .'

'Master Crispin!' The boy seemed exasperated. He rubbed at his beard, a new habit he had acquired since it filled out to a handsome feature on his maturing face. Even the freckles of his childhood seemed to have faded in favor of this new hirsute adornment. 'But Master Gilbert leaving this earth is a long time in the future, sir. And anyway, I *want* to be a Tracker. It might not be as safe as a tavern keeper but it's a fair bit more exciting, isn't it? Isabel can run the tavern while I fulfill my vocation. It's an honor, sir, finding criminals, righting wrongs. To follow in your footsteps, master, is all I ever wanted, all I've trained for. Don't you want me to?'

Crispin's cheeks warmed further. He shrugged on his cote-hardie and began buttoning it. 'Of course I do. And you are quite accomplished at it. I merely thought . . .' He turned to Jack, observed his stoic expression and absorbed it at last. 'Very well. There is sense to having a reserve career. You know very well that this one doesn't pay well.'

'Aye, sir. That's what I was thinking. And I pray that Gilbert and Eleanor have a long and happy life. In the meantime, I have this important work to keep me occupied. When I marry Isabel, I will have an honorable vocation. It won't pay much but maybe Isabel can take on another job to help. There will be three mouths to feed, after all. And before long . . . more.' It was Jack's turn to blush.

Such changes. And just as he thought it, Gyb, the black cat with the white blaze and belly, dropped in from the windowsill. He strode across the floor, tail up, past Crispin and Jack and out of the chamber door.

Crispin looked at Jack and they both smiled. 'It looks as if someone has no stomach for our arguments,' said Crispin.

'Aye. That cat has the sense of it.'

'Find something for him, will you, Jack. A saucer of milk, perhaps.' Crispin secured the belt around his waist, checked his dagger and turned to his apprentice, who was as tall as he and nearly as robust. Still lanky with youth, Jack now cut an intimidating figure. Crispin sometimes could not reconcile that curious boy with the many freckles to this man who now stood before him.

'I am gratified to hear your choice of vocation, Jack. Frankly, I don't know what I would do without you.' That made the boy's cheeks blush deeper. Crispin looked around, somewhat embarrassed. 'Well, then. You are a man now, Jack. It is up to you whether you feel you need to keep up with your Greek. I shall not force you to do it.'

Jack looked resigned. 'But as you always say, sir: *A command of languages gives a man command of his life*. I'll be the best-educated tavern keeper in London, I reckon.' He grinned.

Crispin smiled back and slapped the boy on the shoulder. 'That you will be, Jack.' He left his bedchamber with Jack close behind him. They tromped down the stairs and Crispin grabbed his cloak hanging from its peg by the door. He looked at the sword scabbard hanging from its own peg beside it. He decided to wear it today. It was not often he wore the gift from Henry Bolingbroke, his former charge, but today he felt the need to look like someone worth trusting.

He began to fasten it around his waist when Jack took it out of his hand and did it for him . . . as would any good squire worth his salt. The familiar weight of a sword at his side invigorated him. He pulled open the door. 'Guard the relic, Jack.'

'Yes, master,' came the proud reply.

Crispin trotted out into the street, his smile fading as he thought of the tingle in his hand. He rubbed that hand absently against his hip. Hadn't he encountered the like before? Jack was right. Nothing good ever came from association with relics, at least not for him. It was damnable how they kept turning up at his door.

'*Forget what you think you know . . . Beware of what you find . . .*' The last words of his old friend Abbot Nicholas kept haunting him. What did they mean? The words always brought a chill rippling up his spine. Such words of caution could not bode well. A dying man's words . . .

He shook it off and raised his face to the sunshine. The air smelled fresh, at least now he'd left the Shambles. His mind lighted on the woman and he steeled himself. He'd be all business. Yes. He'd make his coin from her and that would be that. Simple.

A shadowy figure trying to hide his face as he ducked into an alley caught his eye and Crispin swiftly changed direction in pursuit. The man started to run in his queer, loping gait so it was a simple matter to catch up to him. Crispin snagged him by the collar of his ragged coat and yanked him back. 'Lenny! What devilry are you up to?'

Lenny shook off Crispin's hand and pulled his coat to straighten it. 'I'm not pleased to see you, Master Crispin, and that's a fact! You done me wrong last we met, you did.'

'I like that! Did you not perjure yourself in a court of law just to get your revenge on me?' With sudden fury he drew his sword. Lenny cringed back, arms up.

'Jesus mercy!'

Crispin looked at his raised arm and cursed under his breath. What the hell was he doing? For one, Lenny wasn't worth washing the blood from the blade. And for another, he certainly wasn't worth the trouble he'd have with the sheriffs.

Crispin sheathed the weapon smartly. He said nothing more, turned on his heel and marched up the avenue.

Footfalls behind him.

Crispin glanced over his shoulder at Lenny. He stopped again and turned. 'Why are you following me?'

Lenny clutched his coat. Though his old, disgusting coat had been long abandoned it looked as if his new one was on its way to mimicking the old with its stains, patches and strident odor.

'So, we have little to say to one another.' Lenny squinted up at Crispin before dropping his gaze to his dirty fingernails. He examined them with particular care, even biting a cuticle and spitting out the leavings.

The gesture was familiar but the man seemed frailer than he used to be. His skin was pocked and threaded with lines. His eyes sat in dark hollows; little wonder with the life he lived on the street. Barely any hair or teeth left. Only God knew the age of the old thief. Lenny was an untrustworthy man. Loathsome in his disdain for any moral code. But he had proved useful in the past . . .

Crispin could feel his resolve crumbling and he cursed again. He was a fool. A trusting, rash fool.

'I *might* be persuaded to give you a *fifth* chance. It so happens that I might have a job for you. One that could possibly pay, say, a farthing a day.'

Lenny licked his lips and his fingers rubbed his palms. 'Eh? A farthing? A day? So you forgive me, then? Not that . . . er . . . that I did anything wrong. I just forgot, is all. Got confused. You know how it is when you get to be my age.'

'Our Lord admonishes us to turn the other cheek. Can I do so without you stabbing me in the back?'

'Oh aye, Master Crispin! I'd never do that. I told you you'd need old Lenny, didn't I? I told you I could be useful.' He gathered his filthy cloak about him. 'Although, I'm finding m'self awful busy these days, awful busy. Suppose I should have a moment or two to take you up on this offer – not that I will, mind – but what if I did? What would I have to do?'

'Follow me and I'll tell you.'

He drew back and seemed to shrink, folding into his raised shoulder. 'Where are we going?'

'To the Unicorn Inn on Watling Street.'

'I'm not going inside. Besides, the innkeeper tossed me out last year, told me never to show me face in there again. He held a butcher's knife when he said it.' He rubbed his stubbled and blotchy neck.

'You won't need to go inside. You only have to follow me there.'

'Is that all? Just follow you there?'

'Well, there is a bit more to it but you won't have to go in. There is someone I wish for you to follow.'

'Oh aye,' he said, wringing his hands anxiously. 'I can do that. Old Lenny is good at that, isn't he?'

'Precisely why I thought of you. Will you come?'

Crispin knew the man had already decided. The thief could always use coin and honest coin was better for his soul. Lenny nodded and gestured for Crispin to precede him.

They walked together, not exactly side by side but close enough for Crispin to look over at the man as he loped along. The scarred skin where Lenny's left ear had been was partially covered by his gray-brown hair and another tooth was missing from his sneer.

At times such as these, Crispin marveled at the company he kept.

The streets were already busy with the traffic of the cold morning. A young girl with a yoke struggled under her burden of buckets of water, sloshing some of it onto the frozen mud at her feet. Two apprentice boys – no more than ten years old – pushed a cart piled high with ceramic pots and jugs tied together precariously with rope. An old man used a stick to gently coax a boney ox with a ring in its wet nose through the streets, while a priest in dark brown robes cursed at him for leading such a bulky animal through the narrow lane.

The street vendors with meat pies and roasted meat on sticks made Crispin's belly rumble, but he ignored them as they turned the corner at Watling Street.

The sunshine glowed on the pale face of the inn, though the courtyard stank from horse droppings. 'Lenny,' said Crispin, turning to the man. 'If you wait across the lane you will see the lady I am looking after. She is the one I would have you follow. And I would like to know if anyone follows her.'

'I get you, Master Crispin. Old Lenny can hide like a shadow, he can. And well you know it.' Lenny beamed his portcullis smile. 'Right, then!' Off he trotted across the lane and, true to form, melded into the shadows.

He entered the courtyard and pushed open the door to the inn. The innkeeper was a tall man with thinning sandy hair and a prominent nose. He was directing a boy to clean out the ashes in the hearth when he looked up and spied Crispin. His expression darkened.

'Crispin Guest. You are not welcomed here.'

'As much as Lenny,' he muttered. 'Peace, Master Hakeforde. I have no intention of starting a melee again.'

'I never did get just compensation for my broken jugs and chairs.' He pointed a crooked finger at him. 'And if you think you will leave these premises without paying out, you're either dim or mad. Will,' he said to the boy, 'fetch my butcher knife.'

'Now hold, Master Hakeforde . . . and you, too, Will.' The boy stopped in mid-stride. He had a smug look about him and an unpleasant glint in his eye that said he wouldn't mind a show of blood. 'I little recall the event in question' – and he reddened still further reckoning the reason – 'but I have every expectation of compensating you for your loss. It's just, at the moment, I . . . well . . . I—'

'I will pay Master Guest's debt.'

They all turned. Katherine Woodleigh stood on the last step of the staircase. Her smile as she looked at Crispin made his gut flutter.

The innkeeper bowed. 'My lady. So generous. But you do not

know this knave. He's a drunkard and gets into common brawls. He did so only a month ago and tore up my place. This is no alehouse, Guest,' he sneered at Crispin.

His words caused a hot surge of blood to heat Crispin's cheeks. Though he wished to defend himself, he couldn't muster the strength to dispute the man's accusations.

'I will pay nonetheless,' said the lady, and handed the innkeeper several coins. 'I hope this will suffice.'

Hakeforde weighed it in his hand. 'More than enough,' he said. Bowing, he glared daggers at Crispin and made no move to leave. She waved him off and the innkeeper sullenly shuffled away, bowing backward out of the door.

'That was . . . very gracious of you,' said Crispin to the floor. 'Too gracious. You shouldn't have done that.'

'I did not wish to complicate matters. He was best dispatched quickly.'

'I do not need you to pay my debts.'

'Clearly you do.'

Clenching his fists, Crispin continued to stare at the floor. This is not how it should be! Being the Tracker meant that *he* decided what clients he chose. *He* made the decisions. Not some lord or lady throwing around their purses. He scowled and raised his chin. 'I will repay you every coin.'

'That is not necessary. But if you insist . . .'

'I do!'

They were both silent until Will returned with a broom and began sweeping in the far corner of the hall.

'I would speak with you, my lady.' Will eyed him with an unpleasant grin. 'But perhaps not here.'

'If that is your will.'

He motioned her toward the door and they stepped out into the sunshine. Her floral scent of gilly flower touched Crispin's nose and made him forget the last few moments. He couldn't help but sigh at the remembrance of such genteel perfumes in the halls of Westminster.

Mentally, he shook his head and looked at her again. 'You are again without a lady's maid. Perhaps you should call her forth.'

'That will not be necessary. I trust you to be my escort.'

'But . . .' He could not make himself say aloud how entirely unsuitable he was for such an honor. A female courtier, even one not allowed to court, should not be alone with him. 'My lady . . .'

'There are more important things to discuss, Master Guest. We cannot worry over decorum at such a time.'

'If you insist. Shall we go to an alehouse?'

'Of course. There is one next door.'

'I prefer another,' he said. 'If you will indulge me?'

She quirked a brow but allowed him to lead the way back toward the Shambles. They turned at Gutter Lane and, under the sign of the curled tusk, they entered Crispin's favorite haunt. Before he shut the door, Crispin looked behind on the street and spied a familiar form in the shadows outside.

Even with the shutters open, the place felt close and smoky. He glanced at the woman but she didn't seem to care. Questions about her and her family buzzed through his mind.

Few patrons were in the Boar's Tusk at this early hour, but Crispin knew the faces if not the names of the men who sat alone at their tables, a beaker of ale clutched in their hands and their sour, yellowed eyes staring into nothing.

He motioned her to a bench while he slid onto a stool, his back to the wall with a view of the door, just as he preferred it.

'Demoiselle.'

'This place is special to you. You trust it.'

The worn table caught his attention and he rubbed his palms across it. 'An interesting observation. It *is* true.'

A woman, round and pink-faced under her white, starched wimple, emerged from a curtained alcove with a jug in her hand. She smiled warmly at Crispin but eyed his guest with wariness. 'Good day to you, Crispin. Ned did not say you had company but I will bring another goblet.'

Katherine raised her hand faintly. 'No, thank you, good woman. I would rather hear what Master Guest has to ask me with a clear head.'

Crispin took the offering and poured himself a healthy dose of wine. 'Thank you, Eleanor.'

The woman moved away with a brief curtsey, looking back with a subtle shake to her head.

Katherine laughed a light sound. 'She does not like me.'

'Eleanor is the alewife here and has succored me for many years now.' He took a quick gulp of the wine. 'She thinks she is protecting me.'

'No doubt.'

Taking one more drink, Crispin, thinking of Jack's admonition to curtail his drinking, set the bowl down and looked over his client. 'You seem in better spirits today.'

Her eyes dimmed and her lips softened from their smile. 'A bright morning makes the horrors of the night disappear.'

His fingers curved around the rim of the bowl and slowly turned it. He watched the crimson liquid shimmer and reflect the hearthlight. 'Tell me, demoiselle. Why is it that I feel you are lying to me?'

'What?' she said, flustered.

'It was only last night that you were desperately afraid for your niece. You also witnessed the dread result of a murder, yet this morning all is well. Perhaps it is time to tell me the truth.'

She leaned away from the table, arms folded. 'That is an audacious accusation, Master Guest. Can you justify it?'

'You're not denying it.'

She glared at him steadily. Enough time passed for Crispin to take another drink, wiping his mouth with the back of his hand. *Jack be damned.* He leaned back until his shoulder blades rested against the warm plaster wall. 'Well?'

'There is much I may not tell you,' she said, mouth tight.

'Ah.' He poured more and drank again, less this time. 'Then what *can* you tell me? Wait. Let's begin with why you are not staying with kinsmen or even at court. You seem to have no lady's maid with you. This is unthinkable. There must be some drastic reason why you travel alone. I suggest you tell me all or you can leave now.'

The bench squealed back as she jerked to her feet. 'Insolence!' Turning on her heel, she was halfway to the door before he called out, 'Demoiselle!'

She turned. He dropped her coin pouch on the table with a clunk. 'Take back your fee.'

Her face twisted with rage and she stomped to the table, snatched it up and continued on her way out.

Sighing, Crispin raised the bowl to his lips.

'Crispin, Crispin.'

Eleanor sank to the bench beside him and absently wiped the table with a rag. 'That looked to be a very foolish thing you did.'

'Perhaps.'

'She looked like a courtier. Could she make trouble for you?'

'I don't think so. I think that it is she who is in trouble. She won't tell me exactly what or the extent of it. But she'll be back.'

'Courtiers! I think they'd all be happier living simple lives as we do. Everything about them is secrets. I see it all the time. Gentlemen sitting in tight circles, whispering their plots. Delicate ladies with a sly eye. I tell you, Crispin, you are well out of it.'

He refrained from finishing his bowl and set it down with a thump. 'Forgive me if I cannot find the heart to agree with you.'

She made some noncommittal noise in her throat and left him. He couldn't resist the wine bowl's allure and drank a bit more, thinking it might be pleasant to while away the day finishing the jug . . . or two, as he used to do . . . when he pushed the bowl away from him. Bah! This was no good. The woman had paid his debt and the money pouch he'd returned was only a small portion of it. But he knew in his gut that something was amiss, and he'd learned from many years' experience never to ignore his gut.

There was also the problem of a dead man.

Rising, he stretched. He adjusted his coat and sword scabbard, looked back fondly at his wine and left the Boar's Tusk.

The smell of spring was far off. In its place was mildewed plaster and mud. He could recall a time when March meant the opening of spring, when hares went mad and daffodils nodded from snow-wet verges. The road to his long-lost manor house in Sheen had been lined with daffodils and then foxgloves. Hundreds of them, winding the long trail to the gatehouse, opening up to wide, green fields that surrounded the manor . . .

His heart gave a stumble when remembering that it had burned to the ground five years ago.

'Seasons change like a woman's mind,' he muttered.

There was no time to dwell on the past. Several problems now assailed him. One, who was that dead monk and from where did he come? Two, where did that relic come from? And three . . .

'Simon Wynchecombe.' What the hell was he to do about that? He had no desire to ever speak to Wynchecombe again. Too many times he'd suffered humiliation at the man's hands, even as they'd almost seemed to come to terms with each other. The man was an enigma, to be sure. And extremely ambitious. It wouldn't be long till he was elected Lord Mayor. If Crispin had any say in the matter, he preferred to keep out of Wynchecombe's way.

But that dagger spoke much and it had to be dealt with. He supposed it was time to go to Simon's house and have a conversation. But what to say?

He stood in the street, looking up the road. A humid mist rose from the damp streets and with it the smell of mud mixed with horse piss. A man with a dusty red tunic and a tray in his hands was calling out, 'Sheep's hocks! Sheep's hocks!' Crispin was tempted to buy one before he remembered he had given away most of his money to Katherine Woodleigh.

He girded himself. Wynchecombe had a house in London where he conducted his business as an armorer but he knew he had lands elsewhere in another county. With any luck, he'd be at home in town. He headed down the lane toward Candlewick Ward.

It was only a matter of less than a quarter of an hour before he stood before Wynchecombe's place of business. He shook the dread off as he straightened his coat and adjusted his cloak. He felt better with a sword at his side, though he could not dare draw it on the man. Wynchecombe wouldn't be any happier to see him than Crispin was to see the former sheriff but it had to be done. He strode up the flagged stone path and met a servant sweeping the front entrance. He looked up at Crispin and slowed his sweeping until he rested the broom on its bristles.

'Good day to you,' said Crispin with a nod of his head. The young man, nothing more than sticks in oversized clothes, regarded him without a sound. His dark, lank hair ruffled against his cheek from a breeze. The grip tightened on his broomstick.

Crispin stopped a few paces from him. He squinted up the tall building, measuring the plaster and stone of its architecture, scanning the shuttered windows for signs of life. 'Is your master at home?'

'You're Crispin Guest,' the youth said at last.

Crispin rested his hand on his dagger hilt more from habit than threat, or so he told himself. 'Yes.'

'Why would the likes of you want to be talking to Master Wynchecombe?'

'Why not? Perhaps I am in need of armor?'

'Perhaps you aren't. I know who you are. And Master Wynchecombe is not at home.' The broom arced and he viciously swept the dew from the carved granite step directly at Crispin's boots. Crispin looked down at the water beading on the leather and frowned. The boy's face changed from defiance to fear and he stepped hastily back into the entryway, scrambled behind him for the latch and slid inside with a slam of the door.

It would almost be amusing if Crispin hadn't been so annoyed. Undeterred, he made his way to the side of the building and spied an open gate. Without a backward glance, he went through, surveying the yard. A maid was picking her way over the mud, a heavy basket hoisted on her shoulder. Crispin trotted to catch up to her and quickly relieved her of her burden. She seemed startled but he gave her a ready smile. 'Forgive me for frightening you, but it looked too heavy for so fair a maid.'

She brushed a wayward lock over her ear. The rest of her tawny hair was covered by a linen kerchief. She measured Crispin for a moment before smiling. 'And who might you be, my lord?'

'No one in particular. But I am an old acquaintance of Simon Wynchecombe. Can you tell me if he is at home?'

Her smile vanished and her eyes held concern. 'Oh, sir.' They stopped before a side entrance and Crispin set the basket down. 'I fear to tell you that Master Wynchecombe hasn't been nigh in days. Truth to tell . . .' She leaned closer and Crispin followed suit. 'He hasn't been seen by anyone,' she said in a harsh whisper. Her breath smelled of ale. 'Not for some time. They've even sent messengers to his manor in Winchcombe but just got word that he is not there either. The mistress is worried sick, God bless her.'

'That is troubling news. But surely there is nothing sinister about it. Maybe I could speak to the mistress.'

'Oh, sir, if you are a friend that could put her poor heart at ease, you are welcome. Come inside.'

Crispin followed her into a dark corridor that led to a parlor flooded with light from tall reticulated glass windows. 'Wait here. I'll get Madam Alice.'

It was a small deception, he reminded himself as the girl scurried off. He'd made many over the years. One more wouldn't hurt.

He glanced about. It wasn't the first time he had been in Wynchecombe's home but that last time he had been rushed, in a panic. He hadn't had the opportunity to size up the room and its wealth. He knew the former sheriff was well-heeled but he never knew the extent of it until now. Candlesticks of silver sporting beeswax candles. An expensive-looking tapestry hanging on one wall over a sideboard of rich wood and intricate carvings. The glass in the windows was relatively smooth and cut in diamond panes, with heavy, rich drapery hanging on either side of them. The chairs had ornate wooden legs and their cushions were bright with embroidery. Yes, the man had done well over the years with his armor business, being an alderman, as well as the bribes he took as sheriff. Along with a modest estate in Winchcombe, it seemed he would never starve, which reminded Crispin of the many times the man had managed to pry Crispin's hard-earned wage from him. He scowled. The rich stayed that way not by the grace of God but by commonplace greed.

The door swung open and Madam Wynchecombe entered, followed by the maid. The lady was slight with a somewhat plain face and a severe chin. Her eyes were gray and they moved over Crispin with agility. Her hands held tight over a rosary. 'My maid said you were a friend.' She studied Crispin's clothes. Though they weren't the rags he used to wear, they were merely service-able, not tailored from rich fabric. Surely not the clothes of any acquaintance Wynchecombe might have known, though the sight of the sword served to confuse.

She stepped closer. Her face was rigid. 'Who are you?'

'Forgive me, madam,' he said with his lowest courtly bow. 'I am Crispin Guest.'

The maid gasped and threw her hand over her mouth. 'Madam, have mercy on me. I did not know that this was Crispin Guest. I never would have allowed him in. Oh, curse it. Curse you, sir, for your trickery!'

'I ask your forgiveness, too, good maid. But it is important that I speak with your mistress.'

Madam Wynchecombe turned to her maid. 'Call the steward.'

'In all haste!' she cried and left in a rush.

The lady turned slowly to Crispin. 'You are known here, Master Guest.'

'I can well see that,' he said with a flush.

'Will you leave on your own or must my man throw you out?'

'Just a moment of your time is all I crave, madam. Is it true that your husband is missing?'

For a moment, she seemed to have forgotten that they were enemies. Hope flamed in her eyes and she lurched forward, grabbing his arm. 'Have you heard from him? Is that why you are here? Simon told me that you investigated things. Have you found him?'

'I . . .' *Feel like a knave*, he thought. She truly was worried and he had buoyed her hopes without cause. 'I was merely looking to speak with him. I did not know he was . . . missing.'

Her hand fell away and she moved from him, shoulders slumping. With her back turned, it looked as if she wiped at her eyes. When she spun to face him again her anger had returned and she shook her rosary. 'If you are here to cause trouble, Master Guest, you will feel his wrath. For when my husband returns he will see that you are punished for trespassing where you are definitely not wanted.'

'I ask forgiveness again, madam. I meant no disrespect to you or . . . or to your husband. But I must know. How long has he been gone?'

She sniffled, her eyes glancing away. 'Three weeks with not one word. He is not in London and not in the village.'

'The village? You mean Winchcombe in Gloucestershire?'

A step in the doorway made him turn. It was the servant from the front entrance. His mouth was gnarled in a scowl. But it was no broom he brandished this time; it was a club. And he wasn't alone. There were two other men beside him and they each had clubs. 'Our mistress bid you leave, knave,' said the youth.

Crispin wondered if that meant before or after a beating.

He wanted to ask her about any of Wynchecombe's dalliances but didn't think it wise under the circumstances. Maybe under *any* circumstances. Could Wynchecombe be missing because he was in hiding with Katherine Woodleigh's niece?

The men with the clubs took a step into the parlor. It was definitely time for Crispin to depart.

The way was blocked. Nothing for it but to walk through them.

He put his hand on his sword – this time unquestionably in warning – and stepped forward. Miraculously, they stepped aside. Before he reached the entry, he stopped, turned back to the lady with a courteous bow and proceeded to the front entrance. More male servants stood nearby. All looked ready to pounce. Crispin swallowed and strode swiftly through the door and up the lane. He felt the men follow behind him. He kept his pace swift and steady when his foot touched the road. He didn't stop, didn't look back for many yards. When he no longer heard heavy steps behind him, he finally stopped and looked back.

They had gathered at the end of the lane by a stone wall, shaking their clubs in his direction and urging him on with obscene gestures.

Crispin straightened his coat again, nodded politely to the men and hurried on his way.

And so, Wynchecombe was not in London. Not even on his estates in Gloucestershire. Where the hell was he?

Once he was farther away from the manor, Crispin glanced over his shoulder again. The men were still there but now there was some distance and many more people between them. He released the breath he was holding. Close. Too close.

What was he to do with this information? If Wynchecombe had this young niece, where could he hide her? And what was his knife doing in the back of a monk from a cloistered order very far from home? Which posed the question again of the identity of this monk. If the monastery in London wasn't missing a monk, then which one was? Where was the closest Cistercian house? Perhaps that would require another journey to Smithfield to talk to the abbot there. No, the abbot had assured him he would send a missive to the other houses to ascertain who had a missing brother. A dark cloud hovered over this. Killing a monk, stealing an innocent maid, a *married* Simon Wynchecombe.

And the relic.

None of it boded well.

Crispin walked slowly back to the Shambles. As he placed a foot on the step of his threshold, his stomach growled. Why had he been so foolish as to give back that money? So noble! When was he going to learn that he could not afford to be so high-handed?

He pushed open the door. 'Jack?' Nothing. What a surprise. He only hoped the boy was out searching, begging . . . hell, *stealing* something to eat. 'Have I sunk so low?' he muttered. His stomach growled again in answer.

Staring at the empty table did little good. He thought of examining the bloody dagger again but he already knew to whom it belonged.

But that relic. Where did it belong? He didn't recall seeing it before.

He climbed the stairs and headed for his chamber. Kneeling by his bed, he reached under the straw-stuffed mattress for the crystal monstrance when a knock at the door below startled him. He abandoned the mattress, descended the stairs and went to the door.

Katherine Woodleigh blinked up at him, eyes shining with grave sincerity.

'May I come in?'

Crispin stepped aside. She brushed passed him and he inhaled her scent again, vague with blossoms and woman.

Her steps were tentative. Fingers trailed along his table and she sank gingerly onto the chair. She pushed the pouch before her across the table's surface and left it in the center. 'I have come to ask your forgiveness,' she said.

Crispin hesitated before moving to stand above her. 'What for?'

'For my treatment of you. For . . . my own high-handedness.' She chuckled unpleasantly and gestured to herself. 'As you see, I can ill afford it. Surely *you* can understand, with your own history, how it is with a person who has been a wealthy courtier and now has nothing.'

'Nothing? Did you pay the innkeeper with pebbles?'

'I paid him with coin I could ill afford to give. But pride is a sore thing.'

Crispin acknowledged it with the drooping of his head. 'Indeed, it is.'

'I told you before, my father was *Thomas* Woodleigh.' She

waited until the name sank in. It took a moment for Crispin to catch up.

'Thomas Woodleigh? I seem to recall a scandal associated with the name. Something was stolen and then a murder?'

'Yes. To our very great regret. My father was accused . . . but admitted no wrongdoing. It ruined us. He died two years ago, leaving me alone and nearly a pauper. The king graciously granted a stipend to sustain me until I could be wed but because of the scandal and the gambled-away dower, even the king's intercession could provide no offers.' She pushed away from the table and paced. 'And now even that has come to a trickle. It is my shame to bear now. I do not know what will become of me. A nunnery, I suppose.' She held her head up. Though her eyes glistened, her will alone seemed to hold back the tears.

Crispin was on his feet and holding her hand before he realized it.

She smiled. 'You are kind and understanding. Perhaps more than I deserve.'

'We cannot be blamed for the faults of our sires. But I am well familiar with shame, and I know the harm it can do.'

'So you do,' she said, eyes covertly scanning the lowly room that had never quite sloughed off the odor of chickens. She kept her hand in his. It was warm and soft.

'Simon is an old family friend,' she began. 'We both have manors in Winchcombe. At least, I used to. I asked him to help me sell some land for much-needed funds, which he did. But as if his indiscretion with my niece were not enough, he made off with the money and has refused my letters. I have come to London at great personal cost to find her and get back what is mine. I *must* find him.'

'I see.' He surprised himself at his reluctance to release her hand, but he did so. He glanced once at the coin pouch on the table. 'So you seek him to return the money he obtained for you.'

'Yes. I was ashamed to add it to the humiliation he has already rained down upon us.'

'Hmm. Did you know that Simon Wynchecombe is missing?'

'He was not at home at his manor in Gloucestershire.'

'But he has not been at his London home for some three weeks now.'

'What? Where can he be?'

'That is the primary question. I have another. What might he have to do with Cistercian monks?'

'I have no idea. Why . . . why do you ask?' But her eyes flashed in the direction of the stain still marring his floor.

'Just . . . curious.' He stood silently for a moment, letting the pause lengthen. He watched her under the shading locks of his hair. She did not fidget or move at all. She seemed to be waiting. Breath after gentle breath lifted the bosom of her gown, and if he weren't careful he could find himself enchanted by the sight.

'Your niece must be found. What if in so doing I cannot recover your stolen funds?' He nodded toward the money pouch on the table. 'Wynchecombe might very well claim he did no such thing.'

One shoulder rose in a half-hearted shrug. 'I don't know. But I do know this: I am not made for a nunnery. And neither is my niece.'

Unbidden, his eyes roved over each curve beneath her gown. No, she was not.

'Why would Master Wynchecombe, a wealthy alderman in his own right, have need to steal from you?'

She shook her head. 'What motivates greed, Master Guest? You say you have known him. Do you think him capable? And to steal from me, why, he knows I have no recourse, no kinsmen to force him to pay it. I am helpless. As helpless as my dear niece, Sybil. Perhaps this is what motivates him the most.'

Was Simon the sort? he wondered. The man was skilled at taking bribes and skimming the funds from Crispin's own pocket. But was he that much of a knave as to steal a maid? Anything was possible, he supposed.

'Or rather, it is the reason he is missing. Might something have happened to him along the road? Master Wynchecombe is not a man to shirk his responsibilities. He might very well be . . . dead.'

'I hadn't thought of that,' she said. 'Oh, but my kinswoman, my Sybil! If something happened to him, ill might have befallen her! And that I thought such cruel and unkind things about him. Where is my charity?'

'Charitable thoughts when one is so anxious? You do not travel with a maid. You can't afford one?'

'At present,' she admitted with downcast eyes.

Don't be a fool, Crispin. But he was doing it anyway. He took up the coins, tipped a few into his palm and handed her the rest of them.

Her eyes rounded first on him and then on the coins.

'Take it, demoiselle. Pride does not feed our bellies. You are in sore need of it, no?'

'But I would pay you your wage, good sir.'

'I have enough here.' He gestured with the coins in his hand but he well knew there were too few. He slipped them into the pouch at his belt. 'I would have returned it all but I must have funds to search for them. And at any rate, you more than paid my wage when you paid my debts. That was a foolish thing to do on your part, under the circumstances.'

The smile reached her eyes. She leaned over and kissed his cheek, petal soft. He felt a mortifying blush.

'You are too generous, Master Guest. Far too generous.' His own words echoed back to him. 'You will be remembered in my prayers.'

'Yes . . . well.'

She rose and headed for the door. 'I will take my leave, then. I hope you find him soon.'

He bounded forward and opened the door for her.

'Oh. By the way.' She glanced at him over her shoulder. 'Whatever became of that relic?'

'I'm keeping it safe,' he said.

'What was it?'

'I don't know. Some saint's blood, I think.'

'May I . . . may I see it again? I have seldom been so close to one.'

He shrugged and trudged upstairs. He retrieved it from under his mattress and came back downstairs. Carefully, he placed it on the table. The blood oozed from side to side in its beryl monstrance.

She reached forward and touched it with a tentative finger before pulling back. 'Curious,' she whispered. 'So precious a thing. You must shield it away again, Master Guest. Until you find the place it belongs.'

He scooped it up and closed it in his fist.

She nodded and smiled. 'It is in good hands. God keep you, Master Guest.'

'Crispin. Call me . . . Crispin.' As soon as the words left his lips he felt like falling on his blade. What the hell was he doing?

Her smile broadened and she offered him a curtsey. He hadn't been offered that particular gesture in many a day. It felt good.

Once she passed over the threshold he watched her make her way across the lane. But he sobered when he spotted a lone, hunched figure saluting him. He waited for her to disappear before he waved Lenny forward.

Lenny's smell preceded him. It was rancid sweat, old dirt and urine tinged with a touch of cautious anxiety. The man licked his lips. Rat-like eyes darted here and there. There was nothing for him to steal so Crispin relaxed and sat. Lenny caught sight of the wine bowl and gave Crispin a hopeful look. Crispin scowled.

'Well, then,' said Lenny. 'I followed the lady like you said.' He paused.

Crispin waited. 'Get on with it.'

'I don't have me farthing yet, do I.'

Sighing, Crispin reached in his pouch and withdrew the quartered coin. Lenny made to grab it but Crispin held it out of his reach. 'Information first, then the farthing.'

Lenny growled. 'Farthing first and *then* the information. Curse you.'

Crispin chuckled and tossed the quartered coin. Lenny caught it deftly in his knobby fingers. 'Right then. I followed the lady to Westminster. And she was alone, I might add.'

'So . . .?'

'I'm getting to it.' He smacked his lips again. 'Good master, you wouldn't be having a drop of ale or so for old Len, now, would you? It's rough and thirsty work following a soul all over England.'

Crispin frowned. 'No.'

'So it's like that,' he grunted, taking his time securing his farthing in the folds of his grimy coat. When he was satisfied it was safe, he continued. 'She left London for Westminster, then she made heel for the abbey. She talked to one of them monks for a bit, and then she left the church to a courtyard nigh the abbey, and after returned to the Unicorn.'

'She went to this courtyard, did she? Into the abbey? And whom did she meet?'

'Aye. I'm getting to that. Sure you won't spare a small draught of ale?'

'I'm positive. Get on with it.'

'Very well. She met a monk. And spent far too much time alone with him.'

FIVE

After Lenny left him, Crispin secured the relic and considered. Why would a monk allow her in the cloister and spend so much time with her? Did she know him? Her situation was grave, to be sure. The monk might have counseled her on a fitting nunnery, though the thought sat sour in his belly like stale beer.

He stared at the dark patch still staining his floorboards and thought a trip to Newgate was called for. He dreaded talking with the sheriffs but it had to be done.

A scramble at the threshold made him grab for his sword hilt but it was only Jack. 'Well now! Back so soon? We'll talk as we go.'

'Go? Go where?'

'Newgate.'

Jack stumbled. Crispin knew the boy hated the prison. He wasn't fond of it, either. But Jack recovered and followed hard on Crispin's heels. The boy refrained from asking, but he could almost feel him straining not to say anything.

They walked in silence up Newgate Market to the looming tower with its arch and portcullis, now raised, poised like teeth waiting to bite down. Crispin didn't cringe while passing below it, but only just managed.

The porter regarded him with drooping lids. 'Master Guest. Come to see the sheriffs?' As if there was any other reason. He nodded anyway, and the slump-shouldered porter nabbed a page who had been drifting off to sleep. 'Here, Rafe,' said the porter. 'Take Master Guest up to the sheriffs. And be quick about it.'

Rafe, a boy with dirty blond hair down to his collar, didn't wait to see if Crispin followed him. Crispin watched the point of his hood sway back and forth across his shoulders as they made their way up a narrow staircase and to the outer chamber to the sheriff's workroom. He knocked, waited a moment and entered, announcing Crispin and Jack.

John Walcote stood. His eyes narrowed. John Loveney turned from his place by the fire. He, too, seemed displeased to see Crispin.

'Well, Master Guest!' said Walcote, coming round the table, a folded parchment in his hand. 'And his young apprentice, Jack Tucker.' He said the last as if reading it from a tax roll.

Jack shuffled his feet and looked at the floor. 'Aye, my lord.'

Walcote shook the parchment. 'You'll never guess what this is, Master Guest.'

'No, he never will,' said Loveney.

Crispin looked from one to the other. His temple began to throb. 'Don't keep me in suspense.'

'And so!' Walcote straightened it and held it under the candlelit corona hanging from a chain above their heads. 'I have here—'

'*We* have!' said Loveney.

'Yes, yes. *We* have here a missive from the abbot of St Mary Graces. Would you like to know what it says?'

Crispin bit down on what he truly *wanted* to say. 'My lords, if I can be of service then it is best to bring all information into the light of day.'

Sheriff Loveney elbowed Jack, who had been trying to stay back behind Crispin. 'Your master. He's an impatient fellow, is he not?'

'Impatient and anxious to solve this wretched crime against one of God's own, my lords,' said Crispin, keeping his voice as even as he could.

Loveney drew back with a frown. He urged Walcote on with a wave of his hand.

'It is from Abbot William de Warden, who says he received a letter himself the very next day after Master Crispin arrived at their abbey. The letter was from Abbot Robert at Hailes Abbey in Gloucestershire. One of their brothers went missing and they are greatly troubled because, only a sennight before, another of the monks was found dead. What do you make of that?'

Staring at the stone arch of the window behind the sheriff, Crispin considered. 'It seems we have found the identity of our dead monk.'

'Yes, but it still does not tell us who murdered him.'

'No, but . . .' Crispin rubbed his clean-shaven chin and only subtly noticed that everyone had leaned forward with parted lips to listen to his pronouncement as if he were the pope. *God's blood!* 'I have no magical answers for you, good sirs,' he said sternly. 'But it is clear someone must go to Hailes.'

He waited. The sheriffs blinked stupidly at him. He sighed. 'I will go, naturally.'

'Oh, excellent!' Sheriff Walcote clapped his hands together and rubbed. 'We shall, of course, supply you with a horse. No, two! One for young Master Tucker, here.' Jack seemed to swell at that. 'And you must write to us at once upon reaching Hailes, Master Crispin. We are most anxious to hear your tidings.'

'Most anxious,' said an equally excited John Loveney.

God help me. Crispin sighed.

There was a spring in Jack's step as they led their newly acquired horses from Newgate. 'How about that, Master Crispin!' said Jack, winding the horse's lead over his hand. 'They went and offered a horse to me. Called me "Master Tucker." I never thought I'd see the day when a sheriff of London gave me any attention but bad.'

'Yes, it's all very invigorating.'

Jack couldn't seem to help but trot this way and that before him. 'But Master Crispin, it's a golden day. I never in me life been treated so respectful. It's a new day indeed.'

Crispin smiled. How could he begrudge Jack his first taste of it? Due respect had long ago been yanked from Crispin's grasp. He'd earned it back, in a way, from the merchants and waifs of London's streets, but it certainly wasn't the same as he had enjoyed in his former circles at court.

The sheriffs seemed only too glad to send Crispin and Jack

away. What was on their minds? Was it only to distract him, get him out of the way? Or were they genuinely interested? No. That seemed out of character. Nevertheless, it was an opportunity and he needed to snatch those when they presented themselves.

Jack swung his arm – the one leading the horse – and Crispin had to stop him before he wrenched out the bit. They tied the beasts to a post at their threshold. There was not much to pack but the only thing on Crispin's mind was the relic, and that he wrapped carefully and stuffed in a saddle bag. Once it was safely secured, his thoughts fell on Katherine Woodleigh. She would have to be informed that he was leaving London for a sennight at least. He scanned the street of patrons, horses and carts and honking geese. Where was Lenny when he needed him? But a tall woman caught his eye, tall and broad-shouldered with a long, purposeful stride. She walked alongside a man who was taking furtive glances before they both ducked into a dark alley.

'Wait here, Jack.' Crispin hurried to the alley and crossed his arms, leaning his shoulder into the damp plaster. 'John,' he said.

The man looked up and hastily pulled his braies back into place. With head bowed, he quickly shouldered by Crispin without so much as a by-your-leave. Crispin quirked a brow at the disgruntled woman.

'Crispin, by God, you have got to stop doing that! But at least I got my coin first.' She tossed it once in the air and caught it with a long-fingered hand.

'Master Rykener. Whoring under the eye of Newgate? Aren't you tempting fate a little too much?'

John Rykener, in his woman's clothes, sidled close to Crispin and grinned at him. His cote-hardie buttoned down the front all the way to the hem at his feet. His figure mimicked that of a woman, even with curves in the right places, though less so at his chest. 'Well, Crispin, you know me. A maid's got to do what a maid's got to do.'

'Except you are no maid.'

He snorted and smoothed out his skirts. 'That is a certainty!'

Crispin blushed. 'That is not what I meant.' He spun but John grabbed his arm. 'Tut, Master Guest. You did not frighten off my client just for the purpose of a lecture, for you know far better than that. What is it?'

'Well, I was thinking—' He looked the man over, from the plucked brows down his slim form in its woman's gown to his pointed shoes. He might dress as a woman and play the mare for other men but he was a man and Crispin knew him to be a strong individual, hearty of both body and mind. Yes, it was an even better idea than he had at first thought. 'John,' he said, his voice low and keeping his eyes on the street. 'I wish to hire you.'

Rykener's mouth fell open. 'You *do*?'

Feeling his face heat again, Crispin quickly slid away from the man. 'Not like that! God's blood, John!'

Rykener shook his head, the looped braids at his temples swaying under the kerchief. 'For a moment, I—' He laughed. 'You should have seen the look on your face.'

'Yes, very funny.'

'Oh, it was, it was!' He clapped his hands and pressed his fingertips to his smiling lips.

Crispin felt like melting into the wall. If only he could. 'Do you wish the job or not?'

'Coin is coin, Crispin. What is it?'

'I should like you to continue to play "Eleanor". You work as a seamstress, do you not?'

'Embroideress. And a good one, too.'

'Then I should like you to work as a . . . a lady's maid.'

John blinked. 'To a . . . a lady?'

'Yes, to a lady! To whom else would you be a lady's maid?'

'Well, I have played such games before—'

'And I have no desire to hear about them.' Crispin peeked around the corner at Jack, who was stomping the mud next to the horses. The boy was anxious to get going and so was Crispin. 'A lady's maid, John. And also a protector. Such a combination is unique but necessary.'

'A client of yours, Crispin?'

'Yes. The lady in question is staying at the Unicorn Inn on Watling Street. Her name is Katherine Woodleigh.' He reached into his pouch and withdrew some coins, handing them to Rykener only after he was certain no one had noticed them talking. 'Here is your partial fee. I'm afraid it's all I can give you now.' At least he had bargained traveling money and horses from the sheriffs so he and Jack wouldn't starve along the way. 'Watch her well and tell her I sent you. But don't tell her you are a man.'

'Where are you going?'

'I must leave London. I shall be gone for a sennight at least. But I will return as soon as possible. Keep watch of her, John. I fear someone might be after her.'

Rykener grabbed the dagger hilt at his hip. 'You can rely upon me, Crispin. I shall be the perfect lady's maid.'

Looking at his small mouth, pert cheeks and long, straight nose, Crispin was inclined to agree. 'Remember. You are Eleanor.'

'I know that, Crispin. I have been Eleanor for many years.'

'Good. Well. Farewell, then.'

'God speed you, Crispin. And that clever boy, Jack.'

Crispin left the alley and glanced over his shoulder as Rykener made his way down the lane, heading for Watling Street.

'Was that Master Rykener?' asked Jack.

'Yes.'

'And did you just send him to . . . Katherine Woodleigh?' Crispin said nothing. But Jack seemed to reckon what Crispin had schemed without his saying it. 'Oh, Master Crispin,' he said, shaking his head. 'You shouldn't have done that.'

SIX

It seemed to be a great adventure for Jack. The only other journey they had embarked upon together had been to Canterbury and that had not ended well for his young apprentice. Still, Jack was resilient and seemed to have recovered from the events of five years ago. He also seemed to ride better without fighting the horse's gait. Even so, he twisted and turned on the saddle, examining the countryside and each village they passed through with bright, wide eyes.

'Where is the farthest you've traveled, master?'

'I suppose that would be Jerusalem.'

'Blind me! Truly? What's it like?'

'Hot. Dry. Dusty. Full of strange people and customs.'

'But it's where our Lord preached the gospel, isn't it?'

'Yes, Jack. It is also full of churches and holy places. I was with his grace the duke on a pilgrimage and to preserve the streets from the infidel. More or less.'

'You been lots of places, haven't you, master?'

'Yes. A knight ventures to many battlefields.'

Jack fell silent. The rolling rhythm of the horse's gait lulled Crispin and he daydreamed, lids growing heavy. He thought a doze would be very satisfactory about now.

'What do you hope it accomplish at Hailes Abbey, master?'

Or not. Crispin sat up, rolling his shoulders to urge wakefulness. The sky, streaked by long tails of clouds, was just beginning to glow a yellowish rose. Time to find an inn soon. It was their second day on the road. By this time tomorrow, they should see the blocky towers of the abbey and find hospitality there.

'I hope to find the reason a holy brother was killed and to put his slayer in the noose.'

'And what of Demoiselle Katherine's niece?'

Crispin sighed deeply. 'I worry that she might be . . . dead.'

'God's blood. By all the saints, I hope that is not so. What makes you say so, sir?'

'There is precious little known about her. And with the death of two monks and Simon missing . . .' He shook his head sorrowfully. 'I cannot help but think the worst.'

Jack crossed himself. 'I know you are also thinking of Master Wynchecombe. Sort of a strange coincidence him having a manor near Hailes, the place of two dead monks. And with the man's knife hidden back in our lodgings.'

He was thinking that, too. 'If coincidence it is, it is a poor one.'

'Do you think he did it?'

'As I said before, Jack. Though I cannot rule it out, I find it highly suspicious. Since he is missing, I think it far more likely that *he* might be in peril.'

'By the saints, I never thought of all that.'

'Well, think on it. If Tracker you mean to be, you must put aside your prejudices and think with an open mind. It is a puzzle only. *Educating the mind without educating the heart is no education at all.*'

'I was wondering when Aristotle would rear up,' he muttered.

Crispin gripped the reins. 'I do not see why you disparage Aristotle as you do. His thoughts are wise and remarkably apt for most every occasion.'

'Aye, master. I reckon.' Crispin was pleased when Jack fell silent. He thought, with a judicious heaping of Aristotle into the conversation, he had sent Jack to thoughtful pondering. The boy's mind tended to wander. He needed reining in if he was to learn Crispin's skills. After all, the boy was eighteen. At that age, Crispin had accomplished much. Reading and speaking in several languages, martial skills. He had achieved agility in rhetoric and mathematics. Jack needed to immerse in quiet study. Maybe the boy was finally getting the idea.

'How about them sheriffs?' piped Jack suddenly.

So much for quiet contemplation.

'What ails them, anyway?' he went on. 'One moment they are keen on you, the next not.'

Despite his annoyance, Crispin could not hold back a smile. 'You're a mother hen.'

'I am not. I just . . . you get into trouble, master, and no mistaking.'

'True, I suppose. Every pair of sheriffs seems to see me in the same light: that of a nuisance. These are important men, aldermen of the city, some even Members of Parliament. They must make themselves seem more important and they think the way through it is over the backs of others. Only very small men think that way. You must always be kind to servants, Jack. *All virtue is summed up in dealing justly.*'

Out of the corner of his eye, he could see Jack trying out Aristotle's saying with silently moving lips.

They rode into the day until the evening arrived soft and gray around them. An inn with rickety beams and a leaky thatched roof kept the north wind at bay.

In the drizzly morning, they headed down the mud-sticky path onward. By afternoon the rain had not abated and they rode toward the escarpment of Bredon Hill with their hoods hanging low, dripping rain onto their saddles. A steep descent down the scarp took them along a narrow path through the woods, which opened to a wide pitch of green fields toward Hailes at last.

The stone monastery sat in the hollow of a meadow. Its gray walls were streaked dark with rain. Crispin led them up the muddy path to the gatehouse. He leaned down from the saddle and spoke to the porter, who opened the gate for them. They urged their horses across the courtyard and dismounted at the monastery's arched entry. Crispin slid the wrapped relic from its place in his saddlebags and tucked it in his scrip. At first mention of Hailes, Crispin had surmised what the relic was and cradled it carefully as he ascended the wide stairs with Jack in tow.

An old monk dressed in white with a black scapular greeted them at the archway. Crispin told him who he was and why he had come. The monk surveyed him with curious eyes but took it upon himself to lead Crispin to the abbot.

Down a shadowed arcade they went and emerged into a courtyard where buds hung heavy on dark branches. Crispin could see a door through another arch, and that's where the monk led them. A knock or two and they were inside, facing a man in his middle years with graying hair among the dark, with a ring of hair over his temple and his ears. His eyes measured Crispin and Jack and he nodded for the monk to leave them.

'Crispin Guest, you say? I do not know you.'

'I do not know why you should. I am from London. A man who solves puzzles and finds lost objects. For a fee, of course.'

'So why do you come all this way to me, young man?'

'I also work with the Lord Sheriff. Missing persons. Murder.' He presented the folded and sealed parchment the sheriffs had given him.

The monk's face opened with a gasp even as his fingers closed on the parchment. 'Brother Ralph! You have found him. Where is he?'

'His remains are with St Mary Graces in London.'

At the word 'remains' the monk eased back. 'Ah. He is dead. I feared it.'

'Did you? And what of this other dead monk?'

'You seem to know much, Master Guest. Please, sit down. May I pour you wine? I fear these circumstances have stolen my hospitality. I am Abbot Robert.'

Crispin bowed and sat. Jack stood properly behind him.

The monk first opened the parchment and read, looking up at

Crispin with pondering eyes. He left it on his desk and poured two goblets, giving one to Crispin before he, too, sat and faced him. 'Your sheriffs seem to have great confidence in you.'

Crispin raised his brows but said nothing. He could not have known what the parchment revealed without breaking the seal. He felt a measure of satisfaction that it was, at least, complimentary.

'These are ill tidings,' the abbot went on. 'I do not understand what has been happening. Two brothers killed.'

'How did the first die?'

'A knife wound. To the stomach. It took two days for him to die.' He murmured a prayer into his goblet before he looked up again.

'Was he able to say who slew him?'

'Alas, no. He was mercifully unconscious the whole time. He never awoke . . . until it was into the arms of God.'

'A pity. Have you the knife?'

He shook his head. 'There was no knife.'

'Another pity.'

'What of Brother Ralph? How did he—?'

'Also a knife wound, but to the back. Yet he seemed to know who I was, for he came directly to me and called me by my name before he succumbed to his wounds.'

'Did he? Strange. How could he have heard of you?'

'I am not without a certain amount of . . . infamy.'

The abbot looked at him anew, even sparing Jack a long appraisal. 'Well. This . . . is all very disturbing.' His hand massaged his forehead.

'Perhaps,' said Crispin, setting his goblet aside and taking the wrapped relic out of his scrip, 'this will ease some of your grief.'

He unwrapped it and the abbot shot upward from his chair and staggered toward him. 'Holy Mother of God! Where? Where did you find it?' He sunk to his knees before Crispin and took the crystal monstrance in both trembling hands.

'Your Brother Ralph brought it to me. I daresay, risking his life.'

'The Holy Blood of Christ!' He pressed his forehead to it and wept, kneeling on the floor. Jack gasped by Crispin's ear but he ignored him. The blood in the monstrance had once again caused a tingle in Crispin's fingers as he passed it to the cleric, but now that he was free of it he breathed easier.

'Thank you, Lord, for returning Your precious blood to us,' the monk went on.

Crispin grumbled. It wasn't God who'd traveled the rough and muddy road for three days with sparse meals and cold nights.

Abbot Robert wiped his face and rose, clutching the relic to his chest. 'Come, Master Guest. This is bountiful news indeed! We will feast in thankfulness of the relic's return, even as we mourn our dear brother.'

He rang a bell for his chaplain, who entered quickly as if he were listening at the door. Crispin eyed him critically. *Was he listening at the door?*

He bowed before his abbot and Abbot Robert expounded on the return of the relic and news of Brother Ralph. Both elated and concerned, the chaplain exited to tell the rest of the monks.

Abbot Robert refused to relinquish hold of the monstrance. He patted it gently, rocking it as if it were a babe. 'You see, Master Guest, we did not know what to make of the theft and the disappearance of our dear brothers. Not one of us could believe that Brother Ralph could have stolen it, though others have tried.'

'Indeed. I should like to hear of this.'

The abbot seemed overcome and younger now that good news had roused his blood. He sat by the fire again and shook his head, gazing at the relic with glistening eyes.

'In the last few months, the monastery has been burgled. We suspected ruffians from the town, unhappy souls indeed to steal from the church. Other strange events compounded and then the death of Brother Edwin. It threw us into chaos. We are men here, but we are not fighting men. We are trained in peace and the quiet contemplation of the Lord, not in war or defense. Who should break into a monastery and kill one of our brothers? It was a mystery. And then someone tried to steal the relic.'

Jack couldn't help himself and uttered an oath. The abbot ignored it.

'They did not succeed,' he went on. 'But it wasn't more than a few days later that our dear Brother Ralph went missing and the relic, too. You can imagine what we thought. May God forgive us.'

'Indeed,' said Crispin thoughtfully. 'Why would your Brother Ralph have cause to run away with your relic?'

'Greed, of course. Lust, maybe. He was seduced by a Jezebel. And yet, it can hardly be believed of so devout a soul as Brother Ralph.'

'He . . . ran off with a woman?'

'Difficult to say.'

'But if he was running off with a woman *and* the relic, why come to me? If he knew me by name, surely he would know of my reputation and that I would return the relic here.'

The abbot blinked at him silently.

'You mentioned that *brothers* went missing,' Crispin went on. 'Who else was gone?'

'Did I? A slip of the tongue.'

Crispin eyed the abbot as his fingers traced unsteadily over the beryl crystal. He left it for later. 'So this . . . Jezebel,' said Crispin. 'Do you know this woman?'

'A so-called friend of the abbey. Sybil Whitechurch. She has been known to enter the monastery precincts, which is forbidden. We realize that in many orders there is a laxity of the Rule. But in a Cistercian house the gate is a portal to the sin and corruption without. Few are allowed in. That is . . . we have patrons that must, of course, traverse inside for hospitality's sake. We had royal patronage at one time, Master Guest. But those of the outside are not allowed within without proper vetting. Like the two of you. If your request was of a simple nature, you would have been denied.'

'Then how in the world is this woman—?'

'Well . . . as a patroness . . .' He shrugged, troubled.

Crispin could well imagine. Their Rule often warred with their need to make a living. He noticed the dense flocks of sheep in the pasturelands. He knew that Hailes boasted of their sacks of fleeces. But this was no Westminster, and a monastery in the wilderness of England fought for every penny it earned. The relic brought pilgrims who paid. He wondered if the abbot had alerted any of the locals to the theft or kept it quiet, hoping that there would be no cessation of pilgrim fees. It was Canterbury all over again.

'Many a time we discovered her here,' the abbot grumbled.

'Sybil?' He caught Jack's eye. Katherine Woodleigh's niece was called Sybil. These tidings did not bode well. Perhaps she wasn't as innocent as Katherine supposed. Caught in a cloister? Maybe *she* was the one seducing Simon Wynchecombe, not the other way around. 'Do you know where Demoiselle Sybil is now?'

The abbot touched the side of his face. 'On her estates, I expect. They are not far. In Winchcombe.'

'Speaking of Winchcombe, are you acquainted with Simon Wynchecombe, a noble citizen of London and lately sheriff there?'

'Of course. He is one of our most valued patrons.'

'And would you have knowledge as to whether he is present on his estates here or not?'

'You're the second person to ask me that in a sennight.'

'Oh? Who was the other?'

'Sybil Whitechurch.'

Crispin mulled this information before the abbot rose. 'A celebratory mass is in order. Come with us, Master Guest. And bring your young squire. Let us all partake of the Lord's body and blood before we sup.'

Hungry, Crispin nevertheless agreed. He seldom partook of the holy bread of mass these days and it would be good to feed his soul before his flesh.

Crispin and Jack both shrived themselves with the generous ear of the abbot, who gave them both few prayers in penance, and then they followed the abbot to the church.

The monks assembled in the quire and Crispin and Jack were invited to sit in chairs just outside it, like lords.

Crispin knelt to receive the host and Jack followed suit behind him. They prayed silently on their knees until a monk rang a hand bell. The monks arose and Crispin and Jack with them, following them to the chevet in the apse.

There, a shrine sat solemnly between two candles in floor sconces. It was similar to shrines he had seen before, similar even to the shrine of St Thomas Becket in Canterbury. Except at the very top of the shrine was a tower of sorts and a door with a grille. The abbot himself climbed a special ladder that two monks had brought and placed beneath it, unlocked it, placed the relic within and then knelt before it a very long time.

Crispin scanned the other monks, fifteen in all, their faces mostly hidden by their cowls. What had they thought happened to the relic and their brother monk? Or *monks*, plural, for he did not believe there was a slip of the tongue at all. The abbot suspected which of his monks might be a murderer and obviously had no wish to say. Curious. A lack of discipline had allowed Katherine Woodleigh's niece the run of the abbey, and look where it had gotten them all. Crispin wondered how Simon Wynchecombe fitted into it. Had he met Sybil here in the abbey and fallen for her? Was this monk killed because he had witnessed something he shouldn't have? But what of the other who died at Crispin's door? He hadn't been stabbed three days prior and traveled all the way to London with a knife in his back. Someone in London dispatched him. Simon? This other missing brother? And if their reason for murder was to covet the relic, Crispin had seen to it that they did not get it.

Jack elbowed him hard. He squinted at the boy with a scowl. Jack gestured with his head toward the doings at the shrine, and Crispin realized he had been daydreaming without giving proper respect to the proceedings. He nodded, pressed his hands together in prayer and *tried* to contemplate the miracle before him. But his thoughts intruded again, and instead of the prayer he should have been chanting in his head, he worked on the puzzle.

When he looked up, it seemed to be over, and he and Jack held back as the monks filed out. The abbot left, but another monk approached them and bowed. 'I am Brother Thomas. I will show you to the refectory. Come.'

The monk strode forth and Crispin followed with Jack directly behind. Quietly, the monks moved single file to a door within the cloister. Once inside, the monks took their places. The abbot, sitting at the head table, motioned for Crispin and Jack to join him, but no one said a word. Sitting in their places, each monk passed platters and bowls after filling their own wooden bowls with fish, onions and pottage.

Crispin watched the eerie assemblage continue to pass their food, and once all had something on their plates, including he and Jack, the abbot intoned a Latin prayer, all bowed their heads, crossed themselves and commenced eating. Spoons scraped into

60 Jeri Westerson

bowls, benches creaked, cloth brushed cloth, but no voice lifted to break the uncomfortable silence.

Crispin knew that Cistercians, above all other monks, held great store by their silences and unnecessary talk was against the Rule. That was one of the reasons the gate was sacrosanct, why visitors were generally not allowed into the community. The fact that a woman had been present confused Crispin to his marrow.

Jack chewed but his eyes darted from face to face. The boy was not given to silences and though Jack had done a service to Crispin by pretending to be a monk at one time and certainly saw such a meal before, it was clear he held the proceedings in deep suspicion.

The food was good, though, and Crispin ate his with measured poise, finishing the excellent ale before his tablemates.

Once all had finished, the abbot rose, gestured a silent benediction over them and left the hall. He made no indication that he was interested in further discussion with Crispin, at least for the time being.

Brother Thomas, hands hidden under his black scapular, returned to stand beside Crispin. He bowed and turned, indicating Crispin should follow him.

Down the arcade and out of the cloister they went, Jack beside him. They left the cloister precincts toward a collection of cottages where, no doubt, corrodians and visitors found their rest. The monk strode to one set apart from the others and opened the door without going in. He said nothing more before bowing and walking away.

Jack poked his head inside. 'Our baggage, master.'

Crispin entered and saw that their bags were placed carefully by the two spare beds. A small fire burned in the hearth and it was warm inside. He stepped in all the way and closed the door behind him.

'That's friendly, isn't it?' said Jack, walking around the room and peering into the corners and shelves. The room was fairly stark, with only one coffer, two beds with curtains and a table and two chairs. Beyond the shutter of the back window was a privy.

'Very accommodating,' said Crispin, sitting on the bed. The mattress was stiff with straw.

'Cistercians. They don't say much.'

'It is the vow of their order. Talking is to be kept to a minimum.'

'That's a wretched life.'

'Some would say it is better for to contemplate God.'

Jack shrugged, peered into a jug and sniffed its contents. 'Well.' He turned to face his master. 'I assume we'll be investigating. Where to first, sir?'

He smiled. 'To the church, I should imagine.'

They left the warm and cozy confines of the cottage and retraced their steps back to the cloister and into the church.

It was hours before Vespers when the monks would have to return to the quire for the Divine Office, so the church was a good starting place. When they crossed the threshold and entered the cold nave with its dim shadows and distant aroma of incense permeating the stone, Jack whispered, 'What exactly are we looking for, master?'

'I don't know. Surely evidence from the theft is long gone. I should like a better look at the shrine for the relic, however.'

'Didn't you see it enough when we was praying there?'

He eyed the boy with some disdain. 'Well, Jack, I seemed to have been admonished for not paying the proper respects at the time.'

Jack smiled, abashed. 'It's just that you was looking around like some tradesman. I knew you weren't paying no heed and I didn't want that the monks should think less of you.'

Crispin returned the smile. 'I see. You were looking after my welfare, as you always do.'

With his gaze flitting across the church to each alcove and shadowed corner, Crispin led the way as they moved past the quire, past the rood and into the far apse and its chevet, where the shrine stood.

The shrine itself was bejeweled, not quite as fine as the shrine of St Thomas in Canterbury. Surely something as grand as the Blood of Christ should have a greater shrine than that of a saint, no matter how important that saint was, but Crispin well knew that though Hailes was a popular pilgrimage site, none could compete with that of St Thomas Becket, whose story seemed to compel both noble and peasant alike.

Like a very small chapel of its own, the Hailes shrine also

contained a sliver of the cross in its own monstrance. But atop, behind its grilled cage, was the Holy Blood.

Crispin looked about. No monk to guard it. Foolish. He walked up to the shrine without any interference and shook his head.

'You'd think they'd have someone guarding it,' said Jack, speaking aloud Crispin's thoughts.

'You or I would think so.'

The relic was placed high, but even a person of a shorter height would merely have to bring a stool to reach it. Breaking the lock was easy enough with an iron bar, like a poker.

'Do you think it's truly His blood, sir?'

'Is there any way of knowing for certain?'

'Someone important gifted it to the monastery. Isn't that right, Master Crispin? It's their word, then.'

'Oft times the pope verifies, lending authenticity to it.'

'But . . . what do *you* think, sir? You've seen enough of them.'

Crispin peered in through the little grille to the dull crystal housed within. The rusty red inside the beryl crystal shimmered. He shook his head. 'I have seen similar . . . but I know of a few that have been falsified. Red ochre powder mixed with oil or wax. Dry blood may flow, depending on how it is handled. Or sometimes it is goose blood and must be replenished. But this one . . .' He nearly pressed his sharp nose to the grille, recalling how its touch could make his fingers tingle. 'I don't know.'

'It is truly the Holy Blood of our Lord,' said the voice of the abbot behind them, startling them both.

Crispin turned. 'Forgive me, Lord Abbot, but I have seen my share of false relics. I do not fault my apprentice for questioning the veracity of any we encounter. And we have encountered a great deal of them.'

'So I have been told.' The abbot stood before Crispin, somewhat shorter than him, and clasped his hands over his scapular. 'I knew little about you when you first arrived, Master Guest, but I have monks here who are more worldly than I, apparently, and have since made it their task to inform me.'

'Interesting. And in so quiet an order.'

The abbot sniffed but said nothing to that.

'And so. You know I am a man who has come across many a relic.'

'And still you do not believe.'

'Is that what they told you, these silent monks of yours?'

'Is it not true?'

Crispin fixed his thumbs in his belt, flaring his cloak back with his elbows. 'True enough. Relics, for the most part, are the wishes of men who desire to be closer to God . . . without paying the cost of doing the good works that would accomplish the same thing.'

'Oh, I see. Your cynicism comes from a place of experience?'

'You know of me, so you must know my history. I spent much time at court. Make your own conclusions.'

The abbot must have done, for he added nothing.

'The Blood,' said Crispin after a time. 'With similar relics of Christ's blood, it is a dry stain within a crystal. But this one flows. Has it always been so?'

The abbot squinted at him. 'Eh? You've seen it . . . flow?'

'Yes. As it is now.'

Abbot Robert frowned and turned to Jack. 'Do *you* see it flow?'

Jack stepped forward, crushing his hands into fists with a worried expression on his outflung brows. 'Aye, my lord.'

'Well. Master Guest, it is said . . . that true penitents see the Blood in its flowing state. That those guilty of sin do not.'

'And . . . what do those see?' asked Crispin.

'They see it as a dried, rusty stain.'

The hairs on his neck rose and he swallowed, trying to soothe a suddenly dry throat. 'I see.'

The abbot approached and placed a hand on Crispin's chest, searching his eyes. 'Yes. I see you do. Would it interest you to know . . . that very few have seen it flow? Even those . . . that reside here.'

Crispin took a subtle step back so that the abbot's hand would fall away. 'And what, my Lord Abbot, do *you* see?'

The abbot looked back at the relic and lowered his head. He said nothing. He merely gestured a benediction over Crispin and wandered back into the shadows.

SEVEN

John Rykener left Crispin's side and did as bid, making his way to the Unicorn Inn on Watling Street. He looked back at Crispin's retreating figure and sighed deeply. Such an interesting man was Master Guest. And handsome, too, but without the sense that he was aware of it. Yes, a very interesting man. And he had paid John.

With coins in his purse, John did feel better, even after losing a client. And Crispin trusted him to do this job. That was always a precious thing to be prized. People liked helping Crispin. They knew he would treat them honorably.

Strange. He doubted they would have been as eager had he still been a lord.

He felt like whistling but when he was garbed as Eleanor he always took on the persona, which meant a different kind of comportment. He was slim and fine-boned, with pale skin and cloudy gray eyes. He'd watched women all his life – came early into the care and employ of Elizabeth Bronderer, an embroideress, who taught him what he knew of the stitchery trade . . . *and* of the other, though the more extensive tutelage had come from Anna, the whore of a former servant of Sir Thomas Blount. She knew things and taught him such that he could fool any man that he was a woman. Though, admittedly, few men seemed to care that he was a man. Probably even delighted in it. Or so his purse often told him.

Thinking of his purse put him in a mind of practical matters. If he was to be a lady's maid to this woman, this Katherine Woodleigh, then he needed his shaving kit. It wouldn't do to sprout a day's worth of beard if he was to play a woman.

He pivoted sharply and headed toward Candlewick Street to the place atop a wick-maker, the highest attic room with a ladder leaning against the wall its only access. He clutched a rung and glanced around. No one looking. With one hand, he hiked up his skirts and carefully climbed. Once he reached the top, he had to let the skirts fall to grab his key from his girdle. He unlocked the shutter to his entry, pulled it open and climbed clumsily inside. Quickly, he scooped up his toiletries into his scrip, grabbed a bit of embroidery and put some of his money from his purse into the jar he kept on a shelf. After smoothing his gown, he commenced climbing back down.

It was only a bowshot from his lodgings to Watling, first crossing Walbrook Street where Candlewick became Budge Row. He could see the sign of the Unicorn up ahead when Budge became Watling. He straightened himself again, coyly smiling at men who eyed him with a smirking wink. He made a note that there were men a-plenty near the inns who might want a bit of sport and were willing to pay for it.

Raising his chin, he entered the Unicorn and scanned the room. Wide arched beams upheld the roof and the eye was drawn to the large hearth in the center of the back wall. It was wonderfully warm inside and he felt his muscles relax. A man who looked to be the innkeeper approached and John's hand shot up to his veil, pulling it to partially hide his face. His voice naturally lifted to a higher tone when he was Eleanor, and he offered the innkeeper a beguiling smile. 'Good sir, I am looking for Katherine Woodleigh. Could you be so kind as to tell me if she is here?'

'And who would you be, lass?'

'I was hired as her maid.'

He looked John over and decided. 'Aye.' He pointed up the stairs. 'Last door at the end of the gallery.'

'I thank you,' he answered with a curtsey. He strode across the inn and climbed the stairs. Moving with perfect poise and elegance – years ago it had taken many months to master it – he took a sly look back to see the effect on the innkeeper. It was as he suspected. The innkeeper had watched him move all the way up the stairs with a leer still visible on his face.

Those months were not wasted, he thought to himself with a chuckle. It never ceased to amuse him.

He strode to the end of the gallery, postured before the door and knocked.

There was only a moment's pause before it opened.

A woman, with blue eyes, auburn hair and an upturned nose,

stared at him up and down. With an imperious tilt to her chin, she asked, 'Who are you?'

John curtseyed. 'My lady. I am Eleanor. Crispin Guest sent me to be your maid, as it seems . . .' he looked past her shoulder into the empty room, '. . . you have none.'

'He what?'

'Hired me. He had to leave London for a sennight or so, and bid me care for you as your escort and protector.'

She placed a fist at her hip and measured John again under lowered lids. 'Did he? Protector?'

'Indeed. For though I am slight of frame I am stronger than I look.'

'*He* paid you, you say?'

'Yes.'

She began to close the door when he stopped her with his hand. She looked up at him as she pushed harder, but John held it fast. 'Trustworthy as God's own angels is Crispin Guest. If he says he'll do a thing, you can rely upon it that he will. And so when he asks, his friends do.'

The woman's suspicious glare did not abate.

John gave her his most beguiling smile. 'Er . . . may I come in? You can test me, if you'd like.'

'Since *he* paid you,' said the woman, stepping aside, allowing him entrance. It looked to be a very ordinary room: a coffer, a table and two chairs, a bed with curtains and an alcove with a smaller cot for a servant. It wasn't a rich room but it was larger than his own.

He turned to her and rested his hands demurely before him. 'Anything you need, my lady?'

She had a strange look in her eye and the faintest of smiles on her lips replaced her suspicious expression. 'The hearth is lit. Fuel lies beside it. I have water in the bucket and I have just eaten. There seems to be nothing I need . . . at the moment.'

'Would you have me clear the tray, then?'

'Not yet. Tell me, what exactly did Master Guest say? Where was he bound?'

'To Hailes, I think he said.'

She stopped for a moment. 'Hailes? What a curious vocation, has Master Guest.'

'Indeed. I have known him for years.'

'Tell me about yourself, then. How does Master Guest know you?'

'Our acquaintance was so many years ago now. You see . . .' He sidled closer, confidentially. 'When Master Guest was . . . was banished from court,' he said in a loud whisper, 'it was I who took him in, helped him. He was like a lost lamb. He knew nothing of caring for himself, and him completely without funds. It was a sore thing that the king did to him . . . not that treason should be taken lightly. But Master Guest has proven his worth time and time again. And who could truly blame him for wanting his mentor, the Duke of Lancaster, on the throne.'

'Surely King Richard.'

He ducked his head. 'And long live the king,' he muttered.

'Indeed. So you helped him find shelter and an occupation?'

'I helped him with shelter and food, as did others in London. He found his own way to a vocation. He is now the celebrated Tracker, but that wasn't always the case.'

'No? What else did he do?'

'Dear me. He foundered. For he was proud and could not find work with any noble house. He was truly shunned by them. Desperation and hunger drove him to the job of a gong farmer, cleaning the privies along the embankment. And then I think he worked as a henchman – not a very nice task. He worked for a time as a scribe.'

'How did he become a Tracker?'

Katherine's eyes shone with interest and John got even closer, clasping his hands together in excitement. 'Well! I heard that he was hired to find a lost necklace . . . and found that the lady in question – from whom it was stolen – was murdered. He found the necklace *and* the culprit. People started coming to him and he found he liked the work. He even recovered some stolen items for Westminster Abbey. He is clever at what he does.'

'You admire him.'

'Oh, I do.'

'And are a little in love with him.'

John felt his cheeks warm. It wasn't often anyone could make him blush. 'My lady! Well . . . I think every woman who meets him is a little in love with him. Though he is never for the keeping.'

'I see. He's a dallier, is he?'

'That would be telling tales, my lady.'

Katherine smiled but it soon faded. 'I cannot believe he has struck out in the middle of a client's task. My errand is urgent.'

'But my impression was, my lady, that his venturing out of London had everything to do with your mission.'

'Oh. Well, then. I must be patient. But it is a sore thing when so much is at stake.'

'My lady, may I . . . may I enquire of the nature of your mission?'

Her cheeks paled and she cast a glance toward the fire. 'My niece. She ran off with an unsuitable man, a man who also stole my fortune. It is dire that Master Guest succeed or I am ruined and so is my kin. The man is married.'

'Oh! What a cur! My lady, you can be certain that if Crispin Guest is on the trail he will succeed!'

She nodded, wiping a tear from her eye. 'I am gratified to hear it.' She shook her head and sank to one of the chairs by the fire. 'He is my last hope. If he does not succeed, then it is a nunnery for me, for I don't know where else to go.'

John knelt beside her and touched the chair. 'No, my lady. Surely with your beauty a man can be found to marry you.'

'Beauty is one thing, but an impoverished woman to wife? A useless ornament, I would be.'

'Surely a burgess would welcome you. A pretty thing to decorate his shop. You can read and write, can you not?'

She nodded solemnly. 'I can. But my family history . . . there was a scandal at court. The taint of it runs deep.'

John slowly rose. He unbuttoned his cloak and hung it by the door and then unbuttoned his hood and caplet, hanging that on the same peg. He removed a small bit of embroidery from his scrip, careful not to dislodge his shaving things, and sat in the chair opposite her. It was comfortable with its high back. He showed her the embroidery he had started, a series of florets weaving into a long pattern along the edge of some fabric. It was to be the hem of a woman's chemise. 'Well, a nunnery is no place for the likes of you. I can teach you a proper vocation. See here.'

Katherine stood and leaned over him. She smelled faintly of gilly flower. John approved. Some women drenched themselves in odd spices and floral scents, enough to choke an animal. Her scent was subtle and appealing. He thought he'd like to try it.

'What a fine hand you have, Eleanor.'

'Thank you.' His long fingers seemed suited to the needle and thread. 'It is my other vocation . . . besides being a lady's maid.'

'Indeed.' She sighed. 'But I was never good at stitchery and I simply gave it up, except for those repairs that one must do.'

'I could teach you. You would not have to choose a nunnery. A woman must be wise and wily to make her way in the world.'

Her eyes glinted with something like rising hope. 'You are a marvel, aren't you? I can see why Master Guest approves of you.' She scooted her chair closer to John and peered over his shoulder as John pressed the fine needle into the fabric and continued the stitch he had started, patiently teaching it to her.

They had settled in. John coaxed her to talk of her troubles and her family's past as they worked. She mentioned that a former London sheriff was mixed up in it somehow and he ticked his head at the audacity.

He had given her a section of his cloth to work on and, even though he would have to pull the stitches out later, he felt it was worth the time to help Crispin's client. How the nobility suffered in their ignorance! Crispin with his poor knowledge of everyday life and Kat Woodleigh (for she bid John call her so) and her poor understanding of her choices. John considered, for not the first time, that he was glad of his own status, for he seemed always to find work for himself, whether in stitchery or on his back. Though he knew that the older he got, both might not be as viable. Still, there were options. More than once he considered getting *himself* a husband, though that might prove a delicate prospect.

He found, despite Kat's dire circumstances, that she was a merry woman and even got her to admit an interest in Crispin.

'He is a handsome man, true,' she said, 'but as poor a prospect as myself. Sixpence a day – and few scattered days they appear to be – would not sustain a wife and children.'

'That may be true. But when two work it fattens the income.'

'Though,' she said, setting down her bit of cloth and gazing distantly into the corner, 'one need not marry to, er, enjoy the company of a man.'

John laughed and pushed at her lightly. 'Madam, you are a "Kat" indeed!'

'Confess it. You would try it with Master Guest if you could.'

He sighed. 'Aye, 'tis true. I would. But . . . I am not the kind of woman Master Guest prefers.'

'Oh? And what is his preference?'

John smiled and ducked his head beneath his veil. 'Well, truth to tell, *you* are the kind to catch his eye. A clever woman with beauty seems to trap our Master Crispin more often than not.'

'Listen to us. A pair of gossips. We shall have to shrive ourselves.'

'Oh, lady, if I shrived m'self for all my thoughts, I'd be in the confessional still.'

She laughed. It was a good sound. John was glad to take her from her troubles if but for a little while, for soon enough she would remember them again and her smile would fade.

Their days moved on much like the rest. Some sewing, some taking the air in the courtyard, some drinking in the inn hall.

When nightfall came on the fourth day, John slept fitfully on the uncomfortable cot. So it was easy for him to rise early, as was his custom, yawning, to see to the fires.

Kat was softly breathing in her bed when he checked on her. He felt his chin and secretly took up his shaving kit, retreating to the secrecy of the privy to shave in the dark as he did every day, once in the morning and once at night, so as to leave no stubble at all. He did so slowly to avoid nicking himself, but used careful fingers to search out the stubble and smite them with his sharp blade. Satisfied, he tucked blade and soap in his scrip, washed his face in the trough and begged porridge and bread from the innkeeper. He waited for the tray and shared a cup of ale with the innkeeper while the man's wife fetched the food. The man smiled and winked at John enough for him to catch the innkeeper's meaning, but he didn't know if he could reasonably get away from Kat and still act as her protector.

He began to plot just how he could do that when the innkeeper's wife arrived and elbowed her husband. He abruptly moved away and John thanked them both, took up the tray and climbed the stairs.

He shouldered his way into the room and set the tray on the table. Taking up the poker, he urged the fire again and turned to the bed – but she wasn't there. 'Must be at the privy,' he mused, and went to the window to have a look.

She was not at the privy but on her way down the road, heading west.

'What, by all the saints! I'm supposed to be protecting you, lass.'

He grabbed his cloak and hurried down the steps after her. But even as he trotted to catch up, he slowly hung back. 'Now what would Crispin do?' he murmured to himself, sidestepping a sway-backed mule drawing a cart.

The working day had begun but the market bell had not yet rung for business to commence. The sun had barely risen, casting golden light on the shops and houses. Prime had rung in the nearby churches an hour ago at least. Too early for shopping. Where was she bound?

He decided to hang back and merely follow her to see. He was certain this was the correct course.

She disappeared and emerged from the shadows of the towering shops, winding down the crooked streets of London. She never stopped or lingered anywhere, for her destination was clear – wherever that was. John kept her in his sight and stayed back as far as he dared. Though shops weren't open yet, shoppers awaited them and apprentices were busy sweeping steps, fetching piggins and fuel. Street peddlers were milling, calling out their wares, usually food. Many partook of the warm meat pies, skewered meats and ale. John would have stopped, too, but his quarry was moving ahead of him too swiftly.

It was only when she passed through Ludgate that he was certain she was bound for Westminster. At least, it was the only destination he could reckon.

Now it was a little more treacherous keeping out of her sight as there were fewer along the road, but once they reached Charing Cross he could hide himself among the throng. Relieved she didn't enter the palace – for he could not have followed her there – he watched her reach the cloister gate at Westminster Abbey.

He hid himself around the corner of a shop, its rough plaster tugging at the threads of his cloak. At length, a monk arrived at the gate, looked hastily about and unlocked it. He grabbed her hand and tugged her inside, disappearing into the shadows.

'God's nails,' he muttered. What mischief was here? A secret meeting in the cloister? A woman? With a monk? Well, he'd certainly trafficked enough himself in cloisters, with monks, priests and nuns paying for his services. The clerical class kept him fed and housed, to be sure.

But she did not seem to be the sort. Still, a woman had to use every wile she had to make her way in the world.

He shook his head. 'Hush, John,' he admonished himself. Perhaps it was perfectly innocent. She might know this monk. He might be kin. Surely she needed advice on these dread matters. But why didn't she wait for John to escort her? After all, that was why Crispin hired him. But he saw how wily Master Guest was, for perhaps he wasn't hired so much to escort and protect her but to keep an eye on her.

What was he to do now? Wait, he supposed. And so he did. He leaned against the wall, getting as comfortable as he might while keeping an eye on the cloister gate.

His stomach growled after not too much time had passed, but finally he saw her approach again and he slid into the shadows until only a sliver of him might be visible.

The monk bowed to her once he closed the gate behind her and walked away. She made no backward glance as she hurried toward London. John kept pace behind her, wondering if she would make any other stops. Once they passed again through Ludgate and it didn't look as if she were going to stop, he realized he had to get back to the Unicorn before she did.

He picked up his skirts and ran. Ducking up Old Dean's Lane to Paternoster Row, he ran hard along West Cheap toward Mercery. He ignored the stares and oaths as he pushed past people hawking their wares for sale. The market bell had finally rung and shops had opened their window shutters, their little stalls open for business. John skirted past a fat priest and his dogs held on a short leash by a retainer, begging their mercy as he went. He cut down a lane to Watling and scurried up the muddy row to the Unicorn. Shoes now muddy, he stomped up the stairs, skirts lifted high, got to the door and flung it open. Out of breath, he slid out of his shoes, had just enough time to scrape the mud off them out of the window, arranged himself in a chair before the fire and controlled his heavy breathing just as the door opened.

He stood, putting on a face of exasperation. 'My lady! How am I to serve as your escort when you go out of your way to elude me?'

'Oh. I am sorry, Eleanor. I beg your mercy. But . . . there was simply something I had to do and it could not wait.'

'Truly? You were gone for hours.'

'Not hours, surely.'

'Well, nearly so. I was worried. Are you all right?'

'Yes, I am. Don't fret, Eleanor. I will not do it again, I vow it.'

'Good. Well, there lies your mixtum. It is cold now.'

'Forgive me, again.'

'I'll fetch you warm pottage, shall I?'

'Please don't bother. I'll just take the bread and ale.'

John grumbled as he set the board before her, pouring the ale from the jug into a dented metal goblet.

He set to his chores, until later in the day when they ventured downstairs to take the air and perhaps the news from the inn's occupants in the great hall.

Later, as the noon bells rung for sext, they sat in their room, John at his sewing and Kat trying out a stitch on one of her old gowns. The warm room shuttered John's eyes. He let his head fall forward once before jerking it up to rouse himself. But it was of no use. Sleep overtook him and his head drooped.

The scream awoke him. He was nearly to his feet when he heard Kat scream a second time. He tried to turn but a suffocating bag dropped over his head. He struggled when a gag wound round the bag and over his mouth. He yanked at the bag but a rope yanked his arms to his sides against the chair. He struggled, kicking, twisting, but he could do nothing while he listened helplessly to the sounds of Kat fighting and crying out, and finally being smuggled out of the room to a dread fate.

EIGHT

'Haven't we done what we came to do?' said Jack. Crispin was aware that the boy had been watching him a long time as he contemplated the high arches of the apse, the shadows, the entrances. 'Can't we go home now?'

'You, who are ever anxious to travel and see the world, would leave this place?'

'Monasteries,' Jack snorted. 'They make me skittery. Monks creeping about, quiet as shadows. It isn't natural.'

'*To pray is to work, and to work is to pray*, Jack. There is a purpose in it. Do you mean to say that you would not desire to be a corrodian in a monastery?'

'When I retire, I hope that my children will care for me.'

'And so they shall. May you have many.'

Jack always brightened at talk of his betrothed. But that brightness was brief. 'We returned the relic.'

'But have not yet talked to this Sybil Whitechurch. Nor found a reason why Brother Edwin was killed. Or that another monk went missing but the abbot and none of the monks will reveal who.'

'Brother Edwin was killed because whoever wanted to steal the relic caught him there. He encountered the thief, is all.'

'So why was he killed in the cloister and not at the shrine?'

'He staggered there.'

'Leaving no trail of blood.'

'You've only their word there was no blood trail.'

'Why, Jack! So suspicious of holy brothers?'

He pulled himself up and raised his chin. 'Like you, sir, I suspect everyone.'

Crispin nodded. 'It is best to do so. You will find yourself less disappointed later.' Crispin glanced over his shoulder but didn't find any brothers lingering in the shadows. 'We must go to the Woodleigh estates and talk with Sybil's servants. Perhaps they have some idea where she might have gone.'

'And then to Wynchecombe's estates?'

'Yes.'

Crispin was forced to find a monk who could point out the directions to the Woodleigh manor and he and Jack saddled their horses and set out.

It was only a few miles up the northern road, and so they allowed the horses to amble along. Jack was relaxed on the saddle, body rolling gently with the horse's gait. 'Master Crispin, do you think that Master Wynchecombe is *not* guilty of murdering them monks?'

Crispin shook his head and urged his horse down the left fork as instructed. He could see a manor house just beyond the hedgerows but no smoke lingered near its chimneys. 'That, Jack, I have not yet concluded. There isn't enough evidence either way. It's certainly possible, I suppose. Anyone can become angry and Wynchecombe can be baited so easily. But a judicious man stops before he does true harm in his rage. It is the mark of an intelligent man. *Honors and rewards fall to those who show their good qualities in action.*'

'Aristotle,' Jack muttered.

'Yes. Wynchecombe is a man of business. A respected alderman and armorer.'

'Other respected men have been murderers before.'

'True enough.' He fell silent as they crested the last rise of the road that led down to the porter's gate of the Woodleigh estates. The arched stone gateway stood solitary and quiet. No man stood guard there. Crispin proceeded down the lane toward the modest structure. Certainly much smaller than Crispin's own lost estates in Sheen, the whole compound was surrounded by a wall whose gate hung open and broken. A cobblestone courtyard separated the house from the stables. Their horses clattered through the open gate but no one came to greet them.

Jack hopped down from his mount and took both horses' leads. Dismounting, Crispin stood by the well before the house and scanned upward toward the higher storey with its shutters closed tight. There were two chimneys, one at each end of the house. A stone foundation, dark timbers and aged daub between. There was no sound from the structure, no animal in the courtyard.

'I don't like the looks of this, sir,' said Jack.

'Nor do I.' Jack led the horses to a post and wrapped the reins around it. He joined Crispin at the front door. Crispin glanced once at the anxious face of his apprentice before he reached up and knocked.

The hollow sound rang out but even after waiting a respectful time there was no answering sound. He knocked again, louder, but the result was the same. He took hold of the latch and pushed. The door opened easily.

'Careful, sir.'

In answer, Crispin drew his sword. He pushed the door open, letting it swing on its own as he stood poised in the doorway, sword held aloft. 'Hello! Is anyone there?'

The place smelled musty, closed, unused. And was. The floor was covered in dust and what scant furniture there was also lay under a powdering. Even dried leaves were strewn about and there were bird skeletons lying scattered in the fireplace where they had, no doubt, fallen in from the chimney.

He moved forward toward the dark hearth. Touching the stones of the fireplace arch, he could tell they had been cold for some time.

'What is this?'

Katherine Woodleigh had said they were without means but this was more extreme than he had bargained for. No wonder she was so anxious to find Wynchecombe if he had stolen from her. But that made little sense either. Why would he have need to steal from her? Though, if she owed him money, he could well see Wynchecombe exacting his payment in so callous a manner, especially if he harbored a grudge against the family. But surely stealing away her niece would negate such extreme measures, wouldn't it? And what did he expect to do with this niece? He could not offer her the sanctity of marriage, for he was already married. Keep her? But where? Winchcombe, he supposed. Such things were done by noblemen. He had known them. But Wynchecombe was not so wealthy that he could afford to keep both houses running at once.

Crispin moved into the room and stopped. The joists above his head creaked. The glance back at Jack was unnecessary. The boy was at his heels as Crispin made for the stairs. He took them two at a time, stopping at the top to listen. Tilting his head, he heard the floor creak again and moved quickly to the room in question. Casting open the door, he presented the sword first.

An old man, ragged and crooked, screamed and cowered back. Crispin immediately lowered the blade but didn't sheath it. 'Who are you?'

'An old man. A servant here.'

'Where has everyone gone?'

When it didn't look as if Crispin would strike, the old man lowered his hands but still took a shuffling step back. 'Peace, good sir. Mercy.'

Looking down at his blade, Crispin saw the foolishness of keeping it ready and sheathed it smartly. He opened his empty hands. 'I mean you no harm, old man. Tell me. What happened to the Woodleighs?'

'Such a rich house,' he said shakily. His cloudy eyes roved wildly about the empty room. 'Even the king stopped here once. It was a grand thing, that. King Edward. Long live the king.'

Crispin caught Jack's eye as he made his way into the room around its perimeter.

'But the family is not here now,' Crispin insisted. 'Where are they?'

'Scattered to the wind. The scandal,' he whispered, gesturing with a clawed hand.

'Yes, there was a scandal at court. But that was over ten years ago. Where is Sybil Whitechurch? Have you seen her of late?'

He looked at Crispin with even more confusion than he already wore. He squinted and raised those curled fingers to his face. 'Eh? Who did you say?'

'Sybil. She was the younger woman. Katherine Woodleigh's niece.'

The man put a hand to his cheek. 'That must be the child, eh? Such a pretty child.'

'And this is the home of Katherine Woodleigh, is it not?'

'Aye. A strange and quiet mistress,' he said vaguely. 'She comes and she goes. All of them left, didn't they? All the servants but myself. The Pykes, the Harkers, the Howards. All gone. Left me alone.'

Crispin restrained his sigh. 'But the niece, man. When was the last time you saw her?'

'The niece? Dear me. The house is so quiet without the children. And the Pykes were so good with them, weren't they? Such good company. So merry. Where have the other servants gone?'

Stepping forward, Crispin took the man's arm gently, walked him to a chair and carefully prodded him into it. 'Sit, old man. Now, tell me. How long has it been since the servants left?'

'Well . . . let me see. It was Candlemas last. Aye, Candlemas.'

'Are you telling me that all the servants left last month?'

'No, *last* February. It's been over a year I've been alone, tending to the old house m'self.'

The room was cold and dusty. It hadn't been swept in many a day. Maybe since the servants left. Did the old man light any fires? He was wrapped in a cloak, a hood, and another wrap over that. His clawed fingers were red and raw.

'Who waits on Mistress Katherine?'

'She waits on herself, when she is here, which is seldom.'

'And what of Mistress Sybil?'

He dropped his forehead on his palm and rubbed. 'I do not know that name.'

Crispin straightened and looked down at the man, still rubbing his forehead. 'She is the young niece of Mistress Katherine. Perhaps she did not live here in the fullness of the year, but certainly part of it.'

Still rubbing, the old man began to hum.

Impatient now, Crispin tapped his shoulder. 'The girl. When was the last time you saw her?'

'She never stayed long. She'd take what she could from the coffers – clothes and such – and leave. Leave me all alone.'

And left you mad. What a wretched house this is. He felt worse than ever that he had allowed her to pay his debts when she herself was in such dire straits. But he certainly recognized the pride in her. He often wore it himself.

He crouched beside the old man. 'But I'm worried, you see, about the young one. The girl, Sybil. At the monastery; they said she often went there.'

'Oh, no. That is not proper. That cannot be.'

'And yet the monks say it is so.'

'Do they? Well . . . she often . . . left.'

'And the last time. Was there a man with her? Do you know Simon Wynchecombe?'

'The tall one? London alderman?'

'Yes, him. He was with her?'

The man stopped rubbing and looked up, but not at Crispin, not at anything within the room. 'Aye. Sometimes. He was here. And she without a lady's maid.' He ticked his head.

'When was the last time you saw him?'

'The ides.'

That signifies, he thought. That would be about the right time.

'What can you tell me about the girl, Sybil? Was she flirtatious? Cautious? Cunning?'

He turned his head and looked up at Crispin, searching his face with rheumy eyes. 'You keep saying that name and I tell you I have never heard it before.'

'Then what did you call the other woman who spent time here with Mistress Katherine?'

He leaned over to squint at Crispin. 'But that's what I am trying to tell you, young man. There *is* no other woman.'

NINE

For a tantalizing moment, Crispin almost believed the old servant. But spending more time with the man and questioning him proved useless. Crispin had to conclude that the man was addled and simply couldn't answer fully even if he tried. It was maddening.

He had taken Jack aside and sent him to make a search of the house, and his apprentice had concluded that two chambers at least showed signs of recent occupation.

In the courtyard and mounting their horses, Crispin, even as frustrated as he was, felt a bit sorry for the old man. Perhaps he should have sent Jack to fetch the man some firewood . . . but no. He wasn't paid enough for that sort of charity and he longed to leave for London again.

'The man's a fool,' said Jack after they had ridden up the lane past the gatehouse. Once at the main road, they turned southwest toward Winchcombe.

'Is he? He was addled, to be sure. But he seemed to be certain that there was no Sybil Whitechurch.'

'But that cannot be, master. The monks have plainly seen her, and Katherine Woodleigh is in search of her; paid you good silver for that, and she can plainly use the coin. Add to the fact of *two* chambers in use . . .'

'Yes. She is desperate, to be sure. That Wynchecombe would steal from her under these circumstances . . .'

'He's a cruel man,' he said with a scowl. 'This whole adventure leaves a bad taste in me mouth.'

Crispin had to agree, but his thoughts kept drifting toward the monastery and the murder of one monk, a theft and then the death of another in London. What did any of that – if at all – have to do with this business? It seemed an extraordinary coincidence if they were separate affairs. And just as he thought it, Jack voiced the same concerns. The boy was quick, he'd give him that. He wondered if he could see the pride in Crispin's face.

'Why would he kill them monks? And why steal the relic?'

'You think the former sheriff would steal a relic?'

He shrugged. 'Why not? He wasn't put off by murder.'

'But why steal it? Surely a relic such as that would be well known. How could he boast of having it in his household when all would know – his servants, his friends – what it is and from where it came? They'd know him for a thief.'

'You have the right of it. That don't make sense.'

'Unless he would choose not to display it. Keep it as a secret.'

'Does God bestow his gifts to those who steal them?'

'As you know, Jack, that has always been my greatest argument against the power of relics; that God would not allow them to be used by the unfaithful . . .'

'Or unrepentant,' he said quietly.

Crispin glanced sidelong at his apprentice and slowly nodded. 'Perhaps. But we are moving away from the main point, that monk that went all the way to London. And another one missing about which the abbot will not speak. If Wynchecombe intended to steal the relic for whatever reason, why not take it after he stabbed the poor fellow?'

Jack adjusted his seat and absently stroked the long mane. 'Then did the *monk* steal it, or did Master Wynchecombe?'

'Hmm. It would make more sense if the monk had. But why come to London? Just to see me? And to what end?'

'Because the poor bastard knew Master Wynchecombe was on his trail.'

'But why was he on his trail? Because Simon was trying to recover it? But he was already stealing away with Sybil. Why would he waste precious time chasing after a thieving monk? And again, if he was close enough to stab him – in the *back*, mind – why not close enough to take back the relic? Yet this monk, this Brother Ralph, came to me. For protection? To protect the relic?'

Jack shivered. 'It's strange, isn't it, master? Gives me a chill to think on it.'

Crispin rode silently for a time. Thoughts of the relic itself swirled in his head. Quietly, he asked, 'Jack . . . *you* saw the blood flow, did you not? In the crystal.'

Jack's voice dropped to a solemn tenor. 'Aye, master. As sure as I'm seeing you now. Is it true, then? The blood only flows for repentant eyes? Even . . . sinless?'

'The abbot did not see it flow,' he said thoughtfully. 'Odd that he would admit it to me.'

'It's your reputation, sir.'

He twisted on the saddle to look back at the boy. 'What do you mean by that?'

'Nothing bad, Master Crispin. I meant your reputation . . . with relics.'

'Oh.' He turned back toward the road, curling the reins around his hand.

'He knows – as does anyone – that these relics seem to come into your hands, and that you are faithful to them. God trusts you.'

Crispin snorted. He had burned one, and let others fall out of his hands whether knowingly or by those deceiving him. And faithful? He wore about him a healthy cloak of skepticism where they were concerned. Too many false relics had crossed his path to believe in every one of them. And yet . . . He touched his scrip. He kept a certain thorn within, and though he tried not to think about it too often he still felt a strange sense of peace that it was on his person.

'But that is a long way to go to keep it safe,' said Crispin. 'All the way to London. Surely there are others in the district the monk could have gone to for succor.'

'To one like Master Wynchecombe, you mean?'

'You make a compelling argument, Jack.'

Jack drew his cloak about him. 'Travel is interesting, master, but I don't like being so far from home, so far from familiar surroundings.'

'You miss your betrothed, eh? It won't be long now. We'll have gleaned all the information we can, and then get back to London as soon as we might. I should like to know about that missing monk, though. No one will say. Perhaps I *have* gotten it wrong. Perhaps it was merely the slip of the abbot's tongue.'

'It may be so, sir.'

A scattering of houses appeared between the hills and copses. He could hear church bells. Probably the abbey of Winchcombe. He trotted forward anxiously, wanting to get to the former sheriff's estate and get this business over with. He was feeling his years because, like Jack, these days he longed for the comfort of home, such as it was. A real home and hearth was something he now had, for his circumstances had changed for the better only last year. And though not anywhere near what he used to enjoy on his own estates, having more than one room seemed a luxury, something that he never could have imagined for himself just a few scant years ago. A man in disgrace as he was, who had lost all, had no right to be particular. But old habits – and desires – died hard.

He crossed himself, thinking on it, before trotting his mount toward the first house and to the man in the garden, tending to it with his hoe.

'You there, man!' he said in a tone he had always used as a lord. 'Can you tell me which is the house of Simon Wynchecombe, late of London?'

The man looked up. His hood shaded his eyes though little he needed it on so cloudy an afternoon. 'This is Master Wynchecombe's house, m'lord.'

Crispin raised his eyes to the decidedly humble dwelling. It was nothing like Simon's grand house in London. Wynchecombe seemed to have come from modest beginnings . . . and promptly forgot them. Well, a house was a house, and Crispin gave another thought to the derelict Woodleigh estates.

'Is Master Wynchecombe at home?'

The man set one end of the hoe in the dirt and leaned on it. 'Master Wynchecombe has not been at home here, sir, since a sennight. Maybe more.'

'When he is at home, does he make many journeys to Hailes?'

'Aye, sir. That is usually his destination . . . when he is alone.'

'Meaning, when his wife does not accompany him?'

The man licked his lips anxiously, nodding. He glanced over his shoulder toward the direction of Hailes. 'He . . . he is a patron of the abbey.'

'Of course. Does he . . . is he accompanied by anyone else when he returns here?'

The man suddenly looked Crispin over. 'Begging your mercy, m'lord, but who are you to enquire?'

'I am of London myself. I am an old acquaintance of Master Wynchecombe's, in the days he was sheriff.'

'I see.' He scratched his head through his hood. 'Well, sir, he . . . he sometimes had someone with him.'

'A woman?'

The man looked around and slowly nodded.

'Was the woman Sybil Whitechurch?'

He looked at Crispin sidelong and shook his head. 'It was that Woodleigh woman, sir.'

'I see. Well, thank you.'

But before Crispin could turn his horse, the man called out: 'Would you have word of Master Wynchecombe, sir? His wife has sent a missive. He isn't in London.'

'No. In fact, I have been looking for him myself. Is it strange his disappearing?'

The man picked up his hoe and shrugged. 'I only tend to him here, sir. I don't know his London habits. But when he is not here with his wife, he is often gone on some errand. The house is seldom occupied. His son, Sir John, is said to be taking over here soon.'

'I see. Thank you.' He would have offered the man a coin for his time but he had so few of them in his purse. He scolded himself for feeling guilty about it. Instead, he aimed his horse back toward Hailes.

'Are we leaving then?' asked Jack once they turned back up the road.

'Yes, Jack. I would see the relic once more and the place where the monk was killed. And then we can be on our way.'

Jack seemed to trot his mount faster and it was Crispin who had to keep up with him.

When they reached the monastery, Crispin thanked the stableman for taking their horses and moved immediately toward the cloister. Though the monks glared at him with disapproving eyes, none said a word. Crispin had never been so happy for a vow of silence.

He strode to the place the monk was said to have been killed. Stabbed in the belly. It was between two carrels in view of the cloister's greensward. The flagged stone walkway had been scrubbed clean of his blood. But no one had seen anything. It had been right before the Divine Office of sext and most of the monks had already made their way to the quire. Clearly, whoever had done it had chosen a perfect time when they would not be noticed . . . or it was an extraordinary coincidence.

Crispin didn't believe in those.

A cold wind swept through, shuddering the budding trees and herb garden. The grass was wet, as was the flagged stone of the cloister walk from a sprinkling rain. It smelled of damp tombstones.

Brother Edwin would have been unarmed. Even if he meant to attack, a man skilled in fighting, as Wynchecombe likely was, could have fended him off. Why kill him? And why say nothing? He could simply claim it was self-defense, and as a wealthy patron and alderman of London, he would surely be believed.

If Wynchecombe had killed him, there was more to it than this.

A shadow fell over the shiny wet floor. 'Let us see the relic one last time,' he said to Jack, 'and then bid our farewells to the abbot.'

Jack followed as they made their way back into a side door of the church, up the nave, around the quire and to the apse. The candles standing in their floor sconces flickered with a draft. The only other light came from a tall window with glass, painted with a Christ figure. The chevet was cold like stone, permeating the wool of his cote-hardie and his cloak. His gaze traveled up the spiring shrine to the very top where the monstrance stood pride of place. The gold cross atop it gleamed, and the blood, that he could barely see from his position below it, sat as a sluggish deep russet liquid at the bottom of the beryl crystal.

Crispin stared at it, as he had stared at many a relic, wishing it to reveal itself simply by the power of his observation. But was he not already seeing it for what it was? For it was liquid he saw, not the rusty stain Abbot Robert intimated *he* observed.

His shoulders convulsed with a chill. The place was cold, after all.

Turning abruptly, he spat out a, 'Come, Jack,' and headed toward the abbot's chamber while he instructed Jack to see to their things in their lodgings.

The abbot mumbled his muted gratitude again to Crispin but did not escort him to the door, nor did he call for any of his monks to do so. That satisfied, for there was always something uncomfortable about the celibate. Oh, he liked Brother Eric from Westminster Abbey well enough. Years of acquaintance had brushed away his discomfort. And Abbot William de Colchester was growing on him, just as Crispin, apparently, was growing on the staid and serious abbot. But there was a reason that walls surrounded a monastery. Their ways, though pious and humble, were not for everyone.

Crispin drew his cloak about him as he walked through the cloister arcade, out of the arch and toward the gate. He waited there for Jack, and when he heard a step behind him, he turned, expecting his apprentice. Instead, it was a monk in his white habit, head bowed, cowl covering his features.

'You are Crispin Guest,' he said, speaking in a breathy voice and standing some few yards away.

'Yes.'

The monk glanced cautiously over his shoulder but did not approach any closer. 'Then you know of Sybil Whitechurch.'

Crispin moved toward the monk but stopped when the monk took a step back. 'What do you know of her, brother?'

He sighed and looked down, hiding his face completely. 'A
Jezebel. A temptress.'

'Yes, I'm getting that impression.'

Suddenly the man looked up. The reflection of the weakened
sun on the wet walkway flashed across his face. A young face.
Smooth with eyes full of innocence and youth. 'Then you've
talked to the others.'

'Why have you not talked to me before this?'

'It wasn't my place. I am the newest monk here.'

God preserve me. He sighed. 'Well, you are talking to me
now. What have you to say?'

'Only that she cannot be trusted. Beware. Beware that a knife
does not find *you.*'

'I can escape a knife or two . . . and have. Many a time.'

'But her weapon is a face that a man believes he can trust.
Alas.' He lowered his eyes again.

Crispin stepped closer and this time the man did not shy back.
'Brother . . . are you . . . making a confession of sorts to me?'

'She . . . is beguiling.'

'I see. From the information I have, she ran off with one of
your patrons, Simon Wynchecombe. Do these tidings surprise
you?'

Slowly, he shook his head.

'Do you know Simon Wynchecombe?'

'I have served him. As I must serve all our guests.'

'And was *he* particularly . . . beguiled?'

'Indeed he was.'

'Would you have any idea where they have gone?'

'I would have assumed London.'

'One would. Tell me, brother, why do you think Brother Ralph
disappeared with the relic?'

'I couldn't begin to say.'

'Could you speculate? For your insight on the matter is more
informed than mine.'

The monk shook his head. 'He, too, was beguiled. Stole the
relic for her, mayhap.'

'If that were true, why did he bring it to me?'

The monk remained silent and stuffed his hands beneath his
scapular.

'Do you recall any other brother missing for a length of time?'

The monk said nothing. His eyes merely gazed back at Crispin.

After it appeared that the man had nothing more to say, Crispin bowed to him. 'Well . . . thank you, brother. Unless you have anything to add.'

'Only one thing more: beware, Master Guest. Two have died. Two beguiled . . . or possibly *bewitched*. For I do believe the Devil was in this.'

'You may be right.'

The monk jumped at Jack's step behind him. He didn't wait. Hurrying past Crispin back into the cloister, he disappeared into the shadows.

Jack watched him go. 'What was that about, sir?'

'I'll tell you once we've ridden out of here.'

TEN

John Rykener struggled and finally loosened his bonds enough to free himself. The chair fell back when he jerked to his feet.

'God's teeth!' He shook himself, disgusted that he had been surprised like that and that his charge had been taken. 'And Crispin paid me to watch her. What will I do?'

He grabbed his knife and shoved it in his belt. Yanking his hood and cloak from the pegs, he slammed open the door and tore down the stairs. 'You there! Innkeeper!'

The man turned, annoyed at first . . . until he recognized John. His expression softened. 'Aye, lass. What service can I do you?'

Ignoring his salacious tone, John grabbed his arm and dragged him to a lonely corner. But the innkeeper mistook his intent and slipped a hand around John's waist. 'There's no need to be so rough, lass. We have time. The wife has gone out.'

'Oh, for Jesus' sake! *Later*, man. For now, I am looking for my mistress. Did you see her and her abductors?'

'Abductors? What are you on about? It's been a busy morn. I would not have noticed had the king himself come down them stairs.'

'Damn!' He let the innkeeper go, but the innkeeper had other ideas. His arm tightened about John's waist.

'I don't know if "later" will do. Me cod says otherwise.'

John sighed impatiently and shoved the man back. The innkeeper seemed surprised at his strength. 'I said *later*! Your cod will have to wait.' John left the now sour-faced innkeeper and made his way quickly out to the courtyard. A brisk wind swirled around him and he raised his hood, clutching it closed at the neck. Searching, he saw no one. But, of course, it was too late. He had struggled with his bonds for far too long. She had been spirited away before anyone had had a chance to see her.

'By the blessed saints! What am I to do? What *am* I to *do*?' Go to the sheriffs? No, that was a monumentally *bad* idea, especially in his current situation. He'd been arrested before for dressing as a woman. The sheriffs and the Church were not fond of such. Who could he consult? Who would help?

'Oh! That lawyer friend of Crispin's. What was his name? Nigellus something . . . Nigellus . . . Cobmartin! That's it.' He cast about, as if the man would materialize upon his mentioning him. 'Where does that lawyer keep himself? Gray's Inn, of course.' He grabbed his skirts and ran out of the courtyard.

It was quickest to make his way up the Shambles to Holborn. He found Gray's Inn as a collection of boxy structures, three tiers high. Going to the porter, the man explained that he would send a boy to fetch the young lawyer as women were not allowed in the facility.

John paced back and forth within the damp courtyard, gnawing on a thumbnail and looking up from time to time to catch a law student calling to him out of one of the windows. Too distracted to reply, he stared at the cobblestones and the mud puddles, wishing he could have at least discerned in what direction her abductors had taken the Woodleigh woman. He didn't know how Crispin did such things – following culprits, finding lost objects and people – how he figured out half the things he did. The man was a miracle of logical intellect.

At length, someone passed through the arch of the portico and trotted forward, head under a hood and eyes decidedly narrowed with displeasure. His pinched mouth was shut tight until he came upon John and took him by the arm, leading him further away from the portico.

'Mistress "Eleanor."' He exhaled sharply. 'Dear me, dear me. Why did you come here? And in this guise? It is most unwise, mast— uh, mistress. Could you not have sent a missive? It is not proper that I should see you here in these halls, Master Rykener.' He was certain to whisper the last, and even glanced over his shoulder toward the porter. But John was sure he was quite deaf and wasn't even looking in their direction.

'I beg your mercy, Master Cobmartin, but this could not wait. Indeed, we must make haste.'

'What should we make haste about? Did Master Guest send you?'

'In a manner of speaking. For I was working for him on a very important mission. But I have failed miserably, Master Cobmartin. I cannot forgive myself.'

Nigellus looked back again toward the law court. 'Well . . . we cannot speak here in the streets. A tavern?'

'No. Let us back to the Unicorn where I am staying.'

'Very well.' He tugged his cloak over his chest and hurried behind John's longer strides. Woolly sheep, fat with fleeces, blocked the road a good long time and John was obliged to find a circuitous route back to Watling Street. They entered into the warm hall of the inn and John sat Nigellus down on a bench. When the lawyer asked why, John replied, 'My dear Master Cobmartin. You cannot be seen going up to my room with me. But watch which door I pass through. And after a brief time, follow me up. Do you understand?'

The young lawyer blinked up at him. He wore a dark wool cap over his mousy brown hair and there was a smattering of endearing freckles speckling his nose. He was barely older than Jack Tucker but John was suddenly entranced by his features – his gray eyes that gazed at him with such solemn innocence, the curve of his lip, the small, blunt nose.

'Yes, I think I do,' said Nigellus.

'Good. Then I shall see you in but a moment, Master Cobmartin.'

He looked around for the molesting innkeeper but did not see him, and before the man could make an appearance John hurried up the stairs. He glanced down the stairwell to make certain Nigellus was watching him – and watching him he was – before he unlocked the door and pushed inside.

He noticed the state of the room he had so hastily left. The chair was on its back and the sack and ropes were strewn about. The room didn't appear to have been ransacked but there was so little on offer, though some of Kat Woodleigh's personal items seemed to be missing.

'Terrible, terrible,' he muttered as he righted the chair and straightened the rest of the room, piling the sack and ropes upon the table.

Moments later, there was a timid knock on the door. John straightened his gown, his veil, and then opened it.

Nigellus entered with bowed head. 'And so, Master Rykener. Can you *now* please explain your need of me?'

John sank into the chair by the fire and scraped it across the floor toward the table. 'My mistress. I was hired to be her lady's maid and protector . . .'

'Hold!' He held up a hand. 'Do you mean to tell me Master Guest hired *you* to be a lady's maid to this woman? It is diabolical.'

John raised his chin indignantly. 'It's nothing of the sort. I'm a perfectly good lady's maid.'

'Except that you are not a lady!'

'Dear, *dear* Master Cobmartin. Must we split hairs? I was hired, I was a lady's maid, and there's no more to it. Except that I was supposed to protect the lady in question and now she's been abducted and I don't know where she is!'

'Have you gone to Master Guest with this tragedy?'

'No. That's why he hired me. He was leaving London.'

'Bless me.' He rested a hand to his lips. 'Then tell me what happened. *In principio incipere.*'

'I'm afraid I'm not of the clerical class. So save your Latin for someone who can appreciate it.'

Flustered, Nigellus tapped his fingers on the table. 'I only meant that you should . . . Well, begin at the beginning.'

'Oh. Why didn't you just say so?' With a heavy sigh, John began. 'Crispin hired me a sennight ago to protect a client, Katherine Woodleigh. Apparently, she is abroad without the escort of even a lady's maid, and since Crispin also bound me as her protector, I reasoned that she was in some need, the nature of which he didn't care to share with me.' He edged closer, sliding his elbow along the table. 'But the lady herself confided in me, and as you are as close to a confessor as I will get, I imagine I can tell you and have it go no further.'

'Oh, indeed, yes, Master Rykener.'

John's gaze traveled over the fresh, clean-shaven face. 'You know, you can call me John, if you will.'

Nigellus' brittle smile warmed John's heart.

'And so,' John went on, 'she told me she was in pursuit of her niece, who was stolen away by a foul gentleman. A *married* gentleman, who also stole from her. She sought Crispin's help in regaining her missing niece *and* the stolen goods, and that was why Crispin was out of London. But I never expected that someone should boldly break into our lodgings and steal the lady herself away. And here I was, paid good coin to protect her.'

'They broke in, you say?'

'Yes! I was asleep in this chair and, while I was awakening, a sack was closed over me. This one, see?' He fingered the rough sack and the ropes. 'They bound me to the chair and made off with her.'

'How many were there?'

'I don't know. I was bound, hooded and gagged before I could discern aught.'

'How ever did you escape, Master John?'

'The bindings were ill done and I wriggled free. But not in time to catch in what direction they took her.'

'Did you ask downstairs in the hall if anyone had seen her and her abductors?'

'Only the innkeeper, but he hadn't seen anything.'

'Then let us return to the hall and make our enquiries at once!'

Encouraged by Nigellus' ardor, John happily followed him down the stairs. Eschewing the innkeeper, who was nowhere to be found in any case, Nigellus approached some men gathered at a table, drinking and laughing.

'Good sirs,' he said with a bow and pressed a hand to his heart. 'I am the lawyer Nigellus Cobmartin. I am investigating the abduction of a woman from this establishment not more than a few hours ago, at—' He looked to John for confirmation.

'After sext, before none.'

'As the . . . the demoiselle said.'

The men exchanged glances. 'I never seen no abduction,' said a particularly gangly man. His bright ginger beard seemed as disarrayed as his limbs.

A gruff man of barrel shape shook his head after taking a sip from his beaker. 'I'd remember such like if I saw it,' he said.

Another man, with an arm tight around a bundle pressed close to his chest, scowled. He did not appear to appreciate the interruption. 'No one saw aught.'

Nigellus frowned. 'Surely someone would have noticed a man or two men manhandling a woman down yon stairs.'

'From that door?' asked the barrel man, pointing toward Kat's chamber.

'Yes,' said John, pressing forward. 'Did you see anyone? Did you see her?'

'I seen her before. A beauteous lass. But I never saw her with any men. If they made no commotion, none would have noticed. We were at our drinking or games of dice.'

Drooping, John conceded it. He nudged Nigellus to come back with him up the stairs. Once back in the room he sat heavily in the chair. 'What's to be done, Master Nigellus? How can I save her?'

'Have you any idea at all as to how many men took her?' Nigellus stood before the hearth, fingers rubbing over fingers. 'Think, man.'

'None whatsoever. I heard a scuffle, she screamed and the door opened. I have no idea how many feet . . . but thinking on it, I don't believe there were many. Perhaps merely one man? For the footfalls were few.'

'But no one saw. If she knew the man, maybe she would give no trouble. Do you know the identity of the man who had stolen from her? Maybe that is a place to start.'

'She intimated that he was a former sheriff . . . of London.'

'By St Ives! That's a tricky bit. He's an alderman, then, and I well know they keep themselves as a tight enclave. There's no doubt Master Guest already covered that territory. And yet one of this man's henchmen could be the culprit. Dear me, how does Master Guest do it?'

'I was thinking that very thing.'

'That is our Master Crispin: *Ut quocumque paratus.*'

'But this is getting us nowhere.' John rubbed his chin, ignoring the small spot he'd missed in his secretive shave. 'By logic we must work this out. There were two possible directions from the inn. East toward Budge Row or west toward St Paul's, is that not right?'

'Yes.'

'And there are two of us. If we each take a direction and ask the shopkeepers, might we get somewhere?'

'I suppose it's all we have. Tell me fully what the lady looks like.'

John explained in vivid detail her upturned nose, the blue of her eyes and the exact shade of her hair, comparing it to the common squirrel – but more sable than red. He sent Nigellus toward Budge Row while he took the path toward St Paul's.

But it wasn't long after John questioned a man who sold paternosters that Nigellus pounded toward him, lifting the hem of his gown, revealing knobby ankles in blue stockings. 'Master— I mean, *Mistress* Eleanor!'

'Nigellus. What is it, man?'

Out of breath, the lawyer put a hand to his heart, puffing. He gestured behind him. 'A fellow back there – a carpenter – said he'd seen the lady.'

'Lead me.' Each grabbed up their skirts out of the mud and rushed forward. John held back, even though he could easily have sprinted ahead with his longer legs, allowing Nigellus to precede him. The lawyer skidded to a stop before the shop with the carved saw above the door and entered it again with John on his heels.

'You're back,' said the burly carpenter at his bench. His nose and cheeks burned a cheery red, and a scruff of brown hair stuck out beneath the leather cap that came down to cover his ears.

'Master Williams, would you be so kind as to repeat what you just told me to my friend here?'

Williams looked John up and down. He was used to the scrutiny. Some only saw the woman John was projecting, while others instinctively knew just what they were looking at. Master Williams seemed to be the latter.

'Er . . . well. This fellow, this lawyer here,' and he gestured to Nigellus, 'asked me if I'd seen this woman. And I said I had. Round about none, striding down the lane in all haste.'

John pressed closer. 'And how many men were with her?'

'That's what this one asked me, too. And I'm telling you what I told him. There was no one with her. She was walking alone, in haste. Looking back over her shoulder, like she was being followed. That's why I noticed her. Like she was being followed, or trying to get away from someone or something.'

'Walking?' asked John, perplexed. 'Not running?'

'No. A determined look on her face, too. The kind where . . . well. The wife puts on that look. And when she does, I don't cross her, get my meaning?'

John exchanged a glance with Nigellus. 'There was no one with her?'

'I just got done telling you, didn't I?'

'I thank you, good master.' He curtseyed, and then signaled for Nigellus to follow him out of the shop. They stood in front of it looking down the muddy lane at the shoppers crowding the street, with a boy leading an enormous ox pulling a wagon, a girl carrying a small goat over her shoulders as it bleated at passers-by and a woman selling meat skewered on sticks.

'Such a clever woman, then,' John was saying as Nigellus considered. 'She eluded her captors quickly. Very resourceful.'

'Resourceful,' muttered Nigellus. 'More so than we think.'

'How so? What is your meaning, Master Nigellus?'

'Don't you see, my dear Master John? She is crafty, I'll give her that. And as clever as the day is wide.'

John blinked his confusion.

The lawyer got in closer and said more quietly so no one could eavesdrop, 'She staged the whole thing just to elude you. She wasn't abducted at all. There never were any men. I'm certain of it. And now she appears to be gone and we have no knowledge as to where or why.'

He folded his arms and shivered, realizing suddenly that he had forgotten his cloak. But as he turned to march back down the lane, he noticed a man in the shadows, trying to make himself invisible against a wall. He looked familiar, and when John squinted the memory came into focus as well. He stalked toward the man, who looked as if he was trying to decide in which direction he should dart away.

But Nigellus was there, too, and they both cornered him.

'You're Leonard Munch,' said Nigellus, an accusing finger pointed at him. 'You lied about Master Crispin when you were a witness at his trial.'

'Oh, I remember you,' said John.

Lenny sneered. 'And I remember you, right enough.' He spat, nearly at John's feet. 'You're the one that dresses like a lass.'

John raised his chin. 'So I am. What are *you* doing skulking about here?'

'I don't have to tell the likes of you two, do I? Isn't any of your business, is it?'

John snorted in disgust and whirled away from him in a swirl of his skirts.

'Oi! Are you by chance looking for the lady?'

John stopped and Nigellus nearly ran into him. They both turned and glared at Lenny. His greasy hair was stuck to the side of his face and his disgusting coat was frayed and torn. He postured with false dignity.

'There now,' he said, pulling on his mantle. 'Didn't think I knew, did you? Didn't think old Lenny knew what was what. Ha! You don't know aught. For instance, you don't know that Master Crispin hired me to watch the lady. And I done it. And I seen her.'

'Did you see where she went?' asked Nigellus anxiously.

Lenny smiled a toothless grin. 'Maybe I did and maybe I didn't.'

John grabbed him by the shirt and balled it up in his fist. He tried to forget how badly it smelled as he peered into the rustic's face. 'Harken, you rascal.' His voice was low and threatening, just enough so that Lenny alone could hear. 'I know all about you. And if you think I am going to pay you one farthing for this information that Master Crispin is paying *you* for, you are very much mistaken. Now you have exactly to the count of three to tell me or I shall throttle you right here on the street. One . . .'

'Here now!' He swatted ineffectually at John's hand. 'Let me go! Blind me, but you're stronger than you look.'

'*Two* . . .'

'Mercy, Master Rykener! I'll tell you.'

John didn't let go but he slackened his grip.

'She . . . she went toward Candlewick.'

'And what business had she there?'

'She gone there many a time. I seen her. Went stealing over the rooftops, she did. Skirts and all. Secretly watching Master Wynchecombe's house.'

ELEVEN

'So that monk thinks all these men were bewitched by Sybil Whitechurch,' said Jack as their horses left the abbey well behind them. 'And him, too, by the sound of it.'

'Yes. She would seem to be a singular creature, this niece.'

'You best steer clear of her, master. You do have a weakness for the ladies, after all.'

Crispin whipped his head toward his apprentice and caught the tail end of a smile on his lips. He gave him a sharp look in warning but said nothing.

'It still don't explain why that monk came all that way to you in London.'

'No, it doesn't.'

'And now we must face Katherine Woodleigh with the information that her niece is . . . well. A tart.'

'I do hope you do not intend to put it to her in quite that manner.'

''Course not, master. I have more aplomb than that.'

'I am happy to hear it.' But Crispin felt compelled to think on that himself. It could very well be that whatever mischief had transpired, Sybil Whitechurch was the instigator. Did she incite Wynchecombe to kill for her? It was a possibility. Women have done so before. Even gone to war. Would Katherine Woodleigh accept that pronouncement? In the end, she might have to. But in the meantime, he very much wanted to talk to Simon Wynchecombe, and hoped he had returned to London by the time Crispin got back.

The horses, too, seemed anxious to return. Crispin noticed their tread was quicker, their step livelier as they took the road back. He led them on a narrow path that cut through a plain, hoping to shorten their time on the road. Jack stopped his horse to gaze at a strange, long mound.

'I heard of this, sir. It's called Belas Knap. It's a fairy barrow.'

Crispin eyed it, running his gaze along the long, indistinguishable mound. It didn't look particularly auspicious to him. 'A fairy barrow? Now, Jack.'

'You may very well mock,' he said, affronted.

'I might,' Crispin murmured.

'But the monks told me how folk go missing 'round about here. Say it's the fairy folk stealing them away.'

'Preposterous. Have you ever seen fairy folk?'

'Just because I haven't seen it doesn't mean I can't believe. Isn't that what St Augustine says?'

'It was our Lord Jesus who said it, Jack.'

'Well, now. All the more reason to take it to heart.'

Crispin snorted. 'You have the better of me.'

Jack gazed at it for a while before he shivered. 'Makes me come all over in goose flesh. They say that if you see the fairy folk they lead you to their barrow and there's a great feast. But you mustn't eat anything they give you, nor have any drink.'

Amused, Crispin eyed his nervous apprentice as he scanned the mound. 'And why is that?'

'It bespells you, is why. You can't leave after that. And then they make you dance with them, and you dance till you drop dead.'

'Fairy folk don't seem very sensible.'

'They don't have to be, now, do they? They're fairy folk.' Jack halted his horse and cocked his head, listening.

'What are you doing now?'

Jack held his hand up for silence and put his other hand behind his ear. 'Do you hear that?' Jack whispered.

Crispin listened but all he could hear was the wind rushing through the trees, the trickle of water somewhere, the snuffling of the horses and the creak of their saddles. 'I don't hear anything.'

'Music. Muffled music . . . in the barrow!'

Crispin turned his ear toward the mound. He heard nothing. Or did he? Was that the wind rattling through the tree branches or was it the faint sound of a shawm and tabor?

He shook himself and lifted his head. 'Curse you, knave. You've nearly got *me* believing it. Come, Jack.'

'Gladly, sir.'

It must have been the lay of the countryside, the barrow, the surrounding woods, for Crispin could swear he heard another set of hoofs. Fairy folk? The Unseelie Court on their rounds? *Must be the echo of our own horses*, he mused. A better explanation. He turned on the saddle, bracing a hand on the horse's rump and looked behind, expecting the sight of a man on horseback. No one back there. He shrugged and returned forward.

But after more miles, he still heard it. *Now Jack's got me thinking of fairy folk!* But he was a practical man and fairy folk didn't play well in his imagination. Someone following them did.

'Jack,' he said casually. 'Tell me, with your ears peeled, do you hear another's tread?'

'Eh?' Cocking his head like a dog, Jack listened, pushing his hood away from one ear even as he looked behind. 'I don't see no one.'

'Neither do I, but I do hear them.'

'Aye. I do, too, now. Shall I nip back and investigate, sir?'

'Yes. But be stealthy about it. Go the long way around, through those woods.'

Jack kicked his heels into the flank of his beast and trotted up the rise to the clump of trees along the ridge. Crispin urged his mount slowly forward, not wishing to forewarn anyone who might be following.

If they were behind, he reckoned they must be skirting the woods to his left. He kept half an eye on its shadows but couldn't see anything.

His horse moved on and meandered along the main road. But after almost an hour, there was no sign of Jack, nor of the owner of the mysterious hoof falls. As afternoon stole over him and he neared the inn, he worried that Jack still made no appearance. Had their shadow attacked his apprentice? He looked back, saw no one and grunted. Deciding, he turned his horse. 'Where is that rogue?' he muttered, kicking the beast's flanks. Back over the road, over a rise and toward a copse. He kept his ears sharp but the shadows were lengthening, making discerning the wood for the trees difficult.

His head jerked sharply to the right and he drew his sword at the same time a horse cleared the brush with a breaking of branches. Jack pulled his beast to a skidding stop and looked up, surprised at the drawn sword. 'It's only me,' he said, amused.

Not as amused, Crispin snapped the sword back in its scabbard. 'Where the hell were you?'

'Stalking someone, master. But he's a stealthy bastard and he got away from me.'

'Did you see him?'

'Naw. Just the tail end of a horse disappearing into the wood. Highwayman, I'm thinking.'

'Likely.' He peered back the way they had come, eyes narrowing. 'Well, we are close to the inn. Let us to it. I'm starving.'

They clambered down the rise to the main road again and presently came upon the inn. When they had eaten and returned to their room, they doused the light. Stealthily, Crispin opened the shutter a crack and looked out. No one had come to the inn after them and, if they continued to follow, smoke from a campfire might be visible over the treetops. But there was nothing. Either they did not light a fire or their mysterious horseman had been a highwayman as Jack said. Still, there was the other possibility that it had all been innocent. A traveler who had not wanted to encounter *them*.

He let it go, closed the shutter and hunkered down in the curtained bed to sleep.

In the morning, after a quick repast, they were both anxious to get back on the road. The wind whipped up, tossing the still-empty tree branches like clattering bones. They wrapped their cloaks about their shoulders and closed their hoods over chilled faces, speaking very little. Crispin could hear no more hoof beats behind them, either because the wind was so loud or no one was tailing them.

Another day passed, until late afternoon on the third day saw them approaching the gates of London.

'Oh, it's good to be home at last, master.'

Crispin nodded. His horse plodded down Holborn. Newgate was in sight. They'd drop off the horses and report to the sheriffs. What would the sheriffs think of their less-than-helpful journey? Well, best get it out of the way.

They road in under the portcullis arch and dismounted. One of the pages took the reins. Jack lumbered away from the horse, rubbing his backside, and offered Crispin a sheepish grin. 'It takes getting used to,' he said.

Once the horses were led away, another boy took Crispin and Jack to the sheriffs' tower room where the sheriffs' clerk announced them.

John Walcote was writing at the desk and John Loveney was looking over his shoulder. Loveney studied Crispin with narrowed eyes but Walcote didn't bother raising his face from the page. 'What is it, Guest? What have you learned about that damned dead monk?'

Such a difference from their excited anticipation from a sennight ago, Crispin mused. They couldn't wait for him to leave and do the work for them then.

'My lords,' he said, bowing. Only Loveney watched him curiously. 'What I have learned . . . is precious little.'

'That's not like you, Guest,' said Walcote, quill scratching carefully over his parchment.

'Lord Sheriff, I wish I could offer you more. But there was little evidence for me to go on. Except . . .' He glanced at Jack and made the decision. 'My lord, it has come to my attention, that perhaps a former sheriff has something to do with . . . these occurrences.'

The quill stopped and Walcote slowly looked up. 'What?'

Jack took a discreet step back toward the door. Maybe that was a good idea.

Crispin cleared his throat nervously and scuffed the floor with his boot. 'A former sheriff of this office is likely involved in some way. It is not known quite yet how involved he was.'

Walcote rested his arms on the table and Loveney leaned forward. 'Guest, what the hell are you playing at? What nonsense is this? What former sheriff?'

Taking a breath, Crispin steadied himself. 'Simon Wynchecombe, my lords.'

'Simon Wynchecombe?' Walcote leapt from his chair and scrambled around the table. 'This has got to be the worst. Oh, I've heard about you and Wynchecombe. Don't think I haven't. This is your revenge, eh? You think you will accuse him of murder? You think you will use *us* to do it?'

'You've wasted our money, Guest,' said Loveney. 'Ha! Maybe you didn't even go to Hailes.'

'My lords! Do you accuse me of lying?'

'There's no other conclusion I *can* draw,' said Loveney. Toying with his dagger hilt, he rested against Walcote's chair back.

'I can well assure you, my lords, that I was the guest of the abbey, that I investigated, questioned and came to the conclusion that the evidence suggested Wynchecombe's involvement.'

'Proof, Guest?' Loveney shook his head, a disgusted expression marring his face. 'Petty revenge is so unbecoming.'

'His dagger was in the man's back!' cried Jack.

Crispin turned to glare at his apprentice. Jack realized his mistake immediately, clamping a hand over his mouth. It was much too late.

Walcote swooped down on Jack, walking him backward into a corner. 'What did you say?'

'I . . . I . . .'

Walcote grabbed Jack by his collar. 'Repeat what you just said, knave.'

'Lord Sheriff,' Crispin interjected. 'Please allow me to explain.'

Walcote glared daggers at Jack before letting him go. His eyes swept over Crispin with an accusatory expression. 'Well?'

'When the monk from Hailes arrived at our door . . . he did have a dagger in his back. And I recognized it as belonging to Simon Wynchecombe.'

Walcote ruminated before sliding his glance toward Loveney. 'And where is this alleged dagger now?'

'In my lodgings.'

Loveney guffawed. 'As usual, Guest, your reasoning is fouled. He could easily have given the dagger away to a servant, who could have sold it. This is not evidence.'

Crispin knew it would be sufficient to hang *him* if the circumstances were different. But he said nothing.

Loveney chewed on his lip. 'Why did you not present this evidence before now?'

'Before his apprentice spilled it, you mean,' sneered Walcote.

Crispin shook his head. 'I knew that such evidence would be hard for you to believe.'

'And it is.'

'I wanted more proof – if any – before presenting it to you, my lords.'

'And you have found none.'

'Well, Master Wynchecombe has estates near Hailes and has been a patron to the abbey. I, er . . . I'm also investigating a possibly related situation in which Master Wynchecombe might have stolen away with a young lady, a woman who was also a resident of Hailes. I was hired, in fact, to find the two of them.'

Walcote sputtered. 'More and more outlandish! See how he tries to hide his true motives.'

'I have a client staying at the Unicorn Inn on Watling Street, my lords. She has paid me to find her niece, one Sybil Whitechurch of Hailes, whom she claims ran off with Master Wynchecombe.'

'But Wynchecombe is married,' said Loveney.

'I know.'

Both Loveney and Walcote seemed to arrive at the bitter conclusion at the same time. Loveney sidled up to Walcote. 'This is ghastly! Do we believe Master Guest in this?'

It stole across both their faces. Seldom had Crispin been wrong, and they knew it. But this was not information they fancied hearing. 'I, for one,' said Walcote, 'would like to see this so-called evidence. Guest, you will bring that dagger to me forthwith.'

He bowed. 'Yes, my lords.' He spun on his heel before they could say anything else.

He was out from under Newgate's arch and heading up to Newgate Market before Jack finally caught up to him. The lad dragged his leaden feet. 'Master Crispin, I'm so sorry. God's teeth, I never meant to say anything. But they were talking such rubbish to you—'

'As they always do, Jack. Well, it makes no nevermind now. The milk is spilt. Let us get the dagger and be done with it.'

Newgate Market soon enough became the Shambles. He held his anger in check. Jack's mistake was one that Crispin might have made in his own anger. They were baiting him as every sheriff he had ever known had done. It was Jack's inexperience that had allowed the matter to get out of hand. Ah, well. He couldn't hold onto the damned thing forever. Maybe it was a good turn that the cat had gotten out of the bag. The sheriffs might yet believe him and then the investigation might go more smoothly.

Crispin reached for his key when they neared the old poulterer's that they called home, stepped up the granite step and turned the lock.

The place always smelled of chickens when he had absented himself from it for a few days. He supposed it had permeated deeply into the old timbers.

It was also dark and cold. Jack hurried past Crispin to light the hearth with flint and steel.

Stepping toward the coffer where the dagger was kept, Crispin could hear Jack striking the flint, cursing when a spark failed to ignite the bit of straw and fluff he used as kindling. But it was the faint scrape of a boot on his floor that caught his ear, and he stilled. In the darkness of the gloom, something stirred in the far corner.

His sword was out just as the spark caught. Light and steel both flashed in the darkness and Jack's exclamation of satisfaction was temporarily quashed by Crispin's own shout. 'Who is there?'

Jack jerked back and pulled his dagger, standing at Crispin's shoulder.

A tall figure moved in the shadows. With hands raised, he slowly emerged into the sparse light that had caught in the hearth, crackling over the twigs and dried peat. As the shadows fell away, Crispin recognized the gaunt cheeks and haughty brow. He lowered his sword and sheathed it.

Speak of the devil.

Simon Wynchecombe shuffled forward. His boots and clothes were muddy, his hair in disarray, his face and beard dirty. He slowly lowered his hands.

'Master Wynchecombe,' said Crispin, as exasperated as he'd ever been, with surprise dappled atop it. 'I've been looking for you.'

'I know.' His eyes, wide with an unusual emotion, darted toward Jack. 'My God, is that Jack Tucker? I remember when he was no more than a sprig of a lad. And dirtier than I am now.'

'What has happened, Master Wynchecombe? Much must be discussed.'

'Yes, that is true. But there is one thing that must be done first.'

'And what is that, my lord?'

Wynchecombe wrung his hands and staggered toward the fire. Crispin was beginning to wonder if the man was hurt in some way. He wore no hat or hood and his cloak was torn and muddied, like his clothes. Crispin surmised he'd ridden hard from a distance and hadn't had time to change. But why had he come here first before going home?

And where was Sybil Whitechurch?

Crispin girded himself, waiting for the former sheriff's reply. Girding didn't help.

Wynchecombe made the motions of warming his hands before the meager fire. 'God's wounds, Crispin. I never thought I'd say this, but . . . I'm in trouble. And . . . and I need *you* to hide me.'

TWELVE

Crispin stared, unable to scramble the words into something that made sense. 'I . . . what?'

'It's a simple request, isn't it?' he snapped. The irritation tinged with muted panic gave Crispin pause.

'Of course,' he said carefully. Jack's mouth hung open and his hands were balled into fists. 'But . . . can you tell me why I must offer this boon . . . and for how long?'

'Goddammit, Crispin!' His shoulders hunched over his tall frame, curving inward like a protective shell. 'Must I explain myself at every turn? Can you not do this one simple thing I ask of you?'

'Only with an explanation.' He settled his hand on his dagger hilt. For once in his life, he had the better of Wynchecombe, and he intended to savor it.

'You're a knave, do you know that?'

'Yes.'

Wynchecombe turned to glance at him, disbelief in his wild eyes. 'I see.'

But the former sheriff didn't speak any further. Realizing they were at an impasse, Crispin decided enough was enough. 'First, I must ask some questions. Where is Sybil Whitechurch?'

'Sybil Whitechurch? That bitch? I haven't any idea and I don't care.'

Crispin couldn't help but exchange a glance with Jack. He cleared his throat. 'Er . . . Master Wynchecombe, there has been some tears shed over her and the fact that she is missing and believed spirited away . . . by you.'

'By me? I'm married!'

'Yes. It is puzzling.'

'Wait, wait. Are you telling me that you believe I was responsible for . . . for . . . stealing away with that woman?'

'I was hired by her aunt to find her and she had every reason to believe it was you. So she told me. And so I investigated.'

'This is unbelievable! Who is this aunt with all her concern? Where was her concern when that woman was forcing her affections upon me?'

'You are saying that you never abducted her?'

'No, dammit. This is beneath you, Guest.'

'Forgive me, my lord, but . . . well. I'm confused.'

'You're damned right you are.'

'Perhaps it would help matters if you told me where you have been. For you were not at home in London or at your estates in Winchcombe.'

'How do you know about Winchcombe?'

'I have just returned from there.'

'God's wounds.' He lowered himself to a chair and clutched at the arms.

'Have you not been home in Candlewick Ward yet, my lord? Your wife is worried.'

'Alice . . .' He laid his head back and closed his eyes. 'Maybe I'd best tell you all.'

'It might help.'

He opened one eye to stare at Crispin before closing it again. 'Very well. I suppose it's the least I can do.' He sighed and licked his lips. 'I met the damned woman at the abbey some weeks ago. She's a patroness; I am a patron. We both venerate the blood relic at Hailes. We . . . well, dammit. She was beautiful and solicitous, and I was far from London, and . . . For God's sake, do you have any wine?'

Crispin nodded to his other shadow. 'Jack?'

Jack hurried toward the larder. In the darkness, Crispin heard the lad pour liquid into two goblets. He rushed toward Wynchecombe and handed one over first. The former sheriff grabbed it and tipped it to his lips, drinking thirstily, spilling some over the side at his cheek.

Crispin waved off the goblet Jack presented to him.

'Go on,' said Crispin after a pause.

Wynchecombe cradled the now-empty goblet to his bosom. 'How can I say it? I stupidly fell in love. I, at my age, and she such a young thing. I suppose I'm a fool. I believed she loved me, too. Or so I thought. Clearly it was the Devil at work, bewitching me. We met in Winchcombe for dalliance. Then she told me of her family's poverty and I tried to help. I gave her money, jewels. But it was never enough. Her tenants, she told me, were ruined by a flood and could not pay the rents. I believed her and tried to help where I could, but she would never let me come to the estates. Then, one day, I secretly followed her and found them to be derelict. When next I saw her at Hailes, I confronted her. There were no tenants, and it looked as if there hadn't been any for some years. She wept, and yes, my heart fell for it again. There was something she wanted me to do. She was desperate for it. Something she was loath to tell me that would see her saved from poverty. I couldn't imagine what it could be, what would be such a boon to her, but like any eager paramour I agreed to it. That was before I knew what it was.'

'And what was it?'

He opened both eyes and fixed them on Crispin. 'She wanted me to steal the damned blood relic.'

'And did you?'

He jolted to his feet, dashing the wooden goblet to the floor.

He stalked up to Crispin but Crispin didn't waver. He felt the man's hot breath on his face. 'How dare you? How dare you stand there and assume I am guilty.'

'I'm still waiting, my lord.'

Wynchecombe drew back his fist but stopped at Crispin's words: 'I don't *have* to let you stay, my lord. There is little compelling me. To imply that we are friends would be disingenuous to me, surely. I will offer my hospitality on the condition that I believe you. And so I must be informed of every turn of your relationship with the missing woman. I shouldn't like to shield a murderer, after all.'

Slowly, Wynchecombe lowered his hand, his whole body deflating. 'I see.' He suddenly looked around at the still, largely dim room. 'I recall when your circumstances were quite grim,' he said vaguely. 'That squalid one room . . . above a tinker shop, wasn't it?'

Jack caught his attention again and his glance roved over the boy . . . the man, Crispin supposed. Taller than Crispin, older than when Wynchecombe first met him and now with his own ginger beard. Jack was not the frightened orphan he had once been but a man in his own right. And Wynchecombe, who stood as tall as Jack and whose dark beard and mustache were now streaked with gray, seemed frailer than when he was at his full power some years ago. He had never risen to the role of Lord Mayor. Maybe he wasn't as popular an alderman as he liked to think he was. Maybe not as wealthy as he liked to play at, judging by his estates in faraway Winchcombe. Maybe he was never the man Crispin assumed he was.

'And now look at you,' Wynchecombe went on. 'This . . . this new place of yours. That apprentice. Everything is bigger and better. You'll claw your way back, won't you, Guest? One decade at a time. I'll be damned if you don't.'

The words were satisfying but Crispin could find no solace in them. Wynchecombe could only see the outer layer of his life: grand new lodgings with a hall and two rooms, a sword at his side, an adult Jack Tucker. But he did not know what lay beneath – that it was the same harsh circumstances he had left behind when exiled from court. He was still the man who had committed treason, the man who'd been banished from court, who had lost it all and yet still lived.

He examined the man who had harassed him, who had made his life on the Shambles miserable for the year he was Lord Sheriff. Their relationship had been one-sided, antagonistic. He had seen the many faces Wynchecombe had worn, seen for himself the many roles he had played. But Crispin had never seen this face on him before. Fear. He was frightened. And desperate. Why else had he resorted to coming to Crispin, a man he never liked? Perhaps he had harbored a begrudging respect, but he had never treated Crispin with the respect that was his due.

And now he wanted a favor.

Crispin stared him down until it was Wynchecombe who turned away first. His shaking hand found the back of the chair and grasped it. 'I didn't steal the relic.'

'Yet it *was* stolen.'

Those eyes again, haunted, surprised, fearful, fixed on Crispin once more. 'It was?'

'Yes. That's why I rode to Hailes. To return it. And . . . to tell the abbot of the murder of one of his monks at my very door.'

'A murdered monk, you say?'

'Yes. Murdered . . . with your dagger.'

'*My* dagger?' He reached for the sheath that should have hung at his right hip, but it wasn't there. 'Ah.'

'Where is your dagger, my lord?'

'Apparently, it was in the back of a dead monk. Do the sheriffs have it now?'

'No. *I* do. I removed it before they came. And I have it still.'

'Oh, I see. You recognized it, then. And now you intend to do your mischief to me in return for my past treatment of you. Well, and why not? It's the least I deserve, eh?'

Crispin gritted his teeth. 'That is not why I kept it.'

'Isn't it, though?'

'No! Damn you, Simon. You have never understood me. You've betrayed me at every turn, you used me, and yes, ill-treated me. But you have never understood *me*.'

'You're a traitor, Guest. What more is there to know?'

Crispin heaved a hot breath. 'Get out.'

The fear was back and he could see Wynchecombe swallowing his pride. 'Wait . . . I . . . I misspoke . . .'

'Only because you want something from me. But the sheriffs

have requested this dagger, this evidence from me, and we are required to give it to them.'

'Wait, Guest . . . Hold for but a moment.'

'Why? Why should I?' His hand squeezed his own dagger hilt. 'Give me a reason.'

'Because . . . because my life is in danger. Because . . . my dagger was stolen from me and used against me. I killed no one. I didn't take the relic. And I don't know where that damnable woman is.' He approached Crispin but kept far enough away so as not to threaten. 'You've helped others. Some even less deserving than me. Can you . . . can you put aside your animosity to help me? I . . .' He seemed to gird himself. 'I don't know where else to go.'

Sincerity at last. Crispin took a deep breath and gusted it through his nostrils. He loosened his grip on his dagger but kept his hand resting there. 'When did you lose the dagger?'

'I don't know. Over a sennight ago. Possibly a fortnight.'

'Any idea who took it?'

He shook his head. 'I was at the abbey at the time.'

'Were you aware that Sybil Whitechurch garnered the . . . erm, *affections* of some of the monks at Hailes?'

He blinked. His face crumpled before he righted it. Crispin supposed he *had* fallen for the girl. 'The whore,' he muttered.

'That's as may be. Since she couldn't convince you to steal the relic, I surmise that she did convince someone else. And if this other paramour was known to you, it could easily be construed that you killed him out of jealousy.'

'But that's not what happened.'

'But it could be construed so.'

He slumped. 'I'm doomed. There is no way out of this.' The unbelievable was written on his face. 'I'll hang,' he whispered breathlessly.

'Perhaps.'

'We're supposed to give them sheriffs the dagger,' said Jack suddenly.

Wynchecombe seemed to only just remember he was there and turned to face him. Jack had always been fiercely loyal to Crispin, and there'd been many a time when Wynchecombe had left Crispin bruised and bloodied and Jack had been there to pick

up the pieces. Jack certainly had no love for Wynchecombe, but
Crispin had taught him a love of the law and what was morally
right, and he was fairly certain what Jack was going to say next.

'But . . . we can easily lose it for a time,' said Jack. His gaze
was steady on Wynchecombe. Yes, things were certainly different
from seven years ago. Jack was no child and Wynchecombe, at
the moment, had no power at all.

'Yes, Jack. Why don't you return to Newgate and tell them that?'

'I was afraid you were going to say that, Master Crispin.'
He gave Wynchecombe a steady look – a warning – before
Wynchecombe silently deferred to their new positions and stepped
aside for the former cutpurse. Jack stood at the door and grace-
fully bowed – to Crispin, or Wynchecombe? – before slamming
the door shut behind him.

Crispin walked gravely around the former sheriff to stand
before the fire. 'Why do you think someone is out to kill you?'

'Because they are. I've been fleeing for my life for days.'

Eyes sweeping over Wynchecombe's state of dress, Crispin
turned back to the small flames. 'When did you return to London?'

'A few days ago. I've been in hiding. I was waiting for you
to return.'

'I'm flattered.'

'Don't be. I thought no one in their right mind would suspect
I'd hide out with you.'

He nodded. 'Rightly so. Do you suspect anyone in particular?'

'That damned woman. Hired someone, no doubt.'

'What of Katherine Woodleigh?'

'Who?'

A scratch at the back of his thoughts. It made him think of
Jack and fairy barrows. 'Katherine Woodleigh. It was she who
hired me to find her niece, Sybil Whitechurch. She is the one
who told me you stole her niece away. And she is the one who
told me that you cheated her out of some much-needed funds.'

'The gall! The utter gall! I've never heard of her. Unless . . .
The daughter of Thomas Woodleigh . . . of Hailes?'

'The same.'

'God's wounds. Sybil Whitechurch's aunt, you say? The Devil
take all their wretched family. I did nothing of the kind, for I
have never set eyes upon her.'

'You do not know her?'

'No. It's all lies.'

'And I should believe you over her?'

'Yes, damn you.'

A knock at the entrance ceased their barbs and they both stilled, staring at the door. Crispin gestured for Wynchecombe to go up the stairs. The former sheriff released his held breath, nodded and made a quiet exit upward.

Crispin waited till he was out of sight before taking the latch in hand and, using his body to hide the room, opening the door a sliver.

THIRTEEN

'What do you mean she was capering about on rooftops?' asked John Rykener. This Lenny knave was scraping his last nerve. How did he even know if Crispin had truly hired him? The last time he saw the rogue, he had lied in court in order to get Crispin convicted of murder. Would Crispin forgive and forget so easily? It certainly wasn't like him, though if the man proved useful Crispin might still give him a chance. How was John to know?

'That's what I seen,' said Lenny, nodding his head. With his bent posture and skinny neck, he looked like the vulture he was. 'I can't explain it. But as you well know, Master Guest does ally himself with some peculiar characters.'

'Indeed he does,' said John, giving Lenny a particularly dour eye.

'Here now. I know your meaning. Put it away. I tell you that it's the Lord's truth. I seen her up there. And after she got done watching Master Wynchecombe's house, and once night fell, she went scampering along them roofs and snuck herself into a window.'

'Now I know you're lying. I'm going to beat the truth out of you!'

He raised his fist to do just that when Nigellus grabbed his arm. 'Now, Master Rykener, you mustn't call attention to yourself . . . or the law,' he said, the last quietly.

He wrenched his hand free of Nigellus' grip. 'It would be worth it. This miserable son of a whore is accusing this woman of . . . of . . . witchcraft, for all I can tell.'

'It weren't witchcraft,' said Lenny. 'Just common thievery. Saw her come out the usual way through the door. Carrying a sack, mind.'

'A sack of what? The horse shit you are trying to peddle me?'

Lenny folded his arms over his chest, closed his eyes and slowly shook his head. 'I don't expect you to believe me. I don't expect Master Guest to believe me. But I seen it with me own eyes and I'd swear to any priest it's what I saw. So help me God.'

John got in one good clout to the man's ear before Nigellus grabbed at him and pushed him back.

'Ow, sarding, ow!' Lenny rubbed the side of his head. 'Don't hit me again, sodomite, or I'll knife you in the throat.'

'Now see here!' cried Nigellus, getting between them. 'Stop it at once! Master Rykener, you stand there. Master Munch, you stand there. Now.' He wiped his hands down his gown's front that was shiny with grease and speckled with crumbs. 'There is a truth here that may not be readily evident. And as men of intellect . . .' He eyed Lenny and paused. 'W-we . . . we must reason it out. You say she was on the roof,' he said to Lenny.

'Aye, that's what I said and that's what I seen.'

'And *you* say,' he said to John, 'that it is an impossibility. How are we to prove which is right and which is wrong?'

John aimed a finger at Lenny. 'He's wrong because he is a liar.'

'I'm not lying! I seen it.'

'But you say, Master Munch, that she came away with a sack. Master Rykener, have you seen anything of a sack in her possession?'

'Of course not! She is as poor as a cat in a dog kennel.'

'Ah, but this is something we can easily see for ourselves. Let us return to the Unicorn and to the lady's room to see if there is anything there that should not be.'

'But I tell you I have lived side by side with her for the last sennight and if there was anything else there, I'd know it.'

'Then let us prove that point, Master Rykener, and eliminate it as a possibility.'

'All because you cannot dismiss this fool,' he said disgustedly. 'Very well. Very well. We will waste our time.' He swept by Nigellus with a swirl of skirts, deliberately knocking into Lenny as he passed.

Stomping back toward the Unicorn, a litany of curses paraded through his head. What nonsense! Nigellus was just naive, listening to the likes of Lenny. And maybe it hurt a little that he would take Lenny's word over John's. After all, he liked the young lawyer, liked the look of him. Crispin trusted John. He might have paid Lenny, but he doubted Crispin would take Lenny's word over John's.

They entered the inn together but the innkeeper waylaid them when they made for the stairs.

'Here, who's this?' He folded his arms over his wide chest and gestured with his head toward Lenny. John swelled with satisfaction, knowing it wasn't a very Christian attitude but feeling a measure of vindication nonetheless.

'He is our associate, good master,' said Nigellus in his most officious tone. 'We have business to discuss upstairs.'

'Not in my inn, you don't.'

'Tut. Truly, sir.' Nigellus reached into his money pouch and withdrew a silver penny, flourishing it. 'For your trouble.'

'See that he don't leave fleas,' the innkeeper called after them as they climbed the stairwell.

'Got *his* nerve,' Lenny muttered, scratching.

John opened the door with his key and pushed through first. Fists at his hips, he stood in the middle of the room. 'This is all mad. She might be running for her life out there in London, and we are listening to this pintle.'

Lenny swiveled his head from side to side, surveying the room with widened eyes. John wondered when the last time was that the man had seen the inside of a room he wasn't burgling.

'And so,' Nigellus began. 'Where shall we begin? Under the beds, perhaps? Floorboards?'

Lenny dove under the larger bed with only his twitching feet visible in their rag-wrapped boots. John did a cursory investigation among the small bits of luggage. 'The same things are here.

A change of clothing, a few items: a carved wooden spoon, a tin salt cellar. Naught else.'

'Aha!' cried the muffled voice of Lenny under the bed. 'See here! Who's a liar now!'

He wriggled himself free, dragging a small sack with him. Thrusting it toward Nigellus, he sneered at John.

Nigellus took it and peered inside the sack. 'Dear me.' He dumped the sack's contents onto the bed: a silver cup, a gold ring, a candlestick, florins and shillings in silver.

'But . . .' John stared at the bounty with mouth agape. 'What is this?'

'Your mistress' thievery, Rykener,' said Lenny with a deep scowl. 'I told you I seen what I seen.'

John knelt on the floor before the bed, picking up each item and examining them. 'These . . . these could have been collecting on debts. Why . . . how . . . could she steal them?'

'She gone up on the rooftops, I tell you.'

'That I cannot believe.'

'Believe your own eyes, then.'

He rose and stood over the items. 'She said she had no funds.'

A gentle hand rested on his arm. Nigellus' touch was warm. 'Clearly she lied to you. Perhaps there was more to Master Crispin asking you to protect her. Were you also to spy on her?'

'He had not said . . .' He frowned at Lenny. 'I still don't believe you, but you say Crispin hired you to watch her.'

'And never bid me stop. And so I didn't.'

'Nothing will be settled until we talk to Master Guest,' said Nigellus. 'Let us see if he has returned, and we can stop all this speculating.'

John was certain Lenny palmed some of the coins on the bed, but he said nothing. What more was there to say until Crispin cleared it up? They marched down the stairs, past the scowling innkeeper and out to the street. Nigellus stopped Lenny from continuing. 'Since Master Guest is hiring you to watch her, I suggest you remain.'

'Eh? I still have to stay here?'

'If she returns for her bounty, it's best we know where she is going, no?'

'Awww. It's always the same. Old Lenny is treated like a beast of burden.'

'It's better than you deserve,' hissed John.

'Sodomite!' Lenny hissed back.

Nigellus grabbed Rykener again before he smacked the beggar once more. The lawyer pulled John away up the lane, wagging an admonishing finger at him.

They walked until making the turn at Friday Street. A left at West Cheap soon got them to the Shambles, and John was relieved to see a light coming from the nearly closed shutters of Crispin's new lodgings.

'Thank Christ he's back,' he said and trotted ahead of Nigellus to knock on the door.

He heard much shuffling inside and a long pause before Crispin himself answered the door, opening it just a sliver. 'For God's sake, Crispin. It's been too long. May we come in?'

Crispin's gray eye – the only one he would show – darted from here to there, taking in his visitors. Reluctantly, it seemed, he opened the door fully to allow them both in. 'What a merry band is here,' he said, mouth set in a grim line.

FOURTEEN

John Rykener and the lawyer Nigellus Cobmartin walked across his threshold. Crispin closed the door after them, recognizing that such a communion was not to bear good news. And when he turned to face them it was certainly evident on their features.

John sighed dramatically. 'Where to begin?'

'What are you doing here, Master Cobmartin?'

John interjected. 'Well, that's the crux of it, isn't it?'

Nigellus cleared his throat and leaned forward with a raised finger, as he might have done while holding forth at a court of law. 'Your Mistress Woodleigh, Crispin, seems to be . . . well . . .'

'Missing!' piped John.

'Missing? Did I not hire you to protect her, John?'

'And I did. Right well . . . up until several hours ago. She was abducted.'

'Or not,' said Nigellus.

Crispin found the goblet Jack had poured for him and drank it halfway down. 'Someone explain.'

Nigellus nudged John aside and, with a gentle expression, began. 'Firstly, it is good to see you again, Crispin. We should not wait for quarter days. Our acquaintance is not merely tenant and landlord but much more, I hope. Well, Master Rykener here came to me most distressed, saying that the woman you hired him to, er, protect, had been abducted.'

'Stuffed my head into a bag, tied me up,' he said, rubbing his wrists. 'And then I couldn't find her.' He still seemed distressed to Crispin.

'So Master Rykener says. This is how it appeared to him.'

'Appeared?'

'Master Rykener, I beg of you to let me continue. Only by the cold recitation of facts may we ever be able to discern the truth. *Veritas numquam perit.*'

Rykener slammed his arms over his chest and blew a stray strand of hair off his forehead. He was in his woman's clothes. The hem was muddy, as was his cloak, as if he had been tramping all over London. Perhaps he had been.

'Now then,' Nigellus went on, 'when I arrived at the inn the room was in disarray. A struggle had taken place, the lady gone. When we investigated downstairs in the inn's hall, the innkeeper claimed he had seen nothing; the patrons, those that might have noticed the violent struggle of a woman for her life and honor, also claimed to have seen nothing. And when we encountered Master Munch along the road, he had a very different story indeed.'

The man paused, glancing at the goblet in Crispin's grasp. Crispin shook his head. 'Forgive me, Master Cobmartin, Master Rykener. May I offer you wine?'

'I'd be grateful, Crispin, truth to tell,' said Rykener. He sank, exhausted, into a chair.

Nigellus licked his lips. 'Oh, that should be a great relief, Master Crispin.'

Crispin took up the discarded goblet from the floor and brought it to the table. He retrieved the wine jug and another cup – a horn beaker – from the larder and poured into each.

'God save us,' muttered Rykener as he drank his.

'Much thanks,' said Nigellus, taking a delicate sip. 'Now then,' he continued. 'When we encountered Master Munch, he informed us that you had hired him to watch the lady as well. I must say, the whole of it intrigues me. Master Rykener intimated that the lady – a client of yours – is in search of a former sheriff that did her an injustice and absconded with her young niece—'

A sound upstairs made them all glance upward toward the rafters. 'Is that young Jack?' asked Nigellus.

'Er . . . no. Probably that damned cat.'

'Ah! The feline. Clever, they are. But deadly. *Qui ludet cum felibus in Expectat scalpi!*'

Crispin tapped his fingers on his dagger hilt. 'You were saying, Nigellus?'

'Oh, yes! The lady. As I said, Master Rykener went in pursuit of her abductors but far later than was helpful. Not your fault, of course,' he said to John's sour face. 'Being tied up, you could do little. But once we encountered your Master Munch, he told us an interesting tale. For he had indeed seen the lady but she was not in the company of her abductors in fear of her life. No. She was alone. Not in fear but irritated, as he explained it. In a rush. Another witness corroborated this portion of the tale – a shopkeeper. Leonard Munch then followed her to Master Simon Wynchecombe's house, a former sheriff of London of your acquaintance, I do believe. He said she watched the house for signs of him for the better part of the day. And from a most unusual place. Can you even guess?'

'I'm on tenterhooks, Nigellus.'

'On the roof! Can you imagine it? Further, this spy of yours, this Leonard Munch, insisted that she crept along the rooftops until she found entrance in a top-floor window, where later she emerged through a door carrying a sack. All most unusual. Now, I am not one to entirely believe this . . . this spy of yours, but with truth in the balance, I insisted we return to the inn to look for such a sack. And what do you suppose we found?'

'A sack?' said Crispin dryly.

'Indeed, Master Guest! The very same. Under the bed, under the floorboards. And such bounty within it!'

'Truly?'

The lawyer raised his hand. '*Meum est vinculum*. Gold, silver goods and coins.'

'And she said she was poor!' cried Rykener, finishing his wine and pouring more.

'Hold, Nigellus,' said Crispin. 'Are you implying that she was . . . *burgling* a house in order to come away with these goods?'

'That, of course, is speculation. As Master Rykener pointed out but none too convincingly, she could have obtained these goods for some sort of restitution or payment. But it seems unlikely by the nature of her, erm, entrance into the house. If Master Munch can be believed on that point, that is.'

'And where is Master Munch now?' A corner of Crispin's mouth crept upward. He scarcely ever thought of Lenny as 'master' anything.

'I enjoined him to maintain his guard of the inn. After all, with such bounty, it is unlikely the lady would leave them behind. But I fear she will quit the Unicorn now that we are on to her.'

'I fear you are right. Well done, then.' He sat, well aware that upstairs Wynchecombe was likely hearing all of this and making of it what he will. Yet the facts were curious. Why would Lenny make up such a fantastical tale? He had never done so before when working for Crispin. At least that he knew of. Stealing into houses? Katherine Woodleigh? It seemed unlikely but what did he really know of her? The feeling in his gut persisted and he knew that feeling well. It was his very body telling him what a fool he'd been. These Woodleighs and Whitechurches might all very well be thieves and murderers. One trying to coerce Simon, possibly even to extortion, while the other was a common burglar. What was he to make of that? Yet she was well-spoken with estates and a past at court. How could this be?

'I'm having a difficult time reconciling these facts, Master Nigellus, even as thorough as you laid them out—' He gave a nod of recognition to Nigellus, who bowed back in return.

'It's impossible, I tell you,' whined Rykener. 'Quite out of character.'

'And you were with her the whole of the week?'

'I was. I never shirked my duty, Crispin. You know I wouldn't have. And I got to like her, too. She's a wit and just a bit naughty.

But I cannot imagine that she would go about mincing across rooftops.'

Crispin leaned forward on the table, fingers wrapped about his goblet. 'About her abduction. What can you tell me? Did you see anyone, hear anyone? Any voices?'

'None. I was asleep and just as I awoke a sack was thrust down upon me—'

'A sack!' Nigellus cried.

Rykener gave him a withering look. 'And I was tied to my chair,' he said, enunciating each word. 'I heard scuffling and Kat crying out, and then they were out of the door.'

'How many were there?'

'I don't know, Crispin. It all happened so fast. One moment I was just awakening and the next I was stuffed into a sack. I heard the noises but I was struggling, too.'

'So . . . you truly have no proof that anyone was there at all?'

He cocked his head and scowled. 'Not you, too? Are you calling me a liar?'

'No, John, not at all. Just that you perceived the appearance of an abduction. But if I came upon you from behind just as you were awakening from sleep, stuffed a bag on your head and quickly tied you to a chair, I could make convincing enough noises and scuffling to make you *think* I was being abducted . . . couldn't I?'

'That's what I told him!' said Nigellus.

Rykener rose, fury coloring his cheeks. 'That damned woman! What horrible deceit! What lies!'

Nigellus cleared his throat. 'Ahem, Master Rykener, to be completely fair, were you not deceiving just as much, posing as her, er, lady's maid? Perhaps she was fearful of you.'

'That's absurd. I couldn't hurt anyone.'

'But she didn't know that.'

He clucked his tongue. 'Crispin, tell him how absurd that is.'

'I fear there is more to it than that, Nigellus. Why go to elaborate heights to make Master Rykener think she is being abducted? She could have simply walked away. No, there is more to it. And . . . I think I have an inkling as to what.'

But when Crispin said nothing more, John slammed his hand to the table. 'Well? Don't leave us in suspense.'

Cocking an eye ceilingward, he quickly looked away. 'I'm not at liberty to say at the moment.'

'This is damnable. Do you mean to say that you do not fear her fate?'

'I rather think not. At the moment.'

'Well I never!' He sat back, arms folded.

Nigellus finally sat at the table. 'You do involve yourself in such interesting ways, Master Guest. Never a dull moment.'

'Oh, for a dull moment,' Crispin muttered.

A knock on the door caused all three heads to swivel toward the entrance.

'Who the hell is that?' rasped John.

Should he tell them to hide themselves? No, there was already one too many in hiding in his humble lodgings. Instead, he rose and went to the door.

A Cistercian monk stood on his step, hands hidden in his black scapular. Crispin's first thoughts were *God's blood! Not another one.*

'Crispin Guest?' said the man, face hidden under the shadow of his cowl.

'Yes. And who might you be, brother?'

'I am Brother James . . . from Hailes Abbey.'

Am I dreaming? It was the only explanation. 'Brother . . . I have only just come from Hailes. What is your business here?'

'I know. I followed you.' He looked to the street with jerky, nervous movements. 'May I come in?'

With a deep sigh, Crispin opened the door wider and allowed the monk to pass over the threshold. But when he saw Nigellus and Rykener standing by the table, the monk paused.

'Oh. You have guests. I . . . I should come back later.'

'Oh, no, brother. Do come in. I couldn't bear to speculate if you were to leave now.'

Eyeing both men suspiciously, he moved a few feet into the room and stood by the hearth.

'Wine, brother? I have only a bowl left from which to drink out of.'

'No, thank you. I have . . . private matters to discuss.'

Nigellus touched Rykener's arm. 'Perhaps we will wait upstairs until your visitor has departed.'

'No!' He hadn't meant to shout. Actually, he wanted to laugh. 'Apologies, Nigellus. But perhaps I will talk with you and John later.'

'Later?' cried John without trying to mask his voice. The monk's eyes widened. 'Why do *I* have to leave?'

'You both have to leave. I thank you for your information but I must see to this man here. Perhaps, J——, er, Eleanor, you will be so good as to go with Master Cobmartin for the moment.'

Still unhappy, John glanced at Nigellus, who was smiling at him. Somewhat mollified by the lawyer's kind expression, John seemed to soften. 'Very well. But you owe me an explanation.'

'And I shall give it when I know more. Thank you . . . Eleanor.'

He rolled his shoulder at Crispin and followed Nigellus out of the door. The monk watched their progress until the door was closed again.

'And now,' said Crispin, trying to hurry this up. 'I say again, why did you not talk to me when I was at Hailes? Why come all this way to London?'

'Because I feared for the safety of the relic. You were only gone a day before someone tried to steal it again.'

'What!'

'It's true. The abbot was beside himself.'

'Did you catch the culprit?'

'No. He got away.'

'Did you see him?'

He shook his cowled head, black over the white gown. 'Alas. But the abbot bid me go to you, and so I have arrived.'

'And so you have. To bring me these tidings?'

'No. To bring you this.'

Crispin swore as the monk pulled the crystal vial out from under his scapular.

FIFTEEN

od's blood! Then Crispin felt foolish, for his oath suddenly rang true. It was God's Holy Blood right here in his lodgings . . . again.

The monk held out the strange, flattened bowl of glass, the rusty blood lazily rolling from one side of the crystal to the other. Vaguely, he wondered if the monk could see the blood run free.

'And just what does the abbot expect me to do with it?'

'Why . . . protect it, of course.'

Dropping his face into his palm didn't seem like enough somehow. 'Could he not put guards on it?'

'We are few monks at Hailes. Even fewer now with our two deaths.'

Dammit. 'I can think of only one solution, then. We will take it to Westminster Abbey.'

'There? Oh. I shouldn't think that a very good idea, begging your pardon, Master Guest.'

'And why not? They have plenty of monks to guard it.'

Brother James clutched the reliquary. 'You don't understand, Master Guest. They are our biggest rivals.'

'Rivals? An unusual term. How can the abbey be a rival to you? Are you not all men of God?'

'Well, certainly. But . . . surely it cannot be unknown to you how envious they are of our relic of Hailes?'

'I don't understand. Westminster has its own blood relic, given to them by Henry III. The relic of the Holy Blood.'

'Oh, indeed. Yet pilgrims come most often to Hailes to see this one. It is our very livelihood.'

It was true. Old King Henry had hoped that the blood relic he presented to the abbey over one hundred and forty years ago would generate the interest and pilgrim fees as did the holy relic of Hailes, but it was never so. And after all this time, there was still a rivalry?

'Nevertheless, I believe the safest place would be the abbey.'

The monk considered. By his expression, he didn't think much of this plan, but Crispin was already grabbing his cloak and stepping out onto the street. 'Brother?'

The monk moved as urged and Crispin locked the door, hoping Simon would behave himself when left to his own devices.

It would take a good half an hour to reach the abbey, and so Crispin whirled his cloak over his shoulders, buttoned it from the cold and set out toward the Strand. Reluctantly, the monk followed.

Crispin mulled it all through his brain and wasn't liking what he was coming up with. Some of it was making sense while other parts didn't. And then there was Simon. The fool had done everything wrong, but Crispin well knew what a wily woman could do to a man's senses.

There were still many travelers going to and from London and as they arrived at Charing Cross it was just as crowded in the late afternoon as it was in the morning. The spires of the palace rose above the mist but the daunting facade of Westminster Abbey imposed itself in front of their view. Crispin made his way not toward the west door but to the side where the porter's bell hung to welcome visitors to the monastery. Crispin pulled on the rope, letting the chimes die away as he waited, stealing glances at the quiet Cistercian.

A shadow preceded the Benedictine monk as he approached the gate. Brother Eric first greeted Crispin before he noticed the man in white robes beside him. 'This is Brother James from Hailes Abbey, Brother Eric. Is Abbot William available?'

'I will take you to him,' he said with only an inquiring brow raised. Brother Eric walked slower these days, Crispin noticed as they moved along the cloister arcade, and his hair was not as dark as it used to be, marked by gray as it was now. Crispin had found several gray hairs in his own black locks, and little wonder. He was thirty-five now, certainly getting on in years.

Crispin watched his clerical friend as he stole glances at the Cistercian. He knew Brother Eric was trained well and would not enquire, but he must have burned with curiosity. Trying to recall how many years he had known the monk, Crispin reckoned it must have been before his time of banishment. Brother Eric was the faithful servant of Abbot Nicholas de Litlyngton, Abbot

William's predecessor and, as was the way of things, demoted in favor of Abbot William's trusted chaplains. The older gave way to the young. Brother Eric, as expected, never complained.

They reached the abbot's lodgings where Abbot William de Colchester was dictating to his chaplain, Brother John Sandon, something about tithes and the accounting as the monk busily scratched down what his abbot said on a flat parchment, holding the quill tight in his fingers and crouching low over his writing. Both abbot and chaplain looked up upon Crispin's entering.

'Crispin Guest, my Lord Abbot,' announced Brother Eric before bowing and leaving them there.

Abbot William smiled in greeting, but the smile faltered when he spied the Cistercian monk standing uncomfortably behind Crispin's back.

'My dear Master Guest. You have brought . . . a visitor.'

'My Lord Abbot,' said Crispin with a bow. He turned to the Cistercian. 'This is Brother James, late of Hailes Abbey. We have a matter of some importance to discuss with you.' He eyed Brother John pointedly.

'I see. Brother,' he said to his chaplain, 'await me without.'

Silently, the monk set aside his quill and rose from his place at the tall desk. He bowed to all present and then shuffled out of the door, closing it after him.

The abbot never moved from where he was standing beside the fire. 'May I offer you refreshment?'

Crispin always thought that Abbot William had the look of a shopkeeper about him, with his fleshy face and pale blue eyes, unlike the patrician features and ancestry of the late Abbot Nicholas. But he knew the abbot to be a shrewd and clever negotiator, having spent his many years as Westminster's arch-deacon, enviable to other less-educated archdeacons, no doubt, for his expertise in matters of divorce and excommunication, though seldom did he use this expertise on its premises, for he had been mostly sent abroad to Rome to take matters of the king to the pope while Abbot Nicholas presided over Westminster. A patient and judicious man was Abbot de Colchester, and Crispin admired his careful judgment and sedate reasoning.

The monk beside him muttered that he needed no refreshment and Crispin declined the offer as well, wanting to get this over with. 'My Lord Abbot, we need not go over the fine details but we are in need of the services of your monks. This brother has brought to me a precious relic from Hailes. I have been admonished by his abbot to guard it. Alas, I fear I am at a disadvantage to do so, and so I implore you and your good monks to take on this task.'

Abbot William laced his fingers over his belly and, though his expression never changed, his eyes seemed to take on a sparkle when the relic was mentioned. 'Of what relic do you speak, Master Guest?'

'The Holy Blood of Hailes, my lord.'

Abbot William unlaced his fingers, crossed himself then returned his fingers to their repose against his belly. 'I take it this is to remain a secret.'

'Most assuredly, my lord.'

'I beg your mercy, Lord Abbot,' said Brother James suddenly, 'but I objected to Master Guest's bringing the relic here. I told him of the . . . the . . . rivalry.'

'Ah.' The abbot strode to his chair by the fire and carefully sat down. This was Crispin's cue to join him there, and he sat in the chair opposite. 'I find it extraordinary,' said the abbot, 'that our brother here should travel all the way from Hailes just to present the relic to you, Master Guest.' He eyed Crispin sharply. Crispin always felt that when Abbot William did so, he could somehow see into his soul. An absurd notion, but the man's gaze was always particularly acute and he seldom seemed to blink. 'But of course,' he went on, 'there is more to the tale that you *have* not, and perhaps *will* not tell me, no?'

'It is a long tale, my lord,' said Crispin, 'and your chaplain is waiting outside . . . in the cold. Suffice it to say that there are those who have already died for it, one is still in danger of his life, and . . . other mischief afoot.'

The abbot's still form always disconcerted him, but Crispin knew that the man had long practice in it, in his many years as envoy for Westminster, waiting long hours and even days in the halls of the pope's palace to be called to an audience. 'Interesting. I hope that you will satisfy my curiosity . . . someday.'

'Indeed I shall, my Lord Abbot. Someday.' He offered a crooked smile.

'But for now you will house the relic here, under lock and

key. I am loath to hide such a thing. For our Lord gave His precious Blood to us for our sins, and it is proper to venerate, to display His relics.'

'And ordinarily I would agree with you, my lord, but in this case it must not be known where the relic is. At present.'

'I need no convincing, Master Guest. If you say it is so, then I am inclined to believe your word.'

Crispin warmed at the compliment. The abbot so infrequently gave them.

Abbot William turned to the monk still standing behind Crispin. 'I take it you have it on your person?'

'I do, my Lord Abbot.'

'Then we will lock it away in my lodgings. Will that suffice?'

'I think that will do well,' said Crispin.

The abbot rose and approached the Cistercian, who seemed to shy back slightly. The abbot opened his hands. 'Brother, will you surrender it?'

Brother James hesitated but finally brought it out from under his scapular again. But instead of handing it to the abbot – *to the enemy*, Crispin mused – he offered it to Crispin.

Crispin rose and took it. The tingle he had experienced before jolted his hands so much he was afraid he'd drop it. Clutching the beryl crystal, he handed it with a reverential bow to the abbot. The abbot shook his sleeves over his hands and took the crystal with great solemnity.

He looked it over carefully, eyes tracking its every surface. 'The Blood . . . it runs,' he muttered.

Ah, thought Crispin. *A sinless soul.* But then he dismissed it. That was assuming the relic was real, and of that he always harbored his doubts.

Like a mother carrying its babe, the abbot cradled the reliquary and never took his eyes off it as he approached an ambry. He took a key from his belt, unlocked the door and carefully placed it inside, relocking the door once he'd closed it. He gently touched the door, dropped to his knees and murmured a prayer. The monk followed suit, and when the abbot was done Brother James stepped forward, nervous hands rubbing together. 'My Lord Abbot, I do not know whether I should stay here or request hospitality at St Mary Graces . . .'

'Of course you should stay here, brother. If that is your wish.'

'I . . . I do not know, my lord.'

'I think you would feel more comfortable as close to it as you can be. My chaplain will find you quarters, and then you may return here to keep vigil. Will that suffice?'

In answer, the monk looked relieved and bowed low.

The abbot rang a hand bell on his desk and Brother John was quick to enter. 'Brother John, take Brother James to his quarters. He's to be our guest. He will be permitted to come and go to my lodgings while he remains here. However long that is.'

Brother John did not seem to question the abbot's unusual request and led the Cistercian away, even as Brother James kept looking over his shoulder toward the ambry until the door closed it from his view.

The abbot turned narrowed eyes toward Crispin until he strode sedately back to his chair by the fire. 'Master Guest, you do involve yourself so.'

'Why does everyone keep saying that?'

'Because it is true.' He sat and arranged his robes. 'Murder, you say? Danger? Perhaps you would find it safer within the monastery as well.'

'I should find such residence . . . confining, my lord.'

The abbot smiled. 'Is there anything I can offer you? Information, perhaps?'

'What do you know of Westminster's Holy Blood?'

'Shall we go to see it?' He rose again and Crispin was compelled to follow.

They traversed the arcade and through the cloister, somewhere Crispin felt particularly privileged to be. They cut across to the church and entered by a side door. There were many people in the church, as there always was, just as there were in St Paul's back in London. Men looking for work as clerks, as lawyers, and others looking for those men to hire. But the abbot managed to skirt the commerce going on around him and made his way to the tomb of King Henry III.

The latten effigy of the king in repose sat high above his tomb, but Crispin could still see the jewels set in his crown and in the crossed scepters in his hands, his features gleaming in the candle-light. Set in the tomb, in its own modest shrine, was a stepped cabinet of gold topped with a cross. Set within a grille was a crystal vase decorated with gems and gold. Inside the vase was a rusty color.

The abbot knelt, crossed himself and touched the grille, unlocking it. 'The abbot of Westminster has many duties and responsibilities,' he said quietly. He shook down the sleeve of his gown again to cover his hand and take the vase with his cloth-covered fingers. He turned with it to show Crispin, who also knelt and crossed himself. 'But I have also found that one of its rewards is being able to do this.'

Instead of going to Crispin, he allowed Crispin to approach. Crispin looked at it from as many angles as he could manage. It wasn't like the Blood of Hailes at all. Instead of the freely flowing blood, it sat as a reddish swath in cloudy glass. He did not want to go as far as to call it less impressive, but, well. That was the only description he could ascribe to it.

'I know what you're thinking,' said Abbot William. He cocked his head at the relic, even as he turned it in his covered hands. 'Because the Blood is not liquid, it isn't quite as . . . inspiring as the Blood of Hailes, no?'

'Yet some say that they cannot see the *liquid* Blood of Hailes. It is only for the sinless to see it flow.'

'Yes. Isn't that interesting?' His eyes sparkled. 'Did *you* see it flow, Crispin?'

He locked gazes with Abbot William. 'Strangely . . . yes.'

The abbot smiled. 'I thought as much.' He gently returned the reliquary to its cupboard and closed and locked the grille. 'It was a great honor, of course, for King Henry to have bestowed this relic upon the abbey, and so we keep it here at his tomb. And yet, it has not brought the pilgrims to us as he had hoped it would. Why do you suppose that is?'

'The Holy Blood of Hailes is kept in its own magnificent shrine, my lord.'

'Do you think that is the reason? I'm not so certain. You have seen many relics, I daresay, have you not?'

Too many was on his lips, but he changed it to a simple, 'Yes, my lord.'

'And are you of the opinion that this relic is the true blood of our Lord?'

'I cannot say.'

'Ah! So you do doubt.'

'I . . . doubt them all, Abbot William. For without proof, how can a man know?'

'Faith, my dear Crispin. I know you are a man of faith. But in these you doubt. The pope himself has declared it a true relic of our Lord.'

'Then if the pope says so . . .'

The abbot snorted. 'And I know how much you admire the pope.'

Crispin judiciously said nothing.

'But what of the Blood of Hailes? Do you think it is the true relic?'

He couldn't help but rub his fingers together, remembering the tingle in them from handling the reliquary. 'I . . . do not know. Only that . . .' He looked down at his hand. 'I get a strange feeling around it.'

'But not with this one?'

Crispin glanced up to the reliquary behind its grille. Though he hadn't touched it, he felt no strange presence from it, no godly sensation. It was merely a crystal with a stain.

Crispin shrugged. 'I cannot say.'

'You say much when you say nothing,' said the abbot with a gentle smile. 'Relics. God's gifts to us. Or are they a curse? You would say so.'

Again, Crispin remained silent.

The abbot nodded. 'Would you be surprised to learn that I agree with you? Man is not mature enough to accept these gifts, if gifts they are. He would use them for ill purposes. Indeed, you have been a witness to much of that. And is it the same again with this relic of Hailes? You said that one is in danger and some have already died. What is man to do with such beneficence? Is it better to toss them all in a pile and burn the lot of them?'

'So I have thought many a time, Abbot William.'

'I thought you had.' He sighed. 'Man is a wretched creature. He is full of sin and evil. Often he would choose first to do his fellow ill, rather than a kindness. Yes, being abbot here has its rewards but also its curses, for I am firsthand with those of the court. And though I am no traitor . . .' his glance roved over

Crispin, aware of the sting his words inflicted but seeming not to care, '. . . and I speak no ill of the king, I cannot say the same for his courtiers.'

'Surely you do not speak of their confessions.'

'Of course not. I am not permitted by the seal of the confessional to even acknowledge a confession took place. But one need not even hear a confession to know the hearts of some of these men. I tell you true, Crispin, that I sometimes think fondly of my days as prior and archdeacon, for I was far from here oftentimes. That is not to say that I regret this office I now perform. Oh, no. I have kept order here. I have cared for my monks like a stern father. But there are responsibilities that a man of poor reputation might find daunting. A more ambitious man might twist it to his own pleasure. I thank God for making me a humble and forthright man, and for giving my monks the foresight to vote me as their abbot.'

Crispin hid his smile in the shadows. 'And how well you fulfill your destiny.'

'Destiny? Is there such a thing when God grants us free will, Crispin?'

Abbot William was fond of such philosophical discussions, as was Crispin. Abbot Nicholas had been less so, but Crispin found he much preferred Abbot William's thoughtful questions and viewpoint that mirrored his own.

The abbot turned from the shrine and tomb and tucked his hands into his sleeves. Crispin wished his sleeves could accommodate his hands, for it was cold in the church. They walked sedately side by side. 'I have another query for you,' said Crispin as they walked back toward the abbot's lodgings and to the much-appreciated fireplace. 'Do you know a Katherine Woodleigh?'

'The name is unfamiliar to me.'

'A young woman, early twenties, blue eyes, auburn hair. A former courtier.'

The abbot slowly nodded. 'I believe I have seen such a woman talking to one of my monks.'

'And might you know the nature of that conversation, my lord?'

'Does this relate to our relic situation, Crispin?'

'Indeed it does.'

'Well, now. The monk in question is a Brother Rodney Beaton. Do you wish to speak to him?'

'I would be most happy to do so.'

'I will have him brought to my lodgings. By the way, as a consequence of our many discussions on the matter, I have obtained a chess set.' His eyes seem to sparkle with mischief. Crispin couldn't help but smile back. 'I would be pleased to play a game or two with you, if you have the time.'

Abbot Nicholas had left his chess set to Crispin in his will, and when Crispin first met Abbot William he had called it a foolish waste of time. Now he had warmed to the idea of it as he had warmed to Crispin himself. It was endlessly amusing how the man had changed. 'I wish I had the leisure time now, my lord.' And he did wish it. But his thoughts fell to Simon Wynchecombe hiding back at his lodgings, and he dearly needed to find out more about that. 'Alas. I have much work to do to save another life. But I'm certain I can find the time for you at a later date.'

'I would be pleased. I do not believe it is pride to say that I shall likely trounce you.'

'You can certainly try.'

They walked through the enclosed cloister in silence. The shadows of the trefoiled arches cast an intricate pattern across the stone floor. Crispin glanced across the garth. The grass was patchy with many dead spots, but with the spring he was certain the new shoots would push up and in no time the whole of it would be green again.

They passed under the shadow of an arch where a monk stood guard outside the abbot's chamber. The abbot spoke quietly to the monk and the cleric ran off to do his superior's bidding. Entering the chamber again, they found the Cistercian at his post, kneeling by the closed ambry.

Crispin forgot he would be there, but it didn't appear that the abbot had. Crispin doubted he forgot or overlooked much.

They waited until the monk returned with what Crispin could only guess was Brother Rodney Beaton. His hair was dark, and his thick brows and sharp nose gave him a penetrating appearance. His dark brown eyes scrutinized Crispin with intent.

'Brother Rodney,' said the abbot, sitting behind his desk. 'This is Crispin Guest. He is known as the Tracker and he is a friend to this abbey. Please answer his questions.'

The monk looked startled but even more so when he turned his head and saw the Cistercian kneeling silently by the ambry.

'Brother Rodney,' said Crispin without preamble. 'Do you know a Katherine Woodleigh?'

He narrowed his eyes. 'My lord?'

'I am not a lord. Answer the question.'

His eyes darted between Crispin and the expressionless abbot. 'I . . . know her, yes.'

'She came to the monastery recently. What did she talk with you about?'

'She . . . she is worried about her niece.'

'And how is it that you know her?'

The monk slid a glance toward his attentive abbot again. 'I . . . made her acquaintance some years ago.'

'How?'

The monk shrugged. 'I cannot recall. She was in the church and needed a candle, I think.'

'And she sought you out ever since?'

He shrugged again. 'I offered her comfort.'

'Surely she had a confessor for that.'

'She did. At court. But . . . she no longer goes there.'

He nodded. 'How often do you see her?'

'Not often. She came here last week. And before that, months had passed. I do not think she lives in London or Westminster.'

'No, she lives in Hailes.'

Brother James turned his head momentarily toward them but then turned back again.

Crispin kept a steady gaze on Brother Rodney, saying nothing, waiting him out, watching him sweat and fidget under his scrutiny.

'Tell me, brother,' he said suddenly. The monk did not appear to expect it and jumped. 'Do you find her . . . enchanting?'

He blinked and wiped the beads of sweat from his upper lip. 'I am a man of God, sir.'

'But even a man of God can recognize a pretty face.'

Abbot William leaned forward, hands interlaced on the desk before him.

The monk looked his way but was forced by Crispin's nearness to look up at him again.

'Answer the question. Is she enchanting?'

'I do not know your meaning.'

'Of course you do,' said Crispin forcefully. 'You were not born a monk, man. Is she charming? Is she beautiful? Even the pope could answer that.'

Abbot William cleared his throat in warning. Crispin ignored him.

The monk pulled his collar away from his throat. 'Yes. Yes, she is. But I was not bewitched by her, if that is the crux of your meaning. As a man of God, it is my duty to ignore such worldly things, as my abbot instructs.' And he bowed toward his abbot, who nodded back.

'Crispin,' said Abbot William softly. 'Have you got your answers?'

Not even close. How much better would it be to beat it out of the man, for he knew in his gut that the monk was lying. About what, he wasn't certain, but the lies were there. Yet he doubted very much that Abbot William would allow it.

Crispin postured, hand on his dagger hilt, and glared at the monk. 'I haven't gotten satisfactory answers, but that is all for now. Mark me, I'll be back again to ask more.'

The monk looked to the abbot for confirmation and Abbot William flicked his hand. That was enough for Brother Rodney and he scrambled out of the door, letting it fall closed behind him.

'Is that how you usually extract information?' drawled the abbot.

Crispin gave him a withering look. 'Not usually, no.'

'Bless me.' He sighed. 'But even I could see that he was sinning by omission.'

'Yes. He is hiding something. I will return and, by that time, after he stews a bit, he might be more amenable to speak to me.'

'Shall I admonish him as well?'

'It might help.' The Cistercian was still at his prayers. 'Brother James, guard your charge well.'

He raised his head and nodded but said nothing. *Cistercians.* Crispin snorted.

'I bid you farewell, my Lord Abbot.'

'As always, Crispin, it has been . . . intriguing.' He motioned a benediction over him. Crispin accepted it and made his way out of the abbot's lodgings.

Brother John hovered outside. 'I suppose you are free to go in again, Brother John.'

The monk smiled, but before he could get away entirely, Crispin asked, 'Brother, do you know a Katherine Woodleigh?'

He thought for a moment. 'No. Should I?'

'A woman comes into the gate and talks with Rodney Beaton, one of your fellow monks. Young, auburn-haired, blue-eyed. You have not seen her?'

'No.'

Crispin sidled up to him and spoke quietly, even though they appeared to be alone. 'If she should make an appearance, could you get a message to me?'

'I shall do all I can. With my abbot's permission, of course.'

'Thank you.' He turned to go when the monk called him back.

'Master Guest, I do know a Katherine Pyke. She has a similar appearance and has come to the porter's gate before.'

That name sounded familiar but he could not place it. 'She reminds you of my description?'

'Yes. If *she* comes, should I also notify you?'

His eyes roved over the monk, the arches, the shadowed corners. 'Why not? Too many women loitering about the cloisters, eh, brother?'

He left the abbey and stepped onto the muddy street, busy with the traffic of carts and men on horses. Crispin smiled. He had much to say to Katherine Woodleigh when they next met.

He looked back longingly toward the palace and wondered if he could send a message to the duke, but just as quickly dismissed the idea. He was back from his travels but very much doubted he would be pleased to receive a message from Crispin. The king had not warmed to Crispin over the years and, especially after the last escapade with the Coronation Chair, he didn't think Richard would be any more pleased to see him now should he encounter him in the halls of Westminster Palace. And he always seemed to run into him there when he least wanted to see him.

He skirted the carts and riders and many people going to and fro. He turned back to look at the gate and ran right into someone.

With an apology on his lips, he shut them just as quickly. The woman looked at him aghast and pivoted to run, but he snapped his hand out and closed it on her wrist, dragging her close as if he were escorting her.

'My dear demoiselle,' he said to Katherine Woodleigh. She struggled for a moment but then stiffly surrendered. 'How you do get about.'

'How dare you, Crispin Guest,' she snarled. 'How dare you leave me with a *man* dressed as a *woman*!'

'Oh, that.'

'Yes, that! What were you trying to prove?'

'I was trying to protect you the best way I knew how. And yet, you scarce needed his protection. Your "abduction" was a brilliant mummery.'

She raised her chin and he admired the profile as they walked.

'But now I wonder just exactly what it was for. You didn't expect to be watched at all hours of the day. That must have irked. You needed to get rid of him and that sufficed. But I wonder at this capering about on rooftops.'

She stopped and he was forced to stop with her. 'What are you talking about?'

'I have spies, demoiselle. Perhaps you aren't as poor as you let on, what with your larcenous habits.'

Her outrage, etched clearly on her face, suddenly vanished, replaced by a playful smile. She laughed – a merry, ringing sound. He was reminded suddenly again of fairy barrows and changelings. 'You are a damned clever man, Crispin Guest. I've never met the like. Would that I could have met you years ago.'

'I don't think you would have liked me years ago. Believe it or not, I have mellowed with age.'

'Mellowed or not, you are quite extraordinary.'

'Allow me to be more extraordinary. You don't have a niece, do you?'

Her playful smile transformed again into a wide look of shock. 'By God's wounds, you are a match for me.'

'A match? I think not. You are clever, true, but I have not yet discerned the nature. So, there is no Sybil Whitechurch? I want to hear you say it.'

'If that is your desire then I will. There is no niece, there is no Sybil Whitechurch. I am she and she is me, for what it's worth.'

'Then you owe me a tale, demoiselle.'

'I believe I do. Shall we to an alehouse to tell it?'

He led her on, until he found an ale stake leaning into the street. The Cockerel would do. He opened the door for her and she stepped in.

SIXTEEN

Once they had settled with ales in beakers in front of them, she began.

'Much of what I told you was true. About me, that is. Reduced circumstances forced me to make some difficult decisions. A woman alone can only accomplish so much without becoming a whore. I chose to avoid that route.'

'And yet, the men you have left behind you . . .' He ticked his head at her.

She frowned. 'You judge me? You, who have committed treason and then found your way through dubious occupations? Look in a glass, Crispin Guest. If I am a whore, then so are you.'

'Careful, demoiselle. My honor may be tattered but it is still intact. My honor has never been compromised. I have never stolen to live.'

'But you let that servant of yours do so. Oh, I know about you, Master Guest. I've asked. I've listened to the tales. People seem to love to talk about you and your exploits. Before you climb onto that high place, do not be so certain you can look down upon me.'

Perhaps she had a point. Jack had started out life as a cutpurse and thief. Crispin had often enough looked the other way when the larder was empty but Jack had produced his meals nonetheless. He folded his arms huffily over his chest and leaned back against the wall with a scowl. 'So what now? If there is no niece, then who is it that had these affairs? You?'

She teased a circle with her finger on the rough table. 'Naturally.'

'And if you do not whore for a living – and that is debatable given the statements of various monks I have encountered – then what is it you do?'

'I'm surprised you must ask. I'm a burglar.'

He eyed their surroundings once more to make certain no one could hear them. She didn't seem as concerned.

'You jest.'

'I assure you, I do not. No one ever suspects a woman, especially a woman with breeding.'

'You would have me believe that you break into houses and steal?'

'Your own spies confirmed it. My "capering about on rooftops."'

He studied her, poured more ale into her cup then poured more for himself. Yes, she was proud of this feat. Her smile told him so. But she was also an accomplished liar. Was this, too, a lie?

She sipped her ale. 'But I am also invited into these houses. It's how I met Simon Wynchecombe.'

'Did you coerce him to kill for you?'

'Don't be absurd.'

'Demoiselle, the entire circumstances are absurd. And two men are dead.'

'Two?'

'Yes. One you saw at my doorstep. A monk. The other back at Hailes Abbey also a monk.'

She drew back. This was clearly a surprise . . . or more of her theatrics. He couldn't decide which. 'A monk at Hailes, you say?'

'Both monks of Hailes. I think you know Simon Wynchecombe was involved.'

She stood. 'I may have said too much. Consider our agreement dissolved. There is no need to reimburse me for paying your debts. We are even.'

He grabbed her wrist and rasped, 'Sit down.'

She pulled but his grip was tight, perhaps too tight. Her hand whitened. 'Release me.'

'No. Sit the hell down. I'm not done talking to you.'

Narrowing her eyes, she slowly sank to the bench beside him. Crispin unfurled his fingers and let her go. She rubbed her red wrist.

'Now. You will tell me everything. Leave out any details and I begin slapping.'

The indignant expression was back. 'You wouldn't dare.'

He was quick. She must have heard it before she reacted. Her hand went to her face in shock. Other patrons looked but no one seemed to interfere with a man disciplining his wife.

'That's a beginning salvo. Try me and there will be more.'

'I do not like you, Crispin Guest, as much as I first thought.'

He smiled and leaned back, arms folded over his chest again. 'Well?'

Still she said nothing. Her pout was most appealing. Instead of slapping her again, the thought occurred to him to lick that pout.

'Let's begin with why you hired me. You sought Simon Wynchecombe. Why?'

'He had something I needed. Or I thought he had.'

'You were his lover, not this fabled Sybil Whitechurch.'

'As I said.'

'Why the deception? Why not simply be who you are?'

'That is somewhat complicated.'

'I have the time.'

'Perhaps I don't.'

'What did you think Wynchecombe possessed that you needed?'

She studied him and then leaned forward on the table. 'It's strange. If I had had the idea sooner, *I* should have become a Tracker, I think. Not that a man would have hired me. But a woman might . . . Hmm. That bears thinking about.'

'And why do you think you can accomplish what I do?'

'Because it takes cunning. And audacity. I have them both in abundance. And it would require far less "capering about on rooftops."'

'Well,' he said, settling back and appraising her. Her lids had lowered to seductive creases. 'I have my share of dangerous encounters. My dagger and my sword are not mere ornaments.'

'But perhaps it is you who provokes violence. You slapped me in anger.' She raised her face, perhaps to show him the red mark forming on her cheek. He suddenly felt chagrined at doing it. 'As a woman, I do not provoke such violence. Men wish to succor me. Women wish to befriend me. It has always been so. I might prove even better at this tracking than you.'

He laughed.

'There is an envious tinge to your laughter, Master Guest.' She looked into her cup. 'How did you surmise that there was no Sybil Whitechurch?'

'The more I thought about the interchangeability of your appearances at the monastery, the more suspicious I became. And your servant had never heard of her.'

She jerked forward. 'You went to the manor house?' She stopped herself and sat back, feigning insouciance. 'But of course you did.'

'It was easier by the moment to put two and two together.'

'And if you had been wrong?'

'I wasn't.'

'Ah. Perhaps that is how you succeed where a woman would not. Your arrogance gets you farther than all my confidence.'

He frowned. 'Answer the question.'

She sipped her ale. 'Which question was that?'

He rested his hand on the table and curled it into a threatening fist. 'What was it you thought Simon Wynchecombe possessed that you sought?'

Without the least bit of fear, she rested her chin on her hand. 'Do you know what amuses me the most? Your confidence that I wouldn't suss out that Eleanor was a man. Do you think women are so easily deceived? Oh, he is rather good at what he does. And one can only guess what exactly that is. Living in such close proximity, I could plainly tell. But I wasn't worried for my virtue. I was not anyone he would desire.'

Crispin gritted his teeth for a moment before taking up the cup and drinking. 'His name is John Rykener and he is a good and loyal friend to me.'

'They are all loyal. I wonder why.'

'Because I do not deceive.'

'Oh, ho! Except when you want to spy on me.'

He could feel his anger rising. 'I did it to protect you. That was before I suspected what I discovered to be true about you.'

'And what precisely is that?'

'That you are as good as a whore, demoiselle. Spreading your lies and your seductions within a monastery, of all places. Shame on you.'

She didn't do it in fury, but as someone who must take care of business: she dashed her cup's contents at his face. The ale hit him squarely and then cascaded down his cote-hardie. He didn't care much about his face, but his cote-hardie was another matter.

She placed the cup back on the table and took up the jug, pouring more. 'It isn't nice or proper you calling me a whore,' she said calmly. 'I object most strenuously at the characterization.'

He did his best to mop his coat with his cloak. 'Then what would you call it?'

'Resourceful. I had a task to accomplish. And if seducing those poor, naive monks would let me arrive at that end, then it was the most expeditious path.'

'You do have a cold heart.'

'Not at all. Do you wring your hands over every man you stab? Or every woman you slap?'

'Sometimes. If it warrants it.'

'And so, too, do I. So far, it hasn't warranted it.'

He stared down at the table. It troubled him that she might have a point.

'Be that as it may, you still have not answered the question.'

'And by this time, I would have thought that you had reckoned I wasn't going to.'

He smiled. He couldn't help it. 'Yet I would still like to know.'

'Of course you would. So may I go?'

'I have no doubt there are men dead because of you. Did you kill them?'

'Would you believe me if I told you I did not?'

His smile faded, for in truth, he couldn't honestly say.

She nodded to his silence. 'Then what is the point in my saying it?'

'You're a damnable woman, aren't you?'

'I'm the sort of woman that attracts you. Or so your John Rykener said.'

'John talks too much.'

'I daresay he does. It's not his fault. Women talk to me. Even women who are men.'

He had to find solid ground again. He scrambled for it. 'A burglar, then.'

She raised her cup halfway, paused, then brought it up, taking another sip. 'I stay fed, and housed, and clothed. I steal from the wealthy. Like Robin Hood.'

'And give to the poor?'

'Yes. Myself.'

'And what would your father say?'

She frowned. 'Nothing, I expect. He's dead, after all.'

He lowered his face, hiding it in his goblet. A woman alone. What *were* her options?

'Demoiselle. I . . . concede to your circumstances. But I can't allow it to continue.'

'Oh? How do you propose to stop me?'

'There are the sheriffs . . .'

She laughed. It was a sound full of merriment but underneath it was a hint of mockery. 'I can handle them easily.'

He sighed. 'Why did you want Simon Wynchecombe to steal the Hailes relic for you?'

She stilled. 'If you knew,' she said quietly, 'why so insistent on asking me?'

'I wanted to hear it from you. I wanted to understand why such a thing needed to be done. I wanted to understand why men had to die for it. Did Simon kill that monk or did you?'

'I did nothing. If Simon did something bad, it was of his own devising, not mine.'

'A clever way to divert the blame. I wonder if a priest could unwind that in the confessional.'

'I have nothing to confess.'

'Don't you?'

'Don't *you*?'

'But we aren't talking about me.'

'We are now. I think it an infinitely more intriguing subject.' She used two hands to cradle her chin. And the smile was back, just curving her lips in a captivating bow. The sudden swelling of his groin surprised even him. He adjusted his braies under the table.

'Demoiselle . . .'

She stood. He didn't. It would take time for him to feel comfortable rising. 'I have taken enough time.'

'I have more questions.'

'I'm sure you do.'

'What of Brother Rodney Beaton of Westminster Abbey? What has he to do with you? Another pawn?'

She turned her head to the side and breathed deep. 'Meet me back at the Unicorn in an hour's time and find out.'

She swept away from the table. Crispin thought of following – his cloak could cover him, he decided. But the promised interview at the Unicorn – the *private* interview, he thought with another pulsing surge – seemed more advantageous. She was gone in any case by the time he had decided.

He drank the rest of the ale and trudged away from the alehouse, back toward London. He had to talk to Simon, whether he went to the Unicorn or not.

Who was he fooling? Of course he would go.

Down the winding streets, he came upon the Shambles, smelling it before he reached it. He spotted Lenny in the shadows, looking anxious to talk to him, though Crispin wasn't as anxious for that meeting. He ignored him instead and arrived at the poulterer's, stomping the mud from his boots on the granite stoop before entering. Jack Tucker and Simon Wynchecombe were facing off, glaring at each other from across the table. Jack rose as Crispin entered.

'Gentlemen,' said Crispin, moving toward the fire to warm himself. 'Is all civil?'

'Aye, master,' grumbled Jack. He hurried to get the jug of wine in the larder but Crispin waved him off.

'I just had an interesting conversation with Sybil Whitechurch,' he said, his back to Wynchecombe. The former sheriff got to his feet. 'Or should I say, Katherine Woodleigh.'

'What?' said Simon and Jack at the same time.

'She is one and the same. There is no niece, Jack. She invented her to raise our sympathies and to encourage us on our course:

that of finding Master Wynchecombe.' He turned to face Simon. 'You indicated that she requested you steal the relic for her. When she discovered it was taken she must have assumed you had done it. Once she saw you hadn't she was no longer interested, for she knew that *I* had it. Did she ever tell you why she wanted it?'

Simon calmed himself, ran his hand over his beard and slowly sat again. 'To sell, I presumed. To escape her poverty.'

'Did she tell you who this buyer was?'

'No. And I never asked.'

'Then who is trying to kill you?'

'If I knew that I wouldn't be hiding out here, now, would I?'

'Could it be her? Would she hire an assassin to dispatch you, now that you know her and her dealings?'

'And now *you* will be a target since the same could be said of you.'

'Hmm. Possibly. I'll be meeting her again shortly to discuss it. Perhaps she will try to kill me then.'

'Then don't go, master!'

'Don't be absurd, Jack. Of course I will go.' He turned back to Simon. 'Can you tell me how many men have tried to attack you?'

'One. But secretly. Along the road at night. Stealing into my room at the inn I couldn't seem to escape him. I didn't wish to bring it to my door at home, endangering my wife. I tried to spy the rascal in the light of day but he never attacked then.'

'Any clue at all? Anyone you could recognize?'

'No. He wore a long gown. That is all I know. And he was strong. It was most definitely a man.'

'And he did not speak?'

'No. That was perhaps the most terrifying of all.'

Simon was a tall man, intimidating, and not afraid to use his fists. If *he* were frightened of this assassin . . .

'How can you be sure you didn't lead the man here?' gasped Jack.

'I can't be. But I had to risk it.'

'*You* had to risk it?'

'Now, Jack,' said Crispin, laying a placating hand on his apprentice. 'Master Wynchecombe will duly compensate us for our trouble . . .' He turned to him. 'Won't you?'

'So you want a fee?'

'I am offering a service at great personal risk. Of course I want a fee.'

Wynchecombe wrestled with the pouch at his belt and withdrew some coins. He threw them at the table. They scattered, some hitting the floor. 'Here is your Devil's payment then!'

'I will do you the honor of not counting it.' He signaled to Jack, who retrieved all the coins and dropped them into his pouch. 'Now, I do not think it wise you stay here in the hall. Best get you up to Jack's chamber. Since you are discommoding my servant, it seems only proper that you treat him with the respect he deserves.'

Jack scowled. Crispin well knew he wasn't pleased about giving up his chamber for the likes of the former sheriff, but Crispin wasn't about to give up his own bed. Still, Jack bore it well. He didn't think the lad would take any of Simon's abuse anymore.

'I am leaving then. Jack, I'll be at the Unicorn. If John Rykener or Nigellus Cobmartin return, make certain Master Wynchecombe is hidden first.'

'Aye, master. God keep you, sir.'

'And the both of you.' He gave them a stern look. 'Behave yourselves.'

Wynchecombe looked as if he wanted to say something when Crispin turned his back on him and left. It was very satisfying.

He made his way to the Unicorn with too much of a spring in his step. He could very well be walking into a trap. This assassin could be lying in wait for him. He kept his eyes peeled and his ears sharp.

He entered the inn, keeping a low profile when he spotted the innkeeper, and climbed the stairs. He wasn't certain what room she'd be in. He took a chance and knocked on a door.

A male servant answered, and when Crispin asked about the auburn-haired lady, the servant immediately knew. 'She's just there, good master. Two doors down.'

'You recall her.'

The young man smiled. 'Indeed I do, sir.'

Crispin thanked him and turned to the proper door. When he knocked, he braced himself. Would it be the assassin who answered? Would anyone answer?

He didn't wait long until she opened the door herself. She seemed somewhat surprised. 'I half-expected that you would not come, expecting a trap.'

'I still expect a trap.'

'But you came nonetheless. Well, you must come in, then, for your curiosity needs satiating.'

He crossed the threshold and she bolted the door behind him. 'Wine, Master Guest?'

'No, thank you. I prefer a clear head.'

'And one free from poison.'

'Did you plan to poison me?'

'No. Not yet, anyway.' She smiled.

He strode to a chair and sat, leaning back in the seat.

'Make yourself at home,' she muttered, and took the chair opposite.

'And so, demoiselle . . .'

'Please. We are friends now, eh? You must call me Kat.'

'If that is your name.'

'I assure you it is. Now, let's see. What is it you wish to ask me? I know. Did I try to kill Simon Wynchecombe? No, you already asked me that. I know! Why is it I wanted that most valuable and venerable relic from Hailes Abbey? And do I still want it? Well, the answer to that, my dear Crispin, is that there is a great deal of money at stake if I capture it.'

'That I reasoned on my own. What I can't quite reason is who is paying you?'

'It's all very surprising, truly.'

Her mild expression didn't waver. She was clearly toying with him and would not say. He tried a different direction. 'This person clearly wishes it for himself, for to display it means declaring what it is and where it is from. They must be of high rank.'

She merely smiled.

'Never mind that for now. Simon Wynchecombe is more than concerned for his neck and the safety of his family. He does not wish to return home and endanger them. Is there any hope that you can give him that you know who might be out to kill him? Besides yourself, that is.'

'Why should I be out to kill Simon? And just for the record,

I don't care a fig for his dear wife, for he seemed to care little enough for her while he dallied with me.'

He kept his expression neutral. 'He is a witness to your attempted larceny.'

'As I said, I do not fear the sheriffs and I can be out of London like the wind. I have done so before.'

'Strange that I have never heard of your antics before this.'

'Well, here is the truth of it, Crispin. I have dealt before in relics with men in high position and they are reluctant to turn me in for fear of implicating themselves. And so my work goes on without mention, without a whisper.'

'Interesting. How long have you been at this . . . trade . . . Kat?'

'Five years or so. Since I was eighteen.'

'And who is Katherine Pyke?'

That brought her up short, wiping the smug smile from her face. He leaned forward. No ready answer this time.

She slowly sat back. 'I have not heard that name before.'

'Oh, come now, demoiselle. I find that hard to believe. I heard it from one of the monks at Westminster Abbey.' A memory spiked. 'And from your servant back in Hailes. The Pykes were servants there as well. Surely you must know them.'

She made an uncomfortable laugh. 'The name came so out of the blue. I have not seen any of the Pykes in many a day.'

'And yet the monk said you had a similar look to one Katherine Pyke. Woodleigh, Whitechurch, and now . . . Pyke? One has to wonder, demoiselle, if "Woodleigh" is yet another alias.'

She couldn't seem to help the slow crawl of the smile forming on her face. 'Crispin Guest. What a marvel you are. I think it's witchcraft what you do.' Her palace accent slipped. And at its edges were the traces of something coarser.

'You are Katherine Pyke, then?'

She nodded, leaning the chair back so it balanced on its back legs. 'The Woodleighs were a mess. The father died two years ago in shame, leaving Katherine a pauper. She didn't know what to do or how to handle the estates. She relied on me to help her in everything, and so I advised her. The servants left, all but that mad old man. At my say so, she married herself off to the first man who offered, a fat miller in the nearby town. I could have

gone with her. She begged me to but I saw a better way, and
when the servants all left, I stayed. I had, erm, *borrowed*, some
of her things – her clothes, even bits of jewelry I could stash
away. It was easy enough to become her. They were all such
fools. But of course, with no tenants and no means of support,
I still had to earn a living. I managed to cajole Abbot Robert
into dealing with me. I bought fleeces at a reduced rate, offering
to pay him later. I resold them at a higher cost and paid him out
of that. And so it went. Soon I had him convinced that I was a
wealthy patroness, doling back to him what he paid to me. But
I began to consider other more lucrative items to sell. I met a
traveling merchant selling small relics. Oh, I knew they were
fake. Bad ones. But I soon learned how to make my own – much
more convincing. And with such a prestigious lady behind them,
why, they must be genuine.'

Crispin sighed. 'I think I'll have that wine now.'

She rose and went to the sideboard. He noted a silver decanter
and two silver goblets. Those were surely not there before
when John was her attendant. Her skills at larceny were
impressive.

She brought the goblet back to him. He looked it over and
noted a shield of arms carved into it. Neither for Woodleigh, nor
for Pyke, though it was unlikely that the latter would even have
arms. Someone else's entirely then.

He drank, watching her as she sipped and touched her lips to
wipe the wine stain with her fingers.

'You are proud of your accomplishments,' he said.

'And why not? It gives me a special joy to fool my betters,
to force them into positions where they cannot do me harm. I'm
sure you feel the same when *you* get the chance.'

'I certainly don't get the chance as often as you.'

'Your honor prevents that, doesn't it? Your honor. A man carries
such a burden. A woman has honor, too, but too many men are
willing to cast it aside without so much as a glance back. I
wonder. Why is a man's honor so much more important than that
of a woman's?'

'Because men must rule. It is ordained by God.'

She glanced at him sidelong. 'And how well men do it.' He
knew by her tone that she meant the opposite. He set his wine

aside. It was good wine. Almost as good as any he'd had at court. How had she managed that?

'Why are you telling me all this? You say you don't fear the sheriffs but you have no cause not to fear me?'

'Yet somehow I don't fear you.' She stood and walked around the table to stand over him. 'You fascinate me.' She leaned against the table, hips at a seductive angle. 'I don't trust you and you don't trust me. It makes for the perfect partnership.'

'Partnership? For what?'

'Oh, come now.' She smiled . . . and began to slowly unbutton her cote-hardie.

He got to his feet remarkably smoothly for all the rushing in his ears and the heat flashing in his body. He stood over her and watched the unbuttoning until the cloth fell open, revealing the white shift beneath. She toyed with the laces until she seemed certain his gaze was planted there, and pulled one until it released its knot. The linen fell open and loose.

He stepped forward. 'Perhaps I should check under the bed for a hidden assassin. The door is bolted as well as the window. I am effectively trapped in here.'

'Do check,' she said breathily.

He bent and glanced quickly, seeing nothing there. He smiled when he faced her again. 'Suppose I don't find you appealing.'

She pulled the shift open wider. Plump breasts and enticing pink nipples greeted his sight. 'You don't?' she whispered.

Don't do it, Crispin, said a voice in his head remarkably like Jack Tucker's.

He ignored it, grasped her by her shoulders and kissed her hard.

SEVENTEEN

Lying beside him, Kat ran her fingers up his chest, tangling in the hair. 'Just look at the scars on you. Some of these are fighting scars, but the rest . . .'

He grasped her hand and held it against him, stopping its progress. 'The rest I think you know.'

'How did you manage to live when so many others were imperiled by the king?'

He swallowed, not wishing to remember, to take away from the warmth of satisfaction that eased his body and soul from her hands and lips. 'The Duke of Lancaster. He spoke for me. I was one of his household knights.'

'Yes, of course.' She reached up and nibbled his neck, pressing soft kisses there. He let her. 'Strange that King Richard should let you live.'

He eyed her sidelong. 'Do you truly wish to discuss this now?'

She drew back to look at him with a tender expression. 'I'm sorry. Let's talk of other things.'

He relaxed his muscles again, settled in. 'Such as?'

'Why such a man as yourself has no woman in his life.'

He laughed. 'Do you propose filling that gap?'

She tossed her head back. Her cascade of auburn hair showered around her shoulders, curling around her chin, her breasts. 'Well, I might. For you must admit, I am your match, Crispin Guest.'

'Because you are clever and resourceful? It will take more than that, demoiselle.'   ′

'Oh? What else must I be? A paragon of virtue? A maiden? If the latter, then that ship has sailed. If the former, then . . . well. The ship might yet be in the harbor.'

'Are you sure? It seems to me that the mooring was slashed long ago.'

She tossed herself onto her back. 'You wound me.'

He turned on his side and gazed down at her creamy skin. This one was a servant, much like the woman Crispin had loved, possibly still loved, but was married to another. He had let her slip from his fingers because of his own arrogance. But what of Kat? It was possible she was a murderer or at least an accomplice. She was most certainly a thief and unrepentant. But Jack Tucker had been a thief. He had been unrepentant, too. For, like Kat, he had had to make a living. Could she be persuaded to give it up, to live honestly?

He couldn't resist drawing a finger from her throat down to the captivating cleft between her breasts. 'I am a man who lives by his honor and the honor in others,' he said softly. 'What would

I see in the glass in the morning if I looked the other way at how you make your living?'

Her gaze was steady. 'You are a rare one, Master Guest,' she said quietly, sincerely. 'So few men can be relied upon to stand by their principles, especially on the gibbet. For the first time in my life . . . I think I am sorry for what I have become.'

'Every man or woman can be repentant. Any priest can shrive you.'

'But can I go out and sin no more?'

His hand traveled downward, pushing the sheets aside to glide over her belly, making it twitch, then lower to the soft curls at her legs' juncture. 'I am not free of sin,' he admitted. 'Far from it. But I try to earn my coin honestly.'

'What could I possibly do to achieve the same?'

His glance traveled up to her face, to the expression of hopelessness that was briefly there in her eyes before they were shuttered again. She looked away. 'Perhaps we are hopelessly mismatched after all.'

'Are you willing to give up so easily?'

She smiled and turned her head again. Her bright auburn tresses fanned out over the pillow, over her creamy shoulders, the dark against the light. 'We'll see.'

'First . . . you will have to tell me who your patron is.'

She laughed, causing a delightful jiggle to her breasts and belly. She dragged the sheet up to cover herself just as Crispin's interest began to peak again. 'So that was your plan all along in bedding me.'

'Not at all. There was no ulterior motive.'

There was a hurt tilt to her mouth. 'Wasn't there?'

'Kat.' He drifted a hand down her face to her chin and took it between his thumb and fingers. 'You must believe me. I thought we were using each other for pleasure. And in truth, I was on my guard that you would try to beguile me as you have beguiled others . . .'

'This is an apology?'

He was mucking it up. He closed his eyes and sighed. 'A poor one.'

'I realize you are only doing your appointed task. But you must stop asking me, for I cannot tell you.'

His hand dropped away. 'You still intend to get the relic for your patron?'

'It is a great deal of money.'

'Money isn't everything.'

'Why, you dear, naive man. Of course it is.'

Sighing, Crispin took her face in his hands, trying to make her understand. 'You said so yourself. You are canny enough to escape this life for one better. I can help you.'

Her eyes tracked over his face. 'You would, wouldn't you? You are a remarkable man. Yet . . . What makes you think that any promise I gave you now would ever be the truth?'

'Damn you!' He pushed her back and slammed himself back down to the bed. Running his hand through his hair, he huffed a breath. 'You are not irredeemable, Kat.'

'The Lord and I have an understanding. He knows who I am.'

'But I would know you, too. And stop you, for what you do is only leading to more deaths.'

'But surely not innocent men.'

'That is not for you to decide!'

'Then who? You? A judge?' She clutched the sheet tight in her fist at her chest. 'It is so arrogant to claim you know what is in a man's heart.'

'I would stop the killing. For me, that is the only goal.'

'You, who bears a dagger and a sword. You, who have killed.'

'Yes. For I kill in defense and righteously.'

'So any killer believes.'

'No. Only one who kills for gain, a man with no conscience. *A tyrant ruleth only to please a few*. No one else must die for this relic, Kat. Can't you see that?'

She levered upward, leaning against the pillows propped up to the wall. 'With just this one relic, I can live in luxury for years. Don't you understand? Each time I make my way into a household to steal, it is just one more danger for me. One more chance to get caught.' She sighed. 'But of course you returned it to Hailes, didn't you? Now *I* must return there and work my wiles again.'

'It is safe.'

She looked at him closely. 'Hmm. By that I assume it is *not* in Hailes.'

He swore under his breath. He had not meant to give it away. Any other woman would not have caught the nuance of his words.

'And you know where it is.'

He closed his mouth this time.

She reached for him but he shied back. Her hands fell to the mattress. 'Ah, Crispin. You will not tell me by hint or utterance. Tracker, Protector of Relics.'

'It is my curse.'

'Let me lift the curse,' she said, a sly smile fluttering over her lips.

He leaned back against the wall beside her, arms crossed over his chest. 'No.'

'I told you how important this relic was. With it I can live freely for years. Can't you give me that?'

'Not if it means the death of an innocent.'

She flopped down and turned over, showing her smooth back to him. 'Then there is little more to say, I'm afraid.'

'Kat . . .'

'Perhaps you should go.'

He screwed his hands into fists, but in the end let them fall uselessly to his sides. He glared at her shoulder for a long moment before he hurled himself out of the bed and began to dress. 'If you let another die, I shall see to it that you hang.'

'Not the most gracious of farewells,' she murmured.

He buttoned his cote-hardie almost to the top and slapped his belt back on his waist, securing the sheaths for dagger and sword. He cast one last glance at her back before he stomped to the door, unlocked it and threw it open.

He hurried down the inn's steps and out to the courtyard. He hadn't realized how late it had gotten. By the slant of the sun he reckoned it must be near Vespers. He stopped at the corner and looked back at the inn. Disgusted with himself and with her, he stalked into the street, making his way back to the Shambles when he saw two familiar figures approaching.

John Rykener was on Nigellus Cobmartin's arm, and the latter looked as if he didn't seem to mind. Crispin gave them the eye and they slowly broke apart. 'Gentlemen,' he said quietly.

'Lady,' John corrected softly, since he was still garbed so. 'Have you been avoiding us? You never returned to your lodgings and, if I didn't know better, I would say that you were coming from the Unicorn.'

'Well, I . . .' He looked back again and turned to John guiltily.

The man pressed a hand to his hip and tsk-tsked. 'So I see. What did I tell you, Nigellus?'

'Yes, well. Master Guest's time is his own. But I take it that the lady was indeed not abducted?'

'That is correct. And most obstinate. She's a thief and a liar and has no intention of helping me stop those who would try to kill for this relic.'

'Hold,' said John. 'Do you mean to tell me that everything she said is a lie?'

'Including her name. She is actually a servant named Katherine Pyke. She took on the name of her former employer.'

'And there is no Simon Wynchecombe?'

'That there is. And he is still in danger for his life.'

Nigellus moved to get out of the way of a cart slowly making its creaking way down the lane. 'You've seen him then?'

'I have.'

'What of the relic? What is it?'

'The Holy Blood of Hailes.'

Nigellus crossed himself. 'Mother of God,' he muttered. 'And so she stole it from Hailes Abbey?'

'I don't think so. Though she tried mightily to get her paramours to do it, including Simon Wynchecombe. And yet, two monks have brought the relic back to me, one sacrificing his life to do so.'

'Two have brought it back?'

'Yes. It is back again.'

'Oh, dear. But then . . . who has hired her to steal it, for I am certain she must have a patron.'

'She does, but will not tell me who. She still intends to collect.'

'You must have her arrested,' said John.

'And I would, but I fear she is telling me the truth in that she wouldn't stay arrested long. She appears to have the goods on too many men of high rank.'

John stomped his foot. 'What a damnable female.'

'Yes.'

'Where do you go now, Crispin? To find Simon Wynchecombe?'

'I know precisely where he is.'

'Then where do you go?'

He noticed John had slipped his arm into the young lawyer's again.

'I'm returning to Westminster Abbey. If you'd care to come along, I shan't stop you.'

'As gracious an invitation as I've ever heard,' John snorted.

As they walked, Crispin said quietly to Nigellus, 'I'd have a care, Master Cobmartin. There are areas of London where Master Rykener is known.' And he made a point of staring at their joined arms.

Nigellus smiled sheepishly. 'I understand, Master Guest.' And yet, he kept a firmer grip on John's arm, even caressing his hand.

Rolling his eyes, Crispin said nothing more. What was there to say?

The air was soft and still, and the pink of the sky seemed to linger as they passed Charing Cross and moved along the wide avenue to the abbey.

Vespers had not yet rung, and so Crispin knew he still had time to see Abbot William de Colchester, to warn him. Rodney Beaton must know who this patron is. Why else would Kat bother with him? Perhaps he was the intermediary. Of course, she dared not go to court herself, for surely there were those there who knew the real Katherine Woodleigh and would recognize that Kat was not she.

What a damnable situation.

He rang the bell, and the usual quiet sweep of cassocks was nowhere to be found. Instead, he heard a distant and incongruous ruckus of running, of shouts beyond the cloister walls. He clasped the gate and tried to stretch, to see what was happening. He yanked on the bell rope insistently until a young porter finally arrived.

'Bless me, Master Guest! Your appearance is most welcomed at this time.' He unlocked the gate, scarcely noticing John and Nigellus. 'Come at once, sir!'

The monk ran. Crispin ran after him, followed by his companions. With his heart pounding, Crispin realized that they were heading for the abbot's chamber. The young monk gestured for

Crispin to enter, and he jumped up the step and pushed through the heavy chamber door.

The abbot was kneeling beside a man lying upon the floor. By his white cassock, Crispin knew that it was Brother James. And by the blood, he also knew that he was quite dead.

The ambry where the relic had lain was thrown wide open. He did not need to look to know that it was gone.

Abbot William, customarily unshaken and sober, looked up at Crispin with a stunned expression. 'Master Crispin. You are here. I prayed for you to come.'

Crispin knelt on the other side of the corpse, looking first to comfort the abbot and then to study the body. 'I am here,' was all he said. The monk had been hit from behind. His eyes were wide and staring, but staring at nothing of this world. The back of his head sat in a pool of crimson.

'He was slain and the relic taken,' said the abbot with a shudder. 'May God have mercy on us all.'

Crispin rose and stepped around the body to look at the ambry. It had been pried open. There, on the floor, was the iron from the fire, which had been used to great effect. They had known where it was. They had known *what* it was.

It went through his head in quick succession. *It could not have been Kat. She wouldn't have had time. She didn't know where it was*. And then . . .

'Simon!' He turned to the stunned Rykener and Cobmartin. 'You must hurry to my lodgings on the Shambles. Warn Simon Wynchecombe.'

John exchanged glances with Nigellus. 'You mean this former sheriff is there, at your lodgings?'

'Yes. He is in hiding there. They'll be after him next if not already. I pray that Jack is unharmed.'

Nigellus swallowed hard as he stared at the dead monk, but he pressed a shaky yet reassuring hand on Crispin's arm. 'We will go in all haste, Master Guest. God keep you, sir.' He grabbed John's hand and ran with him out of the chamber.

EIGHTEEN

They ran. It wasn't until they reached London's gates that John dragged on Nigellus' hand, slowing him to a stop. 'Wait. I must catch my breath.' He doubled over, resting his hands on his thighs. Nigellus did likewise, breathing hard.

He slowly straightened and locked eyes with the lawyer. When Crispin had sent them away from his Shambles lodgings the first time, they had waited back at John's attic chamber. One thing had led to another and . . . well. John gave him a wary smile.

Nigellus had no such caution. He grinned with a boyish face that seemed more suited to the servants' hall than that of a court of law. Though the smile faded on remembering their mission. 'Are you ready?' he asked.

John nodded, lifted his skirts over the mud and cantered ahead. They soon reached the old poulterer's shop that Crispin called home. A handsome black-and-white cat sat on the high sill, his tail curled under him, yellow eyes watching John and Nigellus curiously.

Pounding on the door, John called out, 'Jack! Jack Tucker, are you there?'

There were footsteps and furniture moving. It took a while but then the door opened a crack. John pushed through, knocking Jack aside.

'Here now!' Jack cried. 'What's this impertinence, Master Rykener?'

He stumbled back as John gained the center of the room. 'Jack Tucker, is Simon Wynchecombe in hiding here?'

Jack looked from John to a stern-faced Nigellus. 'Of course he isn't. Where'd you get a fool notion like that?'

'From your master,' said John. 'Crispin told us he was here. Told us to warn him.'

'Eh? What's this about?'

'Master Tucker,' said Nigellus, more agitated than he'd been on the road, 'we were just in the company of Master Guest at

Westminster Abbey. There has been a murder. A White Monk. And I fear a certain relic that was being kept there is now missing.'

Jack's eyes widened impossibly. 'God's blood,' he gasped. He suddenly looked toward the rafters.

'Crispin believes your sheriff is in danger,' added John.

Jack pressed his hand to his chin, rubbing the neat ginger beard there. 'We've got to get him out of here then. But where to put him now?'

'He can room with me!' said John and Nigellus at the same time. They looked at each other.

Jack's eyes narrowed. 'Truth to tell, I think Master Nigellus' chamber to be more suiting. Though it is very much smaller than here.'

'If necessary,' said Nigellus with a cagey expression, 'I can find lodgings . . . elsewhere. Temporarily.'

John felt his cheeks warm. Interesting, this young lawyer. And even more interesting, Jack was not fooled.

'Blind me,' he muttered, gazing at the two of them. 'It's witchcraft is what it is.' He finally decided. 'Aye, then. I'll just . . . go get him.'

He scrambled up the stairs and disappeared around the landing. There were raised voices – Jack's strident one and another like a low growl.

John wrung his hands. 'Do you think it safe leaving him there alone in your lodgings?'

'Young Master Tucker is right when he says it is small.'

'And so are mine.'

'But two amenable souls can reside so easily together.' The lawyer's young face burnished with suddenly ruddy cheeks and nose. He lowered his eyes abashedly for a moment before raising them again.

'So they can,' said John carefully.

'Temporarily.'

'As you say.'

Thunderous footsteps on the stairs broke them apart and a tall man with a dark beard pushed his way into the hall. He cast his eyes upon them, one, then the other, and scowled.

'Master Wynchecombe!' cried Jack.

'I was supposed to be hidden, Tucker. Your master expected better of you.'

'He expects me to know who my friends are, and I do! This is Master Cobmartin, a lawyer and our landlord, as it happens. And this is . . .' Jack hesitated.

John curtseyed and inclined his head. 'Eleanor, embroideress. And companion to . . . Master Cobmartin.'

Wynchecombe's scowl deepened as he looked John over. '*These* are Crispin's friends. It figures.'

'And they are doing you a courtesy, so I recommend you be polite.'

'You seem to forget that I am your better, Tucker.'

'There is none better than my master. And you are nothing more than an armorer.'

Wynchecombe cocked his arm back to strike when Nigellus hurled himself forward to stand in front of Jack. John saw the absurdity of it: the tall Wynchecombe hovering menacingly over the equally tall Jack Tucker, with the shorter, paler Nigellus standing bravely in between. It was ridiculously endearing.

'Hold, Master Wynchecombe,' said Nigellus, arms out to protect Jack. Tucker glanced at him over Nigellus' shoulder with a mixture of astonishment and annoyance. 'Let us all remember that we are here for the greater good. And that is to save your life, good sir. A mission of God's own mercy. No doubt our good friend Master Tucker here is at his wits' end with worry. Let us calm ourselves and reason it out. *Spes sibi quisque*. Indeed, we are all greater than the sum of our parts. Now. My lodgings are at Gray's Inn, and they are small but protected with walls and a porter. I will take you there, situate you and instruct our servants to bring you food. You must stay within for your own benefit and until we come to tell you all is well. Our only assignment is to keep you safe, sir.'

Wynchecombe looked only mildly contrite, but his arrogance lifted his chin. 'Let's get this over with then.'

John hesitated. 'Should we all go?'

Jack stepped forward. 'Aye. All of us. More eyes on the streets.'

The lad had certainly taken after his master, John noted. Jack took the lead as any captain of an army. He grabbed his cloak, buttoned it hastily and pulled the door open only a crack to search the lane. When all appeared clear, he motioned for John and Nigellus. 'Up with your hood, Master Armorer,' he ordered. Wynchecombe clearly didn't like commands from a servant but he complied nevertheless without another word.

Jack ushered them all out of the door before locking it. 'The fastest route to Gray's Inn, if you please, Master Nigellus.'

Nigellus nodded and hastened up the lane, making a turn at Holborn once they passed Newgate. They neared the respected lawyer's haven with its many storeys. They all reached the outer walled courtyard but Nigellus hastened them under the porter's gate arch. Nigellus pushed his way forward and spoke quietly to the porter – that same deaf old man from before – and before the porter was done speaking, Nigellus grabbed Wynchecombe's arm and pulled him along. John hurried forth and Jack took up the rear, scanning the courtyard and the windows above.

They passed through a busy hall full of the smells of food, which reminded John of how long ago he had eaten. Too long. But there was no time to tarry with Nigellus' insistence of moving forward. Out to a garden and through another building, up the stairs and up and up . . . until they reached his small room. He unlocked the door and pulled Wynchecombe in. They all managed to stuff themselves inside.

'What a ghastly sty this is,' growled the former sheriff.

'You'll be polite about it,' warned Jack, hand on his dagger hilt.

Wynchecombe swiveled toward him. 'Or what?'

'Or I'll make you sorry you said aught.'

'Now, now!' cried John. 'Remember where you are, sir. You are being done a kindness. Remember that we don't have to do any such thing. Keep a civil tongue, or I shall throttle you myself.'

Wynchecombe stared open-mouthed at John, beginning to suspect his true nature since John had forgotten to soften his voice. *That's done it, John*, he admonished himself.

But before Wynchecombe could say anything, Nigellus cut in. 'We all must be very careful. I have told the porter that I will be sequestered in my room and to only send my meals here. And so a servant will come attend to it. You may have to offer the page remuneration to keep silent . . .'

'So now it costs me more money.'

'I'll stay,' said Jack.

'My good sir, Master Tucker. These are close quarters . . .'

'He'll need a civilizing soul here. Besides, he'll still need a guard and I reckon I can do that outside the room for the most part. I shall fetch the food for Master Wynchecombe so as to avoid the need to bribe any servants.'

'What am I to do in the meantime?' asked Wynchecombe.

Jack looked around and picked up one of the many books piled about the place, along with scrolls, parchments and bits of quills and ink pots. 'Read a book, sir.'

Wynchecombe sneered but said nothing.

Nigellus remained silent as he made his way to a coffer beside the door. He grabbed some clothes and stuffed them in his scrip, and then rummaged through his mounds of parchments, carefully choosing those he needed as a bird chooses just the right stick to place into a nest. He nodded to himself and opened the door. 'Then I leave you to it, Master Tucker. I will get word to Master Crispin.'

'I thank you, sir. God keep you.'

'And you.' He glanced at John and his pale cheeks bloomed pink. 'Shall we?'

John said nothing but he pulled Jack with them out of the door and stood with him on the landing. 'Will you be all right? That man seems violent.'

'He's a lord, or thinks he's one. They're a different breed of animal, aren't they?'

'Master Guest was a lord as well.'

'That's why I'm used to it. I was frightened of Wynchecombe when he was sheriff. I was but a small lad then. I'm not anymore.' He hitched up his belt.

'No, you are not. You take care, young Jack.'

Jack eyed Nigellus making his way down the stairs, and then John in his woman's garb. 'And you take care, too, John. And take care of that lawyer so that he don't get into any trouble. Get my meaning?'

'I get it very well. Don't worry. I'm suddenly quite fond of Master Cobmartin and wish him no ill.'

'So I see. God keep you, then.'

John smiled, watched the door close and listened as the bolt was thrown. Down the stairs he went, glancing down below the rickety stairs once and taking a second look at a man in a hood and long gown standing in the shadows. When he looked a third time, he wasn't there. *Must be my mind gone mad*, he thought anxiously.

Back to Candlewick Street they went, neither one of them speaking. John ventured a glance now and again at his companion. The man seemed cheerful, watching the various passers-by and nodding to those who looked his way. He seemed intrigued by all he saw. And hadn't he been intrigued hours ago when they'd been alone in John's quarters? It had all been new to Nigellus. And though he was hesitant, he hadn't shied from any of it. It was quite a new experience for John too, for his usual clients were jaded and used to his custom. Not Nigellus. He was tempted to grasp his hand but he remembered the look on Jack's face as well as his admonishment. John was known on these streets and he didn't wish to taint Nigellus with his comportment, though the man was following swiftly beside him and tongues would wag nonetheless.

They found the candlemaker's shop and the rickety ladder that led up to his lodgings. 'Here, Nigellus. You first. It's not the best of ladders.'

'Yes, I recall it.' He offered a shy smile, hitched up his gown and began to climb.

John followed, and when they'd both made it inside safe and sound, John closed the shutter. He hurried to the fire to stoke it and warmed his hands before the small flames. When he turned, Nigellus stood directly behind him. 'You are most kind to accommodate me. I shall not take your kindness for granted. I can easily sleep on these chairs. I daresay I've done it many a time while studying.'

John sighed. 'Don't be a fool,' he said softly. Was he telling himself that, or the lawyer? He took the young man's face in his hands and, gazing at his smiling mouth, kissed him soundly.

NINETEEN

Jack took up his place in the corner, arms crossed tightly over his chest, and watched as Wynchecombe tried to pace in the small, cramped room.

'This is damnable,' the man grumbled.

'Aye, it is. Me having to listen to you whine.'

'I've had just enough peevishness out of you!' Two steps took him directly in front of Jack. He raised his hand to clout him but Jack caught that hand and held it by the wrist, squeezing tight before he gave it a twist and tossed it back.

'They'll be none of that. I told you I wouldn't put up with no grease from you. Master Crispin might do so by habit but *I'm* not in the practice of suffering fools.'

'How dare you!'

Jack jumped to his feet and got in close, pleased when Wynchecombe stepped back. 'How dare I? How dare *you*, you miserable whoreson. As ungrateful a bastard as I've ever met. Here is Master Crispin and me doing you a mercy and you haven't got the skin to even thank us? Sit yourself down and shut it. I'll have no more of your grousing. Be grateful you're alive and, by my master's mercy, not in a cell in Newgate where you most likely belong.'

'I did not kill that monk,' he rasped between gritted teeth.

'Says you. I seen your dagger in his back. Prove that you didn't, I say.'

'I didn't. I'd had no reason whatsoever to kill that man. And I'd never stab him in the back.'

'My master might believe you, but I don't.'

'Then it's a good thing you're not the Tracker.'

'Oh, you'd like that, wouldn't you? But up till this moment, you thought you could belittle me like you done him. And now you know you can't. Aye, you're an alderman. I know that. And most of them deserve the respect London gives them. But you don't. I'll never give it to you.'

'Aren't you the philosopher, Jack Tucker, the high and mighty. Holding his praise dear for other thieves like him.'

'So I was a thief once – I'm not no more. But once a bastard always a bastard.'

'Do you think for one moment Guest would treat you any differently than how I've treated you if he didn't need you? You'd be only one of the nameless army of servants he once had. If you had dropped dead in the mud of the streets he'd no more mourn you than he would a dog.'

Jack's hands knotted into fists. 'Didn't I tell you to sit there and shut it?'

A smile stole across Wynchecombe's face. 'Yes, he's your Achilles heel right enough. The master and his dog. What's he promised you? I wonder. What *can* he promise you?'

'No more than he is able to give. A roof over our heads, a wage and respect. My master treats me as his own. And you can use all the Devil's words you want – nothing will change that fact.'

Wynchecombe's face altered. He seemed to finally absorb Jack's words and he slumped in his seat, stretching out his long legs and crossing his ankles. 'Very well.' He sighed. 'I seem to be unusually sour and menacing today. You're right, of course. Master Guest seems soft in the head when it comes to you. And perhaps I am just that much envious of it. Of such a rapport. You have the better of me.'

Taken aback by his sudden change of tone, Jack settled in on his perch of books. He rubbed his beard. 'A man don't have to be so sour all the time, Master Wynchecombe. *For what does it profit a man—*'

'Good God. You're not quoting the scriptures to me, are you? Next thing you'll be spouting that Aristotle.'

'Well . . . indeed, as Aristotle said, *A common danger unites even the bitterest enemies.* You must admit, he has a saying for all circumstances.'

Simon laughed. 'I should have known he'd teach you the words of that pagan.'

Jack said nothing. The man's words weren't bitter for a change. They were even commiserating.

After a long pause, Simon asked, 'Tell me something. Am I mad, or was that Eleanor really a man?'

'You're not wrong,' he said, pulling a scroll out to stop it poking him in the arse.

'Crispin does know the most interesting people.'

'Aye, that he does. There is no one more loyal than John Rykener, though.'

'Bless me, that was John Rykener? I think I arrested him myself once.'

'No doubt.'

He looked around the room. 'And this Cobmartin fellow is truly a lawyer?'

'He freed my master when he was up for murder.'

'I heard tell *you* did that with your investigating.'

Jack almost puffed with pride at the statement. How had Wynchecombe heard about that? 'A little of this, a little of that.'

The sheriff laughed. 'I'll be damned. You and Crispin. What a duo you are. It's extraordinary.'

'Which is why you came to us, eh?'

Wynchecombe narrowed his eyes, but more to study Jack than to sneer at him. 'I came to Crispin . . . because I could see no other option.' He slowly shook his head. 'What a pitiful thing I have become,' he said quietly. 'No friends to go to, no trusted lords. Certainly no other aldermen . . . or the sheriffs.' He raised his face. 'I could not trust them. But Crispin, I could.'

'And you treat him most foully.'

'He's a traitor.'

'He . . . he made a mistake. Once. Long ago. He's made up for it since. Can't you give him that?'

'I suppose that's true. And yet he's never lost his arrogance.'

'The pot calling the kettle black,' he muttered.

He smiled grimly. 'You have the better of me again, Tucker.'

Jack leaned forward, arms resting on his thighs. 'So why don't you tell me what you wouldn't tell Master Crispin about this woman, Katherine Woodleigh? Or Sybil Whitechurch. Whatever she called herself. Tell me how you met and what transpired.'

Simon clasped his fingers over his belly and glared at the parchment-littered floor. 'Crispin is a man like me. I didn't have to tell him the details.'

'Well, it cannot have escaped your notice that I am not a man like you. So you'll have to spell it out.'

Simon blinked, eyeing Jack. 'There's something of him in you, isn't there?'

'I take that as a compliment, sir.'

'Maybe it wasn't meant as one.' He shrugged and sat back. 'Well. I met her at Hailes. She introduced herself as Sybil Whitechurch. The monks vouched for her and I took her to be who she said she was. Why wouldn't I? She is comely and solicitous. And I, a man far from home . . . well. A man such as myself might fall for flattery so as to not go to a cold and empty bed at the end of the day. She was willing. And before long . . . I fell for her charms.' He rubbed his own beard, quiet in his thoughts. 'Do you have a woman, Tucker? You're old enough.'

'I do, sir. She's my betrothed.'

'Ah. Getting married, are you? Well, here's a piece of advice—'

'Begging your pardon, sir, but I'd rather not take marriage advice from a man who'd commit adultery.'

Wynchecombe drew back, surprised. And then he laughed heartily. 'A moral thief. Well I never!'

Jack scowled. 'Laugh all you like. But I'd rather my wife knew what her husband was about than worry. What will *your* wife say when you finally make it home, I wonder?'

Wynchecombe's laughter stopped. He perched his chin on his hand. 'I take your point.'

'And so,' prompted Jack. 'Your story?'

'She . . . bewitched me. Soon I was giving her money and trinkets. But they weren't enough. She wanted me to obtain that damned relic for her.'

'Did she say why?'

'She said it would mean a great deal to her livelihood. She explained that her family estates were on hard times. And when I went there on a whim, I saw their state.'

'Aye. So did we.'

'After I refused to get her the relic, she turned cold. Would not speak to me. And it was then that I began to have my suspicions about her. I was leaving Hailes when I was attacked for the first time.'

'Do you have any description of the man at all?'

'None. It was dark.'

'You said for the *first* time.'

'I sent my horse on a dangerous gallop in the countryside at nightfall, just to get away from him and find succor at an inn. That night, he attacked again. I lost my dagger.'

Jack stroked his beard, letting the coarse hairs run through his fingers. 'You say the man was wearing a gown.'

'Yes. And a hood.'

'Could it have been a cassock?'

'Someone from the abbey?'

'Aye. Someone that Sybil – that is Katherine – also beguiled. My master and me met a monk there who accosted us, told us of her. He looked like a sore, jealous sort.'

'He killed those monks because of jealousy?'

'It's possible. Men have killed for far less. He followed you back to London but encountered the other monk, Brother Ralph, who was bringing the relic to my master for safekeeping.'

'But why should he kill him if his mission was for the relic?'

'I know not. But he used your dagger for the purpose of incriminating you.'

'The whoreson!'

'And it would have worked had not my master taken it. So you have him to thank for that as well.'

'And yet the sheriffs still want it.'

Jack shifted. 'That's my fault. I told the sheriffs.'

Wynchecombe raised his head.

'I was angry! What is it about that office that turns them so against Master Crispin? He hasn't done them no harm.'

'I can tell you precisely why. Because an upstart like your master eclipses them. He's too clever by far, and him in his lowly position. It's humiliating.'

Jack clutched at his dagger, but when he realized he was doing it, let his hand fall away. 'You feared him.'

'I still do. Crispin is . . . a singular man. There are not many who can stand taller than he, even in his lowly estate. And it galls, I can tell you.'

'You could stand beside him. You could be his friend. Help him. He'd not turn you away.'

Simon huffed. 'I don't need his friendship.'

'Yet I can tell you, it is good to have it.'

Simon grunted in reply. Why was Jack wasting his time on this? He didn't care if Simon Wynchecombe became Master Crispin's bosom cousin. He only wanted the truth.

'So it is a monk that is after you. Someone missing from the monastery. I wonder why that abbot did not tell us of this. Oh, these secret men! I'd take an honest thief any day over them.'

Simon offered another grim smile.

'Did Katherine Woodleigh tell you for whom she was selling the relic?'

'No. She never mentioned a name. But she did say . . . now let me think.'

Jack waited, tapping his leg.

'London. Something about London. I know not. I . . . I wish I could be more helpful.'

'Well, then.' Jack rose. 'That's not much to go on. Are you hungry? I'll go to the hall and fetch some food for us before night falls completely. You stay here and don't open the door for nobody.'

'I assure you, I will not.'

Jack turned to leave when Simon called out to him. 'Tucker!'

'Aye?' He held the door open a sliver.

'Is it possible to be loyal to a man who does little but shelter you? I mean . . . he has no riches to bestow upon you, does he?'

'Riches. They come in all guises, Lord Sheriff. He taught me to read and write, taught me languages. Taught me to fight with dagger and sword. When was the last time you did the same for one of *your* servants?' He turned away quickly before he was obliged to spit at him.

It was strange, he thought as he thumped down the stairs, that a man like Wynchecombe, obviously educated, could not fathom Christian charity and kindness. He supposed many a man – even clerics – were not fit to be called Christian.

He made his way again through the cloister-like setting of greensward, colonnade and finally into the hall. Servants were clearing the tables. He approached one and asked where the kitchen was. The boy lifted an arm and pointed, and Jack trotted forward. There was a narrow passage between the hall and the kitchens, which were warm and filled with cooking smells. It reminded him somewhat of the kitchens in Westminster Palace, though these were much smaller.

A man with an apron peering into a large kettle hanging from an iron rod over the hearth looked up as Jack neared.

Jack pushed back his hood and bowed to the man. 'Good sir, might you have any victuals for a young lawyer and his servant?'

The stocky man with hair as red as Jack's, though not as thick, looked him over. 'Surely *you* aren't the lawyer?'

Jack chuckled. 'Oh, no, good master. I am just the servant of Nigellus Cobmartin.'

'Cobmartin? He is always working at odd hours. Does the man ever sleep?'

'Rarely, sir.'

He grumbled, but he got a wooden tray and spooned the pottage into two bowls. He gathered the leavings of some round loaves and even found some cheese. 'This will have to do. The day's cooking is over.'

'You are kind, sir.'

'Here. Take this.' He slammed a crockery of ale on the tray and waved his hand. 'Take it to Cobmartin with my blessings. He'll need to mark this on his accountings. I fear he hasn't paid in some time.'

'I'm sure he'll have the funds soon,' Jack said with a bow. *Even if I have to squeeze Wynchecombe like a turnip to get it,* he thought to himself.

He grasped the sides of the tray and walked carefully back through the hall, through the colonnade and up the rickety steps when he heard a shout and a clamor within the room. 'God's blood!' He kicked the door open and stilled as he beheld what was happening within.

A man in a gown – no, a cassock – was assaulting Simon Wynchecombe. They struggled with Wynchecombe below and the man above with a dagger. Jack cast the tray aside on the landing, spilling ale and pottage all over the stairs, and jumped onto the man's back. With both hands, he wrestled the arm with the dagger down until he twisted the weapon from his hand. He tossed it behind him and clamped his arm around the man's neck.

The monk struggled. Jack yanked back and the man had no choice but to follow. Simon snapped to his feet and slammed his fist into the man's face. He fell limp in Jack's arms and Jack let the monk slide to the floor, unconscious.

He glared at Wynchecombe. 'Didn't I tell you not to open the door?'

TWENTY

The man slowly regained his senses. Jack had tied him securely to a chair. The blood from his face had smeared the front of his white cassock. He lifted his head and came back to himself. Yanking on his bindings, he scowled at Jack.

'You're that monk that came to me and Master Crispin at Hailes Abbey. Does your abbot know what you've been about, wandering all over England and murdering his monks?'

'I curse you, minion of Wynchecombe! You are nothing more than his tool.'

Jack postured before him. 'Say that again and you'll get another fist in the face.'

Simon rose and stood over the monk. 'Why have you been after me?'

'Because . . . because of her. You don't deserve her love.'

'Oh, God's teeth!' cried Wynchecombe. 'You jackass! You killed for a *woman*?'

'Not just any woman,' he said miserably.

'But you gone and told my master and me what a witch she was,' said Jack.

'She is a witch. She bewitched me. And now I have sinned.'

Jack nodded. 'All the way, you have, brother. Here. What's your name?'

'Brother Fulk.'

'Well, Brother Fulk. Did you kill the monk at Hailes, there in its cloister? Brother Edwin?'

'No. God help me, but I only killed Brother Ralph here in London.'

'You killed him with Master Wynchecombe's dagger?'

'Yes. Yes, I wanted *you* blamed for it,' he sneered, pulling on his bindings toward Wynchecombe. 'If I couldn't get you myself, then the law would.'

Simon stepped closer. His anger reddened his face. 'Why?'

'Because you didn't deserve her. You wouldn't do as she bid.'

'And steal the relic? Are you mad? What am I saying? Of course you are!'

'And *did* you steal it, Brother Fulk?' said Jack, trying to edge Simon out of the way.

'I tried. But I was caught. Brother Ralph caught me. And then he took it away, all the way to London. But I followed. And then I encountered *him*.' He spat at Wynchecombe's feet.

'Here, now!' squealed Jack, stepping out of the way. 'So you were after Wynchecombe but you found Brother Ralph instead?'

'She wanted the relic. I tried to get it for her since I had failed before.'

'And you tried to kill the sheriff.'

Simon shook out his mane of a head. 'He's already said that, Tucker.'

'But why did you have to kill your fellow monk?'

'Because he desired her, too. And I couldn't have that.'

Jack scratched at his beard. 'Then what of Brother Edwin? You claim you *didn't* kill him.'

'No, I didn't. I found him and told the others.'

'Then who killed *him*?'

'I don't know. Maybe *he* did,' and he jerked his head toward Simon.

Jack looked up at Wynchecombe.

'Of course I didn't,' rasped Simon. 'Why are you listening to this madman?'

Exasperated, Jack jerked away from Wynchecombe to face Fulk again. 'Did you kill the Cistercian at Westminster Abbey?'

'What? What are you talking about?'

'Another monk from Hailes – a Brother James – brought the relic back to London for safekeeping . . . and he was killed.'

'I know nothing of that.'

Jack threw up his arms. 'I give up.'

'You give up too easily, Tucker. You beat the truth out of him.'

'I won't, and neither will you. We'll take him to the sheriffs and then we can quit each other.'

'The first sensible thing you've said.'

Jack untied the bonds from the chair but kept them tight on the man's wrists behind his back. 'Up, then,' he told the monk, and helped by yanking him by his hands to his feet. He pushed him toward the door.

The monk stopped and dug his feet in. 'But what will become of Katherine?'

'No doubt she'll hang . . . for something.'

'But she is innocent of all. Innocent except in her bewitching character. Oh, would that I had never set eyes on her!'

'Amen, brother,' muttered Wynchecombe.

Jack nudged him out of the door and Wynchecombe followed. None of them spoke as they marched into the falling mist back to Newgate. The portcullis was down but the porter recognized Wynchecombe and turned the wheel to raise it. He sent a page to bring the sheriffs' men back to the tower gate and led the three up to the sheriffs' cold and empty chamber to await them.

The monk seemed quiet, even for a Cistercian. Perhaps he was resigned to his fate. As much time as Jack spent in their company – and it had been far too much, he admitted to himself – he would never understand the ways of a cleric, especially a cloistered one. Though this one didn't seem to feel the need to be all that cloistered.

A rumbling at the stairs had him standing at attention and holding tight to the man's bonds.

The sheriffs arrived and looked aghast at the specter of Simon Wynchecombe. Jack had forgotten that the man was in virtual rags and as disheveled as any London citizen had ever seen him. John Walcote took his place behind the desk and John Loveney stood beside him. 'Master Wynchecombe,' said Walcote, fidgeting with his hands and finally settling them, clasped, on top of the table. 'What are you doing here and in this state . . . and with Jack Tucker?'

'So you know him,' grumbled Wynchecombe. 'I should have known. My lords, I have a tale to tell. And this monk,' he gestured behind him toward the sagging cleric, 'is at the heart of it.'

It wasn't the monk they stared at, but at Jack. He tried to stand still and raised his chin to look them in the eye as Master Crispin had taught him.

Wynchecombe told his tale – abbreviating his association with the woman but making it plain what he meant – and then fell to silence.

'Well, brother,' said Walcote to the monk after he'd recovered from a long moment of shock. 'What have you to say for yourself?'

'God will judge me,' said Fulk with a whimper.

'But first, the king's justice will do so. What have you to say?'

He began to weep in earnest. 'My only crime is in loving the spawn of Eve. I succumbed to the Devil's own curse of lust and covetousness.'

'Did you kill this Brother Ralph who came to London?'

He nodded.

'God's wounds,' Walcote gasped.

Their clerk, Hamo Eckington, recorded the pertinent facts before they had the monk taken away to the cells. Jack saw his moment to take his leave. The sheriffs were busy talking in low tones to Wynchecombe, and since Simon was no longer in danger, Jack could be well rid of him.

But there was a rushing at the stairs and Jack scrambled out of the way as another page hastened up to the sheriffs.

'There's been a murder at Westminster Abbey. Crispin Guest is calling for you to come at once.'

'Guest!' the three sheriffs sneered at the same time.

TWENTY-ONE

Crispin kept himself by himself, away from the monks praying, the monks rushing about, the monks trying to care for the body and at the same time trying to leave it alone until the coroner or at least the sheriffs arrived.

Instead, he studied the room dispassionately, taking in the fact that the dead monk was still warm and the blood flowed. He was freshly killed, right under their very noses. In fact, any one of the monks currently making a nuisance of himself could very well be the murderer, hiding amidst the crowd. His gaze took in their shrouded faces of cowled, severe expressions. How many of them did he know? So many faces of men of whom he had no inkling, no point of reference. And why should any of them kill the man? Well, to steal the relic, of course, and conceal their crime. But which crime was the greater? He knew that men obsessed could find a way to justify anything: murder, theft, war . . . treason.

He crossed his arms. His cloak fell over him, like a cocoon. It took a while, but Abbot William finally made his way toward him.

'You are studying the room,' said the abbot. He had regained his composure but Crispin could tell that his calm was thin.

'Yes.'

'And this is what you do . . . how you do it?'

'Yes.'

'I will pray for you, Crispin,' he said with a harsh rasp to his voice, as if by the force of his will – or his prayers – he could suddenly conjure the truth. Oh, how Crispin wished it were only that easy.

He eliminated Kat. It simply couldn't have been her. The timing was all wrong. She would have to have known already where the relic was and she simply could not have known.

What of this other that was after Wynchecombe? A possibility. Though if it were a monk as Crispin suspected it was, he would be a white sheep among the black; another Cistercian among a herd of black Benedictines. Not exactly stealthy. He hoped John had gotten his message to Jack in time to save Wynchecombe. Not that he cared if the former Lord Sheriff lived or died . . . but the man had more answers to give, of that he was certain.

Who, then? Why? If to steal the relic, he knew why, but who would kill for the relic, and what would they do with it?

'You are far away.' The abbot's face was blank but his concern was discernable in those cloudy blue eyes.

'I am following the trail of a crime . . . and know not the end point of it. Where is the relic? Who wanted it this badly?'

'Did you . . . did you know it was in danger here?'

He shook his head. 'I thought this would be the safest place. I was wrong.'

'God forgives mistakes, Crispin.'

'But I do not forgive myself.'

'You are less generous than God? Surely you can see—'

'Forgive me, my lord, but I must excuse myself.' He pushed past the abbot without further comment. It was useless to argue the point. Crispin knew his own limits. He knew his own guilt.

He spotted Brother Eric looking somewhat lost. He couldn't help but sidle up to his old friend. 'Is all well?'

Eric sighed deeply. 'I don't think anything will ever be well again.'

'It can feel that way. But I assure you, from personal experience, that it will.'

Eric looked still older to him then. He'd known the monk since before his disgrace, though never had occasion to speak to him as much as he had after the unfortunate circumstances of his banishment. His face was often shadowed by his cowl, but now Crispin could plainly see in the firelight that it was scored by the fine lines of time. He had never known Eric's history; who he truly was, his family, the reason for his vocation. And he realized that he knew few men's histories. There were far too few men whom he could call his friend.

'Will word have to get out, I wonder?' said the monk in a scratchy voice. 'The abbey . . . there must not be scandal.'

'I'm afraid that cat is very much out of the bag.'

He closed his eyes, murmuring a prayer. 'But the abbey is a symbol of God's greatness. London has St Paul's but this is the seat of the king. Westminster's spiritual home is here. It must always be perceived as the greatest, without blemish.'

'Well . . . I shouldn't think this will change anything.'

'Don't you?'

'God knows what is His, Brother Eric. He decides what is great and what is not.'

Eric frowned. 'You, who hate His relics, can say this.'

Surprised at the monk's sudden emotion, Crispin studied the dark monk. 'I have never professed to *hate* His relics. Only to doubt them.'

'It is much the same.'

'I don't see it that way. But as you can now see, Man cannot be trusted with their guardianship if murder is the result.'

'Perhaps the . . . the killer was protecting it.'

'And was not Brother James doing that service?'

Eric wrestled his hands beneath his scapular. 'He was hiding it. A relic should never be hidden. It should be out where all can see, in a mighty place of honor.'

'I agree.'

'Will you search for it?'

'Naturally.'

Monks moving side by side approached and Brother Eric bowed to Crispin. 'I must go. God keep you, Crispin.'

'And you.'

But the monk was already moving away with his brethren. Crispin watched him go. Abbots he had known. Seldom had they been changed by their office, for they had prepared, had groomed themselves for it in most situations. But the monks themselves . . . It was a harsh life to accustom oneself to, he supposed.

The abbot's sedate steps came up behind him once more. 'I never meant to offend you,' he said.

Crispin turned to face him. 'You did not. I never meant to give you that impression.'

He sighed. 'I am a . . . blunt man, Crispin. I take a problem and lay out my assessment, point by point. That is why I was much favored to travel to Rome. My logic has always been appreciated by the cardinals. My dispassion much prized.'

'And your monks here, too, appreciate your stoic protection.'

'I have always thought so. Now . . . I am not so sure.'

'You mustn't take this murder so personally. There was a specific reason for it and it had nothing to do with you.'

'I wonder. I am responsible for all the souls within these walls.'

'You have been at your charge for only a few years but I have been at mine for over a decade. And I tell you, this had nothing to do with you. Ease your mind on it.'

'I trust your judgment. You are wise in this.'

'Judgment I have. Wisdom . . . well.'

'Master!'

Relief flooded Crispin's heart when he heard the voice of his apprentice. He turned gratefully and saw him rush forward. 'Jack. Thank God. Is Wynchecombe well?'

'I have much to say, but gird yourself. For here he comes.'

Not only was Wynchecombe pushing his way forth, he was followed by the other two sheriffs. 'It's a nightmare,' Crispin whispered.

They made straight for him.

He bowed but Walcote waved him off. 'None of that. What is this, Guest?'

'Another monk murdered, my Lord Sheriff.'

'Yes,' he replied, 'and we have the culprit in chains.'

He looked to Jack before squaring with Walcote. 'The culprit?'

Wynchecombe moved in, thrusting his thumbs into his belt. 'Yes, that damnable monk from Hailes. He was the one after me. Almost got me, too, if it hadn't been for this young lad of yours.'

Again, Crispin looked at Jack. The boy's pale skin flushed with embarrassment.

'And the whoreson confessed to killing that monk that brought you the relic,' Wynchecombe went on.

'Brother James?' He cast his glance toward the body on the floor, covered with a sheet.

'What? Him? No! The other one. The first one.'

'I see. And did he say why?'

'For the love of that damnable woman!'

'Katherine Pyke?'

'Pyke? No, Whitechurch.'

'She isn't Sybil Whitechurch or Katherine Woodleigh. She's Katherine Pyke.'

'What do I care what her damn name is? He killed for her.'

Crispin blinked with confusion. 'What of the monk at Hailes? The murdered one.'

Wynchecombe shook his head. 'He will not confess to that one. Said he found him dead.'

'He did not kill Brother Edwin?'

'So he says. Did he kill this one?'

'No time,' Jack cut in. 'He couldn't have and found you, too.'

Wynchecombe snorted. 'Of course he could have! He murdered this monk and followed your friends right to me!'

Jack slapped one hand into his other. 'How could he slay this monk, steal and hide the relic, and *then* go after me without my seeing him? I was looking all about for someone following me.

Don't you think I would have noticed a starched white Cistercian on my tail?'

'The lad is right,' said Crispin, rather proud of the boy for his logic and for standing up to the former sheriff. 'And he would have been noticed within the cloister. Surely no Benedictine brother would have left out having seen him.'

'Well, then . . . who did kill him?'

Crispin glared.

'Oh, here it comes again. Won't do your Christian duty unless you are paid your thirty pieces of silver.'

'Thirty? If only that were so.'

'See how the greed bites into him,' said Wynchecombe to his compatriots.

Walcote and Loveney nodded sagely, eyeing Crispin with disdain.

I don't have to take this. 'Then I leave it to you, my lords.' He bowed low and started to stalk away.

'Hold, Guest!' cried Loveney. 'Where do you think you're going?'

'My lord armorer accuses me of the sin of greed, merely for requiring my just compensation for my work. Do you not expect to be paid to repair a breastplate or a poulaine? My results are ethereal, not something to be held in the hand, yet they are nonetheless just as valuable. But as you are plainly not willing, I shan't stay.'

'Dammit, Guest, you are much too hasty. This is Westminster Abbey. Isn't it your obligation to take on such an investigation? I mean, you are friends with Abbot William, are you not?'

Crispin glanced toward the quiet abbot standing in the shadows. The man stepped forward, regal in his bearing as he bowed slightly to each man. 'As it happens,' said the abbot, 'I think it fitting for the king's servants to foot the bill.'

'What?' said Loveney. 'Us?'

'Well, it's only proper.'

Wynchecombe laughed. 'Forget it, boys. He's got you. He'll always get you. He's a sly one is Master Guest.'

'But I'm confused,' said Loveney. 'Just what was supposed to have been stolen?'

'The Holy Blood of Hailes,' said Crispin.

The sheriffs stared at him, mouths agape. Crispin turned to Wynchecombe. 'Did you not tell them?'

'At the time, it seemed the least of it.'

'I am very much afraid it is the *heart* of it.'

'That woman! She did it.'

'No. I had only just left her. She didn't know where it was hidden. She didn't have time to get here before me. And could never have . . .' Crispin paused. He had been about to say that she couldn't have gotten into the cloister. But that was not true, for she had done so before.

'My Lord Abbot, call in Brother Rodney Beaton.'

TWENTY-TWO

B rother Rodney walked slowly into the abbot's chamber and stood. His cowl covered his face, shadowing his down-turned eyes. Crispin wanted to slap it back off his face, to look at him squarely, but he didn't think Abbot William would approve.

While the sheriffs were busy with the arrival of the coroner, Crispin took the opportunity to question the monk. 'You allowed Katherine Pyke into this monastery,' he said in a low growl.

'I know of no Katherine Pyke,' he said, never looking directly at Crispin.

'Katherine Woodleigh, then. She goes by many names.'

'I do not understand.'

'Did you let her in?'

'Yes.'

'Why?'

'She . . . she asked for help most piteously.'

'I'm certain she did. At first. And then she wormed her way into your heart, didn't she? What did she want?'

'Nothing.'

'You're lying. And here is the thing of it, brother. Do you see yon sheriffs? If I let them at you, they will take you back to Newgate where they will torture the answers out of you. They won't be polite and ask. They will simply bring out the red-hot brands, the screws to bore into your toes. Shall I let them . . . or will you talk to *me*?'

His lip trembled and his eyes filled with tears. He looked at Crispin and whispered, 'Yes.'

'Then why was she here?'

'I . . . I hired her.'

'*You* hired her? Forgive me, brother, but are not all monks to give up their worldly possessions?'

'In a fashion. But Abbot Nicholas had let me keep my family jewels – the rings and such. I have them still. I hired her, or the person I thought I was hiring.'

'To what end?'

The tears fell freely down his pale cheeks. His mouth worked but no sound emerged. He licked his lips and tried again. 'To steal the relic of Hailes.'

'You hired a thief.'

'She said she was a thief. I did not believe her at first. And then she stole something from the abbot to prove it to me.'

'Do I want to know what that is?'

'I made her return it.'

'How noble. Why did you want the relic of Hailes?'

'Because . . . the abbey should be the place of pilgrims, not that wretched Cistercian house in the wilderness. Why should they be celebrated? This is Westminster!'

'And for this, you would kill?'

His reddened eyes widened. The tears grew to great crystals before they spilled from his eyes. 'No! I never killed.'

'And yet Brother James is dead.'

'I never said anyone should be harmed in this. That is not what I've paid for!'

'But pay you will. You caused the death of Brother James as clearly as if you cracked his head open yourself.'

'No! NO!'

The sheriffs turned at the monk's sharp denial. They looked at one another and excused themselves from the coroner to approach.

'What have we here, Guest?' asked Walcote.

'The villain behind all of these events, Lord Sheriff. Brother

Rodney here hired our thief to steal the Holy Blood of Hailes and caused those events to unfold.'

'He murdered the monk.'

'No. Or so he claims.'

'But he is guilty of a conspiracy,' said Wynchecombe. 'And what the devil? Why is it that a monk has the wherewithal to hire anybody?'

'You must know, my lord,' offered Crispin, 'that a clever man can get around any oath he swears. At least, he can appear to get around it. God is never fooled, after all.'

'I should slap you for that, Guest.'

'I shouldn't try it, my lord,' said Crispin in a low voice.

Simon seemed taken aback. 'You've changed. You don't fear me as you did.'

'I feared your office. I've learned a lot since then.'

Wynchecombe narrowed his eyes and scowled. 'So you have. Then what of this?' He gestured toward the monk.

'He did not kill Brother James.'

'You are quick to believe these criminals, Guest.'

'I have a sense of them. I generally know when someone is lying to me.'

'Aren't you the miracle. Well, brother. Should I believe you, too?'

'Oh, yes!' he said urgently. 'It is as Master Guest has said. I killed no one. I only hired that woman to steal for me.'

'For the greater glory of Westminster,' added Crispin.

'What nonsense!' Wynchecombe glanced at Jack. 'Do you believe him?'

'I believe Master Crispin . . . *whatever* he says.'

'Somehow I knew you would say that.'

Crispin loured over the weeping monk. 'Where is the relic now?'

'I don't know.'

'He was murdered while guarding it and you don't know where it's gone?'

He shook his head.

'My lord,' said Crispin, turning to Wynchecombe, 'if for nothing else, he is still guilty of the theft from Hailes. He must be taken to Newgate.'

'Oh, he will be. Loveney! Walcote! Here is your prisoner. Though as Master Guest here vouchsafes, he is only a conspirator, not a murderer.'

Loveney approached and looked the monk over. The man was trembling now. 'Oh? We'll see about that.'

'I swear, my lords! I never sought to harm anyone!'

Crispin grasped his arm. 'Do you have an accomplice? Someone who has no such qualms?'

'No, no. Just the woman. God help me. She was . . . more than I expected.'

'And quite more than you bargained for.'

The sheriffs signaled to their bailiffs to take the monk away. Crispin thought Abbot William would put up a fight about it, but he stood silent and stiff in the deepening shadows. The bell had rung a while ago for Vespers and still the abbot had not quit the scene. Crispin had seen other abbots in similar circumstances proceed with the Divine Office even as corpses cooled around them. But not this abbot.

Crispin wished the abbot could be more helpful. In the end, he and Jack simply watched the three sheriffs spirit the monk away – watched him from the abbot's window as he bent over and wept as they bound his hands and trailed him behind their horses in the courtyard.

The monks were bearing the dead Cistercian on a bier and carrying him away, while others cleaned the paving stones of his blood and brains.

The abbot remained at the window until the sounds of horses receded away into the noises of Westminster shutting down for the night. He turned toward Crispin, his face unreadable. 'What now, Master Guest?'

Indeed. What now?

'Master Crispin,' said Jack in hushed tones, stealing glances at the abbot. 'I'm confused. There are too many monks in this pie.'

He nodded. 'You're right. There are altogether too many monks to consider. We know that Brother Fulk killed Brother Ralph and tried to blame Wynchecombe for it with his stolen knife. And we know that Brother Rodney hired Kat to steal the relic, starting this whole chain of events in the first place. But we don't know who killed Brother Edwin in the cloister of Hailes and we don't know who killed Brother James in Abbot William's chamber.'

'I've a mind to think it is that Pyke woman.'

'The timeline is too dear. I cannot see her having the time to kill Brother James.'

'Maybe she hired someone to. If it looked like the hunters were closing in to get rid of any dangling threads . . . I mean, why else would you think she was innocent—' Jack studied him a little too closely. 'God's blood, master! You didn't!'

'Didn't what?'

'You lay with her, didn't you? That's how you know she couldn't have been here so fast.'

'I . . . might have.'

Jack threw up his arms.

'Now look, Tucker. I will not have you judging me like this.'

'I'm not judging you, Master Crispin. I'm just . . . Well. Sometimes I despair of you.'

'Oh, you have gone smug since you've gotten betrothed.'

'It isn't that. Well . . . perhaps a little. You should get yourself a regular woman, sir. It tames a man. In a good way.'

'I'm not so sure of that.'

'Anyway, we must get back to the problem. She must be arrested for her part in it. Maybe she can tell us more about Brother Rodney, if she had beguiled him enough to kill. Unless you do believe him.'

'I'm afraid I do. And you are right, of course. I'm letting my better judgment fall to the wayside again because of some damned woman.'

'You can't help it, sir. There are just some men who are led more by their cods than by their heads.'

Crispin slowly turned his head to stare at his apprentice. 'What did you just say to me?'

'I don't blame you, sir. I was foolish like that once or twice.'

'I can't believe my ears.'

'It's the taming, sir. It makes a man think.'

Crispin pressed his fists into his hips. 'It does, does it?'

'Aye, sir. You'll see. When Isabel comes to live with us, you'll be tamed, too.'

Good God. He hadn't thought of that. Was he to be tormented for the rest of his life by a slip of a girl, half his age? *And* his apprentice? How was it to be borne?

'It hasn't happened yet,' he grumbled.

'Should we go, sir? Should we go and apprehend this Katherine Pyke?'

'Yes.' *Anything to get out of here.*

TWENTY-THREE

They didn't hurry, even as the lingering light faded and failed to paint the sides of the houses and shops down row on row of Westminster's streets and when they got to London's gates. Heading to the Unicorn, Crispin expected that Kat would have fled. *I certainly would have.* And if she had, he did not know where to go from there. Did he believe Wynchecombe? Well, it was plain he hadn't killed Brother Ralph, but had he killed Brother Edwin back in Hailes? And was Crispin too quick to entertain the fact that Kat couldn't have gotten to Westminster before him? She could have. He knew that now. She was nimble and clever. She could have done it. Hell, the woman seemed capable of anything.

'Jack,' he said carefully before slowing to a stop.

Jack stopped with him, standing under the eaves of a blacksmith's. The shop was shuttered but it felt warm there, as if the furnace was still in front of them. 'Aye, sir?'

'Perhaps . . . my judgment where the woman is concerned is . . . compromised.'

Jack folded his arms over his chest. 'Well, then.'

'I didn't think her capable of getting to Westminster before me, but now I see how I could have been terribly wrong.' He gestured toward the Unicorn ahead of them. 'I think that maybe you should go up and see if she is there.'

'Me, sir? Alone?'

'Yes. You seem incapable of being charmed.'

Jack pulled tightly at his tunic to straighten it and squared his shoulders, as if he was marching off to war. 'Aye, sir.' He stalked forward over the mud and passed through to the inn yard.

Crispin sighed, cursing himself. What a fool. And the damnable thing of it was it wasn't the first time. Maybe there was something to this celibacy that clerics were supposed to be doing. No women meant less confusion. He leaned his shoulder into the wall and grumbled. He never seemed to learn this lesson. But dammit. Women were . . . pleasant and soft and most enticing. He looked around to the empty streets darkening with the night and adjusted himself. Maybe he did think too much with his cod.

Something caught the corner of his eye. A movement up on the inn's roof. He turned and squinted into the gloom. Definitely a figure up there. And oddly, it looked like a woman with hiked-up skirts . . .

'Kat!' He hurried to follow below but she was making good speed up there. 'Damn the woman!' He had to join her or he would soon lose her. She had already leapt like a deer to another roof. He searched for a place to climb. The London houses and shops shouldered one another, sometimes holding the other up. It was as if they were one continuous roof. But to climb would take some means.

There! A barrel against a wall with a jutting window. He ran for it and leapt up to the barrel, nimbly jumping to the window and up to the eaves. Fingers digging into the clay tiles, he pulled himself up by the strength of his arms, threw his leg up over the roof, and rolled the rest of the way. He popped up to his feet and just caught the shadowy figure disappearing behind some chimneys. He hastened after her.

Some of the clay tiles snapped under his feet, loosened and careened down the slant of the roof, shattering below on the cobblestones. He ignored the muffled shouts from below and pursued.

Kat stopped beside a chimney and listened, looking back. Crispin threw himself against a wall and hid in the shadows.

She did not seem to be looking to get down anytime soon. She was rather accomplished with this, he thought. Being smaller and weighing less was an advantage. He was certain each of his heavy steps could be plainly heard by the residents below him.

She moved ahead again and he peeled himself away from the

wall to follow. She took several more steps and suddenly spun. 'Crispin?'

He froze but it was of no use. Even with the darkness sheltering him she had plainly spotted him.

'Crispin. Why are you pursuing me?'

He could barely see her face but the moon's light caught one of her cheeks, the sharp brightness of her eyes. He huffed a breath. 'Maybe I enjoy it.'

She laughed. 'I very much doubt that.'

'You ran from my apprentice.'

'So I did. It seems someone wishes to arrest me.'

He shook his head, angry with her, with himself. 'Kat, you knew it would end this way. You knew I would have to turn you in. Why were you still there at the Unicorn?'

'Because I knew you'd be back.'

He took a step forward. She took one away from him.

'This is foolish, woman! You must turn yourself in to me.'

'But I don't wish to be arrested. I feel it would be a detriment to my health.'

'Kat . . . can't we get off this damned roof and talk about it?'

'And be nabbed by your apprentice? I don't think so.'

In a flash, she disappeared. He realized that she had turned and her dark cloak gave the illusion that she had vanished into thin air. But his ears picked up her movement instead and he followed, leaping over the spine of a roof.

'Stop pursuing me, Crispin,' she called over her shoulder.

'I won't. You know I won't.'

She sighed and stopped again, keeping a decent distance between them. He sensed this anyway and stopped. She tilted her head when she gazed at him. He remembered that about her, how she had angled her head, offering her neck for him to kiss and nuzzle.

'You truly must stop pursuing me. I shan't surrender myself to you.'

'Did you steal the relic?'

'No.'

'Did you kill the monk?'

He heard the small gasp. Was it more mummery? 'Who was killed?'

'A Cistercian monk who brought the relic back to me.'

'I am sorry. But no, I did not. Where did this happen?'

'Don't you know?'

She gusted an exasperated breath. 'No, I don't. I never killed anyone and I didn't take the relic. But I would have, for I still need to be paid.'

'That won't happen now. Brother Rodney has been arrested for conspiracy.'

'God's teeth!' she swore under her breath.

'So you see, it is useless to run.'

'Not if the sheriffs wish to accuse me of murder and thievery.'

'Do you swear to God that you didn't kill him?'

'I swear, Crispin. I did not. What did . . . what did Rodney say?'

'What they all seem to say. That you captivated him. That he wished to hire a thief and was surprised it was you.'

'Such a little fool.'

'Did you lie with him, too?' He hadn't meant it to come out as harshly as it had, but . . . well. There it was.

Her silhouetted face looked down. 'Does it matter so much to you?'

'No.'

She laughed. It galled. 'I didn't, as it happens. He was flushed like a child. I've no doubt he'd never experienced such feelings before, didn't know what to do with them. But he was willing to do almost anything for me. Except pay me first.'

'Do you think he killed the Cistercian?'

'Rodney? Oh, no. Someone else, surely. What of that fellow after Simon?'

'No. He only had his murderous heart set on killing Simon. Almost would have if it weren't for my apprentice.'

'He is a handy fellow is your Jack Tucker.'

He looked off between the rooftops to the lane below, where a cat was making its stealthy way along the path, picking delicately over the mud. 'Brother Fulk was so besotted with you he killed Brother Ralph with Simon's dagger to make it look as if he had done it. Then he pursued the poor man to kill him. All for love of you.'

'Dear me. Well, I do confess I did sleep with the man. I thought he would do what I wished afterwards but he hesitated. Simon, too. It didn't stop Fulk from killing, though, did it? Or Simon from being the weakling he is. Only you, Crispin, seems to have kept his head and his integrity intact.'

'Is that supposed to be a compliment?'

'In my way.'

'Is Fulk lying? He said he didn't kill Brother Edwin at Hailes.'

'What difference does it all make, Crispin? You have your culprits. Of the relic . . . well . . .'

'I don't have my culprits. I don't know who killed Brother James or Brother Edwin, and the relic is lost again.'

'And I am without my fee.' She took a cautious step closer. The gap between the roofs was the span of a lane and cut their path in two. One false step and it was a good fifteen feet down. 'We could partner. Suppose I get half your fee if I help you.'

'You do recall how meager my fee is.'

'That's right.' She ruminated, tapping her chin. 'And I already expended money paying your debts. Perhaps I should get *all* the fee.'

It was his turn to laugh. 'You are a ridiculous woman.'

'Nothing of the kind. I'm pragmatic.'

'What makes you think I can trust you? You've done nothing but lie to me.'

'Crispin, Crispin. Those were all necessary lies. But as your partner, I certainly wouldn't lie to you then. How could we help each other otherwise?'

'Why is it I feel you are only out to help Kat?'

'Ah, wounded again. Your barbs are sharp, my dear.'

He firmed his stance on the slanted surface. He could suddenly see a star-filled sky above without the looming buildings blocking his view. Strangely, it somehow made their conversation seem that much more intimate. 'Maybe I can't trust you to find a murderer when you may very well be one . . . but I do need you to help me find the relic.'

'I would give it my all.'

'Why? Do you have another buyer?'

She feigned shock. 'Why, Crispin Guest! You don't believe I would do this out of my own obligation to make things right?'

'Not even a little.'

She laughed. 'There is no veil covering your eyes, is there.'

'None whatsoever.'

She stopped to ponder, becoming as still as the other shadows spilling down the pitch of the roof. 'And yet,' she said softly, almost too softly for him to hear, 'I would help you. But I have a price.'

'Of course. What is it?'

'That you don't turn me in to the sheriffs. When all is said and done and I have helped you, you allow me to walk away.'

'What of *my* reputation, demoiselle? I always bring thieves and murderers to justice.'

She shook her head. 'Not this time.'

He tried to make out her face in the darkness, but night had fully draped around them and all he could discern was her figure in the moonlight. He recalled intimately each curve he could now barely see. 'You drive a hard bargain.'

'So I have been told.'

He gave one nod. 'Done.'

There was the flash of a smile. 'Then off we go.' She spread out her arms like Christ on a cross and slowly fell backward off the roof.

'Kat!' He ran and leapt across the space between the roofs. He got to the edge and looked down. A hay cart stood below. But there was no sign of Kat.

'Damnable woman,' he growled. Yet he was smiling.

He returned to the Unicorn where Jack was waiting. 'Where've you been?' said Jack.

'I've been in pursuit of our thief. But I've made an agreement with her. She helps us find the relic and . . . and I let her go.'

'What sort of sarding agreement is that?'

'She hasn't another buyer. At least, I don't think so. And she is clever. She can help.'

'Very well.' He folded his arms over his chest and scowled. 'Where is she, then?'

'Right here!'

She landed hard behind Jack and, when he whirled and grabbed at his dagger, he was more than displeased to discover that it was already in *her* hand.

She waved it a bit before tossing it in the air and catching it blade first so to offer the hilt to Jack. He took it without thanks, yanking it out of her hands.

'Careful, young Master Tucker. You could have cut me.'

'Only if you wanted me to, for I fear there is little that happens that you haven't plotted beforehand.'

She moued. 'This one takes after you, Crispin.'

'And aren't we lucky he does. The relic was being kept at Westminster Abbey, Kat. The Cistercian monk guarding it was slain where he was. In the abbot's chamber.'

'Blessed Virgin! Someone has the audacity. But he also has the means.'

'*You* would have the audacity.'

'But not the means . . . or the cruelty. I get my men out of the way by other tactics . . . as you know.'

'Yes,' he said sourly.

She merely smiled. 'Any theories?'

'You,' said Jack, keeping his hand on his dagger's pommel.

'Ah, dear Jack, but I did not. I did not kill and I did not get my hands upon the relic. Not this time. And my buyer has been taken to prison. If he didn't do it, then I am at a loss.'

'I would love to say it was Master Wynchecombe,' said Jack, 'but he was with me the whole time.'

'That was my next question,' said Kat.

'Not your buyer, Brother Rodney,' said Crispin, 'not Simon and not you. And not Fulk, for he only cared to kill Simon. There are no more players as far as I know.'

'But there must be,' she said, laying a finger to her lips, tapping their plumpness. Crispin tore his eyes away from those lips that had done maddening things to him.

'Perhaps whoever it was that killed Brother Edwin,' said Jack. 'Seems all them monks were coming and going from Hailes without a so much as a by-your-leave to the abbot, and him not saying much about it.'

'If that is true,' said Crispin, 'and that killer is here in London with us, however will we find him?'

'Look for a stray Cistercian?'

'You're assuming it's a monk,' she said. She pulled her cloak about her.

'Shall we return to my lodgings? Jack, hadn't you better get a message to Nigellus Cobmartin, telling him that his own lodgings are free again?'

'In the morning, master. I have a feeling it isn't an urgency and he might object to the, uh . . . interruption.'

'As you will,' he muttered.

They kept an eye out for signs of the watch and made it to the Shambles without incident. Jack rushed ahead and unlocked the door. He commenced stoking the fire as Crispin took Kat's cloak and hung it on the peg by the door. He unbuttoned his own and hung it next to hers.

'Please sit,' he said, gesturing to the table in the center of the room.

A black-and-white cat suddenly appeared out of the gloom and wound his way around her feet. 'And who is this?' She knelt and picked him up, holding him close to her chest.

'That rascal is Gyb and I'm surprised he is allowing you such liberties.'

She stroked his head and pressed her cheek against his fur. 'Oh, but he's a sweet thing. All men are alike. They only need the right sort of coddling.' She petted the cat for a few more moments before letting him go. 'You see? They like their stroking, but in the end they prefer to be free.'

Jack snorted by the fire.

Crispin sat as Kat found her seat. She looked from one to the other. 'This partnership of yours. It works well.'

'It's Master Crispin's doing,' said Jack, straightening. He stood by the fire, hands behind his back. 'He's taught me everything I know.'

'Not everything,' she said. 'I hear tell you were an accomplished thief when he found you.'

'A man's got to eat, demoiselle.'

'So does a woman. And the world is a much crueler place to a woman, Master Tucker. We learn what we learn to get by.'

He sniffed but stayed before the fire, as if guarding it. Or was he guarding Crispin?

Crispin steepled his hands. 'The relic must be returned to Hailes. That is the first order of business.'

'I didn't agree to that. I agreed to help you find it.'

'Confound it, woman! I did not agree to partner with you only for you to steal it and sell it to the highest bidder. Our agreement is nullified if that is your intention.'

'Fine,' she said, rolling her eyes. 'It returns to Hailes. And you let me go.'

'Fine.'

Jack began to rock on his heels. 'I don't suppose anyone cares what I have to say on it.'

No one spoke.

Jack sighed. 'Well, I do have a question. Are we looking for the same person who killed Brother Edwin, then?'

'I suppose that follows,' said Crispin, staring down at the table, trying not to look at Kat's animated features.

'But it doesn't,' she said.

'And why not?'

'Because the relic was taken by someone who knew it was there. Do you think this culprit could see through walls? It must have been someone at Westminster Abbey.'

'Aye,' said Jack. 'Rodney Beaton. Why'd he want it anyway?'

'For the glory of the abbey,' said Crispin, leaning back.

Jack absently rubbed his backside before the fire. 'But what good would that do? It's not as if he could display it. The best he could do would be to make sure it never returned to Hailes.'

Kat pressed forward against the table. 'He wouldn't destroy it, would he?'

Crispin gazed up into the rafters in thought. 'No. But he'd keep it hidden. He'd keep it . . .' He slammed his hand to the table. 'I know where it is.' He rose and went to his cloak by the door.

'Master Crispin, we're not going back to Westminster again, are we?'

'*I* am, if you've no stomach for it.'

Jack straightened his cloak, which he had not taken off, and stretched his back till it cracked. 'No, master, I'll accompany you.'

Kat smiled. 'And am I allowed to come?'

'I highly recommend it.' He grabbed her cloak and tossed it toward her. She caught it easily and began to draw it on.

TWENTY-FOUR

K at seemed unafraid of the night. Since she was a thief, he expected as much. The misty darkness seemed to follow them, before and aft, encasing their steps. Both London and Westminster had gone to their rest. There was candlelight here and there behind shutters and curtains. Fires were banked for the night, yet some smoke still curled from chimneys and crept over the rooftops.

Spring had not seemed to have permeated the night, for it was icy cold. Crispin drew his heavy cloak over his arms. He glanced at Kat. Her cloak did not seem as heavy and he almost offered his own to her before thinking better of it. Best not to appear more of a fool than he'd already made himself out to be. It was all a game to her. Bedding Crispin was only part of it. And yet he'd done the same to countless other women. Why did it sting so much when it had happened to him?

Charing Cross suddenly loomed out of the mist and he followed the torchlight toward the abbey. The burning cressets glowed outside the north door. Crispin led them around toward the Thames at the entrance of the cloisters. Knowing it was far too late, he nevertheless rang the bell.

It wasn't long before the sedate stride of a black-cowled monk appeared at an arched doorway. When he reached the barred entrance, Crispin could see that it was Brother Eric, and he was none too pleased to see Crispin. 'It is late, Master Guest. Very late.'

'I know.'

The monk's gaze took in Jack and then Kat. It lingered on her before returning to Crispin. 'The abbot is abed.'

'I do not wish to disturb Abbot William . . . just yet. May I . . . may *we* come into the cloister?'

'You are allowed many liberties, Crispin. But this woman . . .'

'Who has been in the cloister many a time before,' said Kat, approaching the bars.

'And who should not have been,' countered Brother Eric.

She shrugged. 'That's as may be, but the point is moot now.'

'Two crimes have been committed, brother,' said Crispin. 'You know why I am here.'

He studied Crispin carefully. 'My brothers are in repose. They deserve their rest.'

'We shall be as quiet as we may.'

In resignation, Eric unlocked the gate, pulled it open and stood behind it, the shadows from the bars falling over his face. 'You can leave by the church.'

'If that is your will.'

Eric said nothing more as he locked the gate again, turned and shuffled back into the cloister.

Crispin led them through the colonnade. The garth was a gathering of ghostly trees whispering in the mist. They seemed to disappear as they passed them, one coming out of the gloom just as others receded into it. An owl hooted from somewhere over a rooftop and the squeal of bats swooped over them, catching fluttering moths. But there was no other sound from the heavy stone structure of church and monastery.

They soon came to a door. Crispin pushed it open and they entered into the dim church.

'How is it, Crispin,' asked Kat, 'that you have been granted this singular honor of free egress throughout the abbey?'

'Years ago, I gained the trust of the former abbot, Nicholas de Litlyngton. He was my longtime friend. I have since befriended the current abbot, William de Colchester. He knows my needs – that I sometimes must be in the church and cloister for my investigating. And he has faith that I will not allow any harm to come to his monks or his church . . . or anything within it.'

She pressed a hand to her throat. 'Never fear, Crispin. I heard that warning as if it were shouted from the rooftops.'

He said nothing more as he moved easily between the pillars, the many tombs like a village, and found his way to the tomb of King Henry III fixed between two columns.

The golden effigy of the king sat high atop the tomb under a gabled canopy just over the royal head, with jewels set in his crown, crossed scepters in his hands and the lions of England at his feet. Purbeck marble made up the sides of the tomb, and below it in arched niches were shrines. One held a stepped cabinet of gold topped with a cross. Set within its grille was a crystal vase decorated with gems and gold. The vase inside held what was left of the Holy Blood.

Jack read the French inscription aloud: '*Here lies Henry, formerly King of England, Lord of Ireland and Duke of Aquitaine, son of King John, formerly King of England, to whom God grant mercy. Amen.*'

They all crossed themselves.

Crispin gestured toward the three niches. 'In this,' he said quietly, pointing toward the left, 'is a piece of the cross. And in this on the right is the Virgin's girdle. And this in the center . . . is the Holy Blood of Westminster.'

'Relics.' Kat sighed. 'There isn't much to them, is there? I used to make and sell them all the time. But I hear tell that you don't put much store in them.'

'I don't. Generally. But some . . . are special in their way. It is more for what they represent than for what they are, I suppose. At least, Abbot Nicholas used to tell me that.'

'They don't belong to us,' said Jack. He stood beside Crispin, almost guarding the little golden shrine. Crispin was certain Jack imagined Kat would grab and make off with it the moment Crispin opened the grille. *The boy might be right at that.*

Crispin looked over the grille and its small lock. 'Ah, but Jack, you are wrong. The relics belong to all. God has gifted them to all of mankind.'

'Then why do only them monasteries get their gold from it?'

'Well, someone must house them.'

Kat peered in, staring at the crystal vase.

Crispin watched her. 'Have you ever seen the Holy Blood of Hailes?'

'Of course. Many a time. And it was strange, I suppose. That blood . . . rolling from side to side as it did. Gave me chills.'

He exchanged a quick and surprised glance with Jack. 'You saw the blood flow?'

'Yes. What else would it be? No wonder the Blood of Hailes was more prized than this old stain. It might as well be paint. It might very well be.'

Crispin reached and, with the aiglet of the lace at his shirt and the point of his dagger, he unlocked the grille.

Kat smiled. 'I see you are accomplished at larceny as well, Crispin.'

Silently, he reached in . . .

'What are you doing?' she said, suddenly alarmed.

Still he said nothing. He took the vase and moved it aside before reaching further into the shrine behind the vase and pulling out the beryl crystal of the Holy Blood of Hailes.

'Blessed Virgin,' she breathed.

He tucked it under his arm, moved the vase to the center once more and closed the grille.

'How did you know it was there?' Her eyes were shining as she gazed at it. He was gratified that she did not reach for it. He handed it carefully to Jack, who slipped it into his scrip. His fingers tingled unpleasantly.

'Because, as you said, they could not display it, nor could they destroy such a holy thing. Everyone would know from whence it came. The only course was to keep it from Hailes. To make Westminster the prime location for pilgrimages. And what better place to hide it than in Westminster's Holy Blood shrine?'

'I suppose that's what Brother Rodney intended. But if not him then who killed Brother James?'

Crispin locked the grille but kept his hand on it. He supposed he had not wanted to think too carefully about it because it had dawned on him some time ago that he knew of at least one other person who had the same philosophy as Brother Rodney. Yet he did not want it to be true, for then that man would be a murderer.

'Jack, Kat, you must remain here for a while. Or perhaps . . . it's best you go home. There is someone I must talk to.'

'Master Crispin?'

He let his eyes rest on Jack's. 'Guard the relic,' was all he said. He hoped that his gaze had conveyed all he needed to say.

Sluggishly, he moved within the cloister, his heart aching with the revelation suddenly upon him. This was the last thing he wanted to do, the last person he had wanted to accuse, and yet it made sense, if anything did. Except he wasn't sure where to find him.

The cloister was dead quiet. The wet stone smelled of mauso-leums in a churchyard. The monks must all be at their beds, their prayers all done for the day until they rose at midnight to continue their Divine Office. They slept in their innocence and their ignorance of what was to come.

Shadows stretched long across the flagged-stone walkway of the cloister. Each carrel was a black hole of gloom, not the sheltered study cell in which the monks read their scriptures in the holy light of day. Their arches facing the garth cast irregular shapes over his steps. All was still and silent.

Until one shadow moved.

The voice echoed over the lonely stones. 'I suppose . . . you are looking for me.'

Crispin *could* turn around. He *could* leave. The sheriffs would never figure this out as he had. He might be able to forget it with enough cups of wine.

'I am.' Crispin had known a while ago, or thought he had. But now his soul wrenched with the certainty. He was aware of his dagger and prayed he would not need it.

The man sighed. Crispin could see his puff of breath in the cold. 'I knew you would be. It would be impossible to hide from you.'

'And yet you killed Brother James anyway.'

A slight gasp. 'I didn't mean to. I struck him too hard. God forgive me.'

'Why, Brother Eric? Why did you do it at all?'

Eric stepped onto the walkway. The moonlight touched the edges of his silhouette and softened it with silver. Tears gleamed on his face.

'Perhaps it is difficult for someone like you to understand. You are such a worldly man, Crispin, full of worldly thoughts. But *this* is my world.' He raised his hand to the cloister, the spired arches of the church, the dim walkway. 'I am limited by these walls, you see. And they have come to mean *everything* to me. They are the sunrise of my day, the sunset of my night. The very stones are permeated with my all my prayers, my heart, my hope . . . my eternity. Can you understand that?'

Crispin bit his lip and nodded. He tried to look away but Eric's ruined face compelled him. There was more emotion on his face now than Crispin had ever seen in a decade of knowing the man.

'So when I overheard Brother Rodney speaking to the woman,' Eric went on, 'I knew he had plotted with her to steal the Hailes relic. At first I was appalled. I even moved toward the abbot's lodgings to tell him, to report it. But suddenly I stopped. And then . . . I began to consider. Few come to Westminster to venerate our relics. Few pilgrims come to this greatest of churches. We have the tombs of the world's most feared monarchs under our roof. And still they don't come.'

'How can one force what is in the heart, brother?'

'Force? Perhaps not. Redirect their course, maybe.'

'I don't understand. Westminster is still Westminster. As you say, monarchs are buried here. They are crowned here. What more fame does it need?'

'Pilgrims, Crispin. Those seeking solace. Those who wish to touch the hand of God. This is a temple of our Lord. We need the faithful to sustain the walls.'

'Oh, Eric. What have you done?'

The monk blinked away his tears, swathed his face with his sleeve. 'Yes. I know. I never meant to kill. It was an accident.'

Crispin stilled. He watched the emotion ripple over Eric's face.

'Maybe you don't believe me.'

'I have no choice but to believe you, for I have known you too long not to.'

A new pain seared across the monk's face. 'God have mercy,' he whispered. 'I've betrayed everything, haven't I? I only meant to help the abbey but sin breeds sin.' He touched his forehead with a trembling hand. 'Where has my judgment gone? I used to be valued for my judgment. But of course, Abbot William has his own chaplains. I was Abbot Nicholas'. . .' He looked down at his hands, rubbing one over the other. 'I'm not sure what to do. Should I . . . should I take my own life, do you think? A life for a life, an eye for an eye? Would that be less scandalous? Or is it the coward's way? Crispin, I tell you, I'd rather go with you to the sheriffs now than face Abbot William. It will break his heart.'

Swallowing kept his own tears at bay. How long had he known this man, trusted him? His throat hurt, his stomach soured. 'Very well. I will take you if that is your choice.'

'You found the relic, didn't you?'

'Yes.'

He chuckled. 'I knew you would.'

Crispin's voice was gravel. 'Will you come with me now?'

Eric glanced around the cloister, eyes looking one last time at the stone walls, the columns, the carrels. 'Yes. I will come with you.'

TWENTY-FIVE

Hours later in the dead of night, Crispin returned to his lodgings and slumped into a chair. Jack and Kat had left Westminster just as long ago and had been waiting for him.

Jack silently moved about the hall, stoking the fire and placing warmed wine in front of Crispin. Crispin took up the goblet, put it to his lips and drank gratefully of the spices and warmth.

Kat gazed at him kindly. She seemed soft and vulnerable in the golden light. 'It was a friend, wasn't it?'

Crispin nodded. When he lowered his goblet, Jack was there, filling it again. 'That was the most miserable thing I have ever had to do.'

Jack stood beside him, cradling the jug to his chest. 'Wh-who was it, sir?'

Closing his eyes, Crispin said, 'Brother Eric.'

'No!'

Crispin drank down the wine again. He stared into the fire till his eyes blurred. 'He had not meant to kill . . .'

'He went with you willingly to the sheriffs?'

Crispin nodded.

'God have mercy.' He crossed himself.

'And now there is only one final thing to finish.' Crispin turned weary, bloodshot eyes toward Kat. 'You killed Brother Edwin, did you not?'

Kat gazed at him, breathing deeply, nostrils flaring. Out of the corner of his eye, Crispin saw Jack stare from one to the other.

Finally, Kat settled back in her chair. 'How did you know?'

'It is the only logical answer. Simon didn't do it. Fulk didn't do it. Who was left?'

She slowly nodded. 'But it isn't what you think,' she said softly.

He silenced the angry screaming in his head. 'What is it I think?' he said carefully.

'That I murdered him. I didn't. I was defending myself. Yes, he was another whom I had bewitched. He was like a lap dog, wanting to help me, wanting to do for me. And yet he would not steal for me. And he, too, was jealous of Simon. He did not know about Brother Fulk. If he had . . . well, I don't know. It seems that the lap dog was becoming rabid. He struck out at me. Threatened me. That if I did not leave Simon he would make sure I was with no one. I could no longer control him. And on that day, he had a dagger. He held my arm and would not let me go. I feared for my life, Crispin – that is the truth of it. And I pulled my own dagger and struck. When he fell with all that blood . . .' She shook her head and swallowed. 'I did not know what to do. Should I tell someone, the abbot? Ultimately, I was a coward and I fled. That is the truth. But I will not go to the sheriffs to tell them.' She stood, clutching the skirts of her cote-hardie. 'This will be the last you see of me. I will be gone and out of your life, whether you believe me or not. But for God's sake . . . please. Believe me.'

He kept his eyes on the fire. 'Why should I? Why is it important that I do?'

'Usually it isn't. But you . . . I want *you* to believe me.'

'I don't know that I can.'

'I understand. Still, I will not surrender myself. What possible chance would a woman like me have?'

'You will have justice.'

She laughed – a cold, brittle sound. 'Do you truly believe that?'

The goblet felt numb in his hand. He realized he was still wearing his cloak, but he was cold and did not wish to remove it. 'I don't know,' he whispered.

She walked to the door and took her cloak down from its peg. 'I'm leaving. Leaving London.'

'Will you return to Hailes?'

'I don't know. I don't think so. Most likely I will have to start again.'

'With yet a different name?'

'Who knows? You will let me leave?'

'We had a bargain.'

'And you are a man of your word.'

'If I have not that, I have nothing.'

She clutched her cloak to her and nodded. 'Farewell, Master Tucker. Take care of your master.'

'I will. God keep you, demoiselle.'

'I think He has.' She stood in front of Crispin until he looked up at her. 'God keep *you*, Crispin.'

He said nothing. He merely gazed at her, watched her walk back to the door and then pass through it.

Crispin snapped awake. He was still sitting before the fire in the hall. Jack was sitting on the hearth, the iron in his hand, but he was fast asleep with his head resting on his chest.

The fire had burned nearly down to ash. Crispin rose, shivered and stacked the peat within the fireplace, casting sticks upon it to catch the flames. Soon, they all burned.

He gently nudged Jack's boot. The lad snuffled awake, looking around with a squinted expression. 'Oh, it's morn.'

'Yes.' Crispin stretched. His muscles ached from sitting up all night, but he was grateful to his apprentice for letting him sleep. 'Why don't you fetch the water to heat?'

'Aye, sir.' Jack unfolded himself and grabbed a pot, taking it to the bucket and filling it. He hung the pot over the fire and rubbed his backside before the flames. 'Should I get us a loaf from the baker, sir?'

'And perhaps a sausage or two. We have the funds. The sheriffs paid me.'

He suddenly stopped and slapped his forehead. 'Oh, Lord! I forgot. The relic. I still have it in me scrip! At least . . .' He ran to where it hung by the door and checked it, sighing in relief. 'Thank God. I thought for a moment that Kat might have—'

Crispin didn't have to acknowledge Jack's words. He didn't have to acknowledge that *he* had suddenly thought the same thing.

'We'll deliver it later to St Mary Graces and let them deal with it.'

'That's a good idea, sir. Then I'll . . . I'll take your scrip instead.'

He waved the boy off and settled before the fire. The door slammed closed and, seemingly out of nowhere, the cat emerged from the shadows. He hopped up on Crispin's lap and settled in. Crispin stroked the beast absently. 'Is this your way of offering comfort? Well, I thank you for it.'

The cat purred and Crispin relaxed in the soft sound. But soon the water boiled in the pot and he brushed the cat off him to rise and go to the hearth. With a wadded rag, he took the pot and lifted it off the fire, setting it on the stone hearth. He went about the mechanical task of getting his basin, filling it with the hot water and taking it up the stairs to his shaving things when a knock sounded on the door. He stopped halfway up the stairs and looked back. Gyb the cat stared at him enquiringly. 'I don't suppose you'd answer it.'

The cat yowled and trotted up the stairs.

'I didn't think so.' He turned and descended the stairs, leaving the basin on the table. He went to the door and opened it.

Simon Wynchecombe stood on his threshold. He was groomed again and garbed in proper attire, nothing that was torn or muddy. He looked the man Crispin had known.

'What do *you* want?'

'That's not a very polite greeting, Crispin.'

'No, it's not.' He bowed. 'My apologies.'

'May I come in?'

Crispin swept out of his way and let him enter before he closed the chill out.

Simon stood in the hall, looking about. 'You've made a decent home for yourself.'

Crispin raised his brows. 'Er . . . yes.'

Simon blew an exasperated breath. 'Dammit, Crispin. I'm here to thank you.'

Pressing his hands to his back, Crispin faced the taller man. 'I see.'

'Yes, well. What I mean to say is . . . thank you. You saved my life. That is . . . your knave of an apprentice did. But you offered me sanctuary. For a fee, mind.' He waggled a finger in his face. 'And . . . I have yet to pay it.' He thrust his hand into his scrip and pulled out a small pouch. He set it on the table. 'I gave you some but there was more that needed paying. You can give some to that landlord of yours. That villain who attacked me might have ruined some of his parchments in his lodgings.' He stood with his hands dangling uncomfortably. 'When you are an alderman – or a lord, I suppose,' he began softly, 'men don't want your friendship. They want favors. Not many men have been kind to me purely out of charity. I don't know how to be truly grateful but I suppose that's a start.'

Crispin nodded, remembering. 'I see your point. Life is different down here among the rushes rather than on the crest of the hill. Perhaps that is why our Lord admonished us to be with the humble and lowly. I have always found far more charity among those who could ill afford it than with any grand prince or duke.'

'Strange company you keep.' Simon rocked on his heels before he moved toward the fire. 'I just wanted to . . . well, to thank you, is all. We have not had the best history together.'

'You were a right bastard to me.'

Simon laughed until it filtered to something uncomfortable. 'Yes, I suppose I was. It wasn't easy dealing with you. You had been so much higher in rank before. You had fallen so much lower and yet the citizens didn't spit on you. They respected you. I resented it.'

'Why is it I suddenly feel like apologizing to *you*?'

'Because it's your breeding, Crispin. Nobility will out.'

'Perhaps.'

'I hear you got your killers.'

'Yes. All of them.'

'I'm curious. Was the woman one of them?'

Crispin rubbed the knot between his brows. 'No.'

'Hmm. I would have wagered good coin on it. And what of the relic? Recovered?'

'It's here, as a matter of fact. Would you like to see it?'

'Please.'

Crispin went to the peg where Jack had left his scrip and took it down. Bringing it to the table, he opened the flap and took out the beryl crystal. The familiar tingle shot up his hand as he set it down on the scrip.

'Strange, isn't it?'

'What is, Simon?'

'That such a thing should be so venerated . . . and be responsible for such mischief. It's only a stain, after all.'

Crispin glanced at the sheriff and burst out laughing.

'What the devil are you laughing at?'

He wiped at his eyes and stuffed the relic back into the scrip. 'Nothing. Nothing at all.'

'You'll return it, of course.'

'Of course. What would *I* want with it?'

'These objects do plague you, don't they? Do you ever wonder?'

He rubbed his scruffy chin and thought of his delayed shave. 'Wonder what?'

'Why they come into your hands? It's . . . odd.'

'Yes. But I suppose one must not wonder too much at what the Almighty chooses to do.'

'That is wisest. Well!' He strode back toward the door. 'I've said my piece. I bid you farewell.'

'Offer my salutations to your wife.'

Simon stopped. 'Oh . . . I have set her aright as concerns you. Should you need to come to my shop again, you will be greeted civilly.'

'Should I have the need. I thank you.'

'God and all his saints keep you, Crispin. It already seems that they do.'

'Farewell, Simon.'

He shut the door, wondering just what he had done to gain God's scrutiny as he had.

Crispin had finally gotten his shave – though his water had gone cold rather quickly – and was just setting about to leave for St Mary Graces when a knock sounded on his door a second time.

He was surprised to see Nigellus Cobmartin and John Rykener when he opened it. They rushed in before he could say anything.

'Crispin,' said John, now dressed properly as a man. 'Is everything all right? I haven't gotten a wink of sleep worrying over you.'

'Yes,' said Nigellus. 'It's been so distressful.'

'I'm glad you're both here. I wanted to thank you for your generosity toward Jack and Simon Wynchecombe, though the latter scarce deserves it.'

John frowned. 'He's a sour fellow, isn't he?'

He felt the weight of the new coins in his money pouch at his side. 'He's mellowing.'

'So all is well?' asked the lawyer.

'Yes. I suppose it could be characterized that way.'

'Oh, dear. All is not well?'

'The murderers were found. The relic is recovered. I have money in my pouch. That's as well as can be expected.'

'Oh, Crispin,' said John with an irritated sigh. 'You've no right to be so melancholy.'

A surge of anger rumbled up, coiled amid all the other frustrated emotions. 'I have every right to be as angry as I please. Was there anything else?'

Nigellus touched John's arm. 'Perhaps Master Guest would like to be alone for now.'

John sneered. 'Perhaps Master Guest would like to pitch a fit all by himself.'

That stabbed at his heart, opening a hole in his shame. 'I'm sorry,' he grumbled. 'And Nigellus, Master Wynchecombe offered me some compensation to you, to replace some of the parchments he might have damaged.'

'That's very kind indeed.'

Crispin handed over the coins.

'That will do very well. I'm looking for new lodgings at any rate. It was fine for a student but I need bigger lodgings these days. After all, I need enough for two.' He smiled shyly at John.

'Let us know when you're in a better mood,' said John, pulling on the lawyer's arm. 'And let yourself celebrate a bit. Even if the woman has left you, for I know why you are being so sour. I'm not an idiot, you know.'

'I'm sorry, John.'

He paused at the door and cocked his head. 'And so am I. You liked her, didn't you?'

He shrugged, looking down at the scrip on the table. He didn't want to speak about Brother Eric. The wound was still fresh, the hurt of it still throbbing.

'Come along, Nigellus. We have new accommodations to search for.'

He watched them leave with some small amount of discomfiture. He *had* been in a sour mood and it hadn't been their fault. It seemed he was always apologizing these days for his ill-temper. Well, there had been a day when he had had no one to apologize to. 'Here's to better days,' he muttered, shouldering the scrip with the relic within.

He stepped outside his lodgings and locked the door. He didn't suppose St Mary Graces would be pleased to receive the relic and have to transport it to Hailes themselves but he didn't want to go back there himself. Not so close to Winchcombe.

He took a step onto the muddy Shambles when he noticed a figure in the shadows. 'God's blood!' he chafed.

Lenny shuffled forward. 'There have been some comings and goings from here, haven't there?'

'Yes. And it's none of your business. What do you want?'

'Well, I like that! Here old Lenny has done you a service for the last sennight and more and what does he get? No thanks at all. And where's them coins he was promised, I wonder? It isn't like you, Master Crispin, to go back on a promise. At least tell me I can stop following her now.'

'Blessed saints, I forgot about that. Yes, you can stop. Here's what I owe you.' He dropped some coins into the old thief's grimy hand.

'Aw, now. That's better. I thank you kindly, Master Crispin. Any time you need old Lenny, he'll be nigh. You just call out to him and he'll come running.'

'Good. Now you can go.'

'Well I would, Master Crispin, except for one thing.'

'Good God, man. What?'

He pointed upward. 'It's just that she's right there.'

Crispin turned. The woman sat on the top of his roof in broad daylight, her skirts hitched up almost to her knees.

TWENTY-SIX

'What in Heaven's name are you doing up there?' Crispin cast about, not wishing to call attention to her, though the people on the street weren't blind. They had already noticed her and were talking among themselves about it.

'Enjoying the view,' she said. 'Will you join me?'

'Don't be absurd. Come down!'

'No. You come up.'

Lenny chuckled and saluted. 'Good luck with the lady, Master Crispin.'

Crispin ignored him as the man limped away. Hitching the scrip over his shoulder, he scrutinized the wall. Lots of handholds but he hated to make a spectacle of himself. There were lots of passers-by on the street, after all. Still, what was the use in denying what he wanted to do?

He placed his foot on his sill and climbed. He tried not to think about the gossips on the lane observing him as he reached for each handhold. Once he'd pulled himself fully up to the roof and sat, straddling the spine as she was doing, he looked down. He saw the butcher, Roger Lymon, standing in front of his stall, staring at Crispin and scratching his head.

'Care to go further . . . where we may not be observed?' he asked. More on the street and in their stalls were looking up toward him with quizzical expressions.

She smiled and turned. He noticed that the back of her skirts were brought up between her legs and tucked into her belt. 'It's disgraceful what you're wearing,' he muttered.

'Better this than to trip over one's skirts, slip down the roof, and die. You have no idea how inconvenient a woman's skirts are.'

He followed her further until they were out of view of the street below. But they could see the goings-on in high windows.

'I thought we'd already said our farewells,' he said.

'We did. But . . . I couldn't leave it at that.'

'And why not?'

She reached over and took his face in her hands. Before he could stop her, she came closer and kissed him. It wasn't a long kiss but it was a tender one. He couldn't seem to stop himself from capturing her waist, clutching her against him and kissing her back.

That kiss took more time. She added to it with the tilt of her head, the savoring of his mouth, the flick of a tongue. When she drew back, her breath coming quickly, she traced her hand down the side of his face, touching his bottom lip with her thumb. Her smile softened her features. 'You should have a woman. That woman should be me.'

'But you're leaving London.'

'Perhaps not. There are ways to hide myself. A change of hair color, a hardening of an accent.' The last had her sounding like Jack. He wondered if that was how she truly talked.

'It is dangerous for you.'

'Only from you. And Simon Wynchecombe. And I somehow think that you both travel in different circles.' She leaned in and took another quick kiss.

'Kat . . .'

'Oh, I love my name on your tongue.'

When she spoke of tongues . . . 'Kat, it might be unwise to stay.'

'No one knows me. Only your friend John, and I daresay he won't speak ill of me. Well, not too much anyway. I hope he's not upset for my deception. He was an amusing companion.'

'He was upset, running all over London looking for you.'

'Wasn't that sweet of him. But that's *your* fault. You're the one who sent a man to do a woman's task.'

'Yes. I apologize.'

'That's not necessary. As I said, he was most amusing. And useful. He taught me how to embroider.'

Crispin gusted a sigh. And still he couldn't resist touching her hair, tucking a stray strand of it behind her ear. He liked the color of it and hoped she wouldn't change it. 'What will you do? Where will you go?'

'I told you. I might stay in London . . . or somewhere close to it. I should like to see you again.'

'What would be the point?'

'The point, my dear Crispin, is that you need a woman to tend to you. In all the ways a woman can.'

He gave her a lopsided grin. 'Oh?'

'Yes.' She slid into his arms again. 'You are in great need of . . . attention.'

'Am I?' He had to admit, it was exciting, her lithe body against him on their precarious perch where at any moment a flurry of wind could send them to their doom. 'What if I prefer my solitude?'

'Nonsense. You are a lusty man. A man like yourself – a man who climbs up onto a roof just to talk to a girl – needs my kind of attention.'

'I don't think you are the kind of girl who likes being tied down to one man.'

'What a dreadful thing to say.'

'But it is the truth. You must admit it.'

'But I've never met a man like you. Perhaps you're just what I need to tame me.'

'Tame *you*? Even I don't have bollocks that big.'

She threw back her head and laughed. It rolled up and down the rooftops and echoed back to him. He feared that her posture would undo her and he clasped her tighter.

She looked up at him through her lashes. Softly, she said, 'You see. You don't want to let me go.'

'I don't want you to fall to your death.'

She seemed to be studying his face, perhaps trying to memorize it. She stepped back incrementally, enough so she was out of his arms. 'You are sending me away.'

'Not . . . too far, I hope.'

'Ah! So you do want me.'

'I don't *not* want you.'

'You are a puzzle. And a joy. I would like to try to figure you out.'

'That may take some time.'

She smiled and stepped up to the slant of the roof, dislodging some shingles without even a twitch. She glanced back at him over his shoulder. 'I'm counting on it.'

Before he could say anything more, she scampered away,

sliding, trotting and finally leaping to the next roof across a narrow lane until she disappeared.

He stood looking after her a long time before he suddenly felt foolish and got himself to the edge, then carefully climbed down.

When he leaped to the ground, he turned and encountered Jack Tucker, staring at him skeptically. 'Something up there worth looking at?' he asked.

'There was,' he said, trying to hide his smile. 'But it's gone now. Shall we go to St Mary Graces and get rid of this relic once and for all?'

'A pleasure, master.'

They walked up the lane together as the working day began.

AFTERWORD

T he Holy Blood of Christ. In the medieval mind, this was *the* relic of relics. After all, in the daily mass, the mystic transubstantiation of the Body and Blood of the Savior into bread and wine to be consumed was the central character of religious life. To possess the *actual* blood of the Son of God was not only a relic to be cherished and venerated but, let's face it, the monastery that had it stood to make a lot of pilgrimage money, and that was nothing to sneeze at. To be fair, having pilgrims traipse in and out of your church, day in and day out, takes a toll on the premises. Naturally upkeep must be maintained. It doesn't mean that a little extra profit isn't skimmed off the top, though.

And so this book concerns itself with two blood relics. One in Hailes and one in Westminster. Let's take Hailes first.

As with any relic, it has a history as convoluted as any mystery plot. It is only a little over a hundred years before Crispin's day, in 1267, that the Blood Relic of Hailes begins. Richard, first Earl of Cornwall, became King of the Romans, which meant he was elected by various princes to be in line for the Holy Roman Empire. His son Edmund went with him to Germany to accept this honor and young Edmund struck up a friendship with Roger, the son of the steward of Castle Trevelyan where they were staying.

Intrigued by the stores of riches there, Edmund was supposedly particularly taken by a relic of the Blood of Christ. Edmund pleaded with Roger to be given a small portion of this blood – cheeky, wasn't he? – and it was so given. Edmund took it back to England and decided to give a portion of it to Hailes monastery where his mother was buried, and which his father founded only twenty-two years earlier.

But how did this blood relic make its way in the first place from Jerusalem to Germany?

As the story goes, a Jew, a Christian convert, snuck over to watch the crucifixion and managed to get himself a bit of blood from Jesus on the cross. Imagine the crowd looking for the same exact thing! Joseph of Arimathea grabbing his bit in what was to become the Holy Grail, this unnamed Jew with his little bottle, countless others waiting in line for a chance at *their* blood relics – a real zoo. In any case, the Jews of Jerusalem, discovering what this fellow had done and well aware of the prohibition of Jews touching human blood, imprisoned him in a little stone house outside the walls with his relic and left him there to rot. Seems like a lot of trouble. But miraculously, he survived on nothing but the presence of the blood. He was there for forty-two years, in fact, until the emperors Titus and Vespasian besieged Jerusalem, reducing it to rubble. But they noticed the little stone house outside the city that had been spared, asked what it was, and went to explore it for themselves. The Jew was still there and they demanded the relic. He refused, and then they just grabbed it out of his hand. Immediately, the Jew 'lost both syght and speech and fell in powder as dead as stone,' according to *A Little Treatise of Divers Miracles Shewed for the Portion of Christ's Blood in Hayles* from Richard Pynson in the fifteenth century.

Returning to Rome, the leaders placed the blood relic and the foreskin of the circumcision they just happened to pick up along the way into the Temple of Peace where the relics remained until Charlemagne entered the city and took them back to Germany. And that is how it supposedly got to Castle Trevelyan and Edmund took a fancy to it.

However, there is another version – as there always is – that seems more logical. Edmund *bought* the relic from Count Florenz V of Holland after it had been brought to Europe by his predecessor, Count William II, along with that all-important seal of authenticity from Pope Urban IV, who was also a Cistercian monk, no doubt enough of a seal of approval for the Cistercian monks of Hailes.

That's not the only blood relic. The other less famous one resided in Westminster Abbey. The Holy Blood of Westminster was originally given to Henry III by the Patriarch of Jerusalem in 1247. Originally it was stored in the Church of the Holy Sepulchre in London before being translated, with much pomp and ceremony, to Westminster Abbey. Strangely, no one knows quite where it was kept in the church. It did not seem to have its own bejeweled shrine as the Holy Blood did at Hailes, but was possibly kept by/in the high altar or near the tomb of Henry III. And, because it is no longer with us and there was a deplorable dearth of photography back then during Henry VIII's reign, we don't know what the reliquary looked like. At some point, it was described as a *cuppe of gold with stonys with ye blode of oure lord*, but later descriptions by Matthew Paris, no less, didn't call it a cup, but a pyx of crystal (*pixis cristallina*) or a 'most handsome crystal vase' (*vasum cristallinum venustissimum*). One illustration by Matthew Paris makes it look like a salt cellar.

King Henry expected it to become a great money-maker for the abbey, but it never turned out to be as popular as Hailes' relic, for some reason.

Fast forward to 1538. King Henry VIII's commissioners on the abuses of monasteries started making the rounds in the country. The original mission of the investigators was to find 'abuses' – that is, misbehaving monks wasting monastery funds on wine, women and song, and idolatry (the veneration of relics that, heretofore, Henry VIII seemed to love). But the not-so-secret intent was to shutter the monasteries and seize the land for the crown. And so, systematically, the commissioners set about turning out the monks and nuns, dissolving the monasteries, seizing the lands and destroying shrines. No relic or shrine was spared, from Canterbury's bones of St Thomas Becket to the Holy Blood of Hailes. Latimer, Bishop of Worcester, reported to the Chancellor Thomas Cromwell, the devisor of the commissions, that the relic of the Holy Blood seemed to consist of 'an unctuous gum and a compound of many things.' Once it was sent to London, Hilsey, Bishop of Rochester, pronounced that the Blood of Hailes was made of 'honey clarified and coloured with saffron.' And so the word came down from on high to not only destroy the relic but the shrine that housed it 'lest it should minister occasion for stumbling to the weak.' The Monastery of Hailes was dissolved, its relic destroyed, its shrine no more.

Westminster Abbey didn't fare much better. Because it was the king's church of high estate (and even deemed a cathedral for a brief period), it was spared destruction. But the monks – as happened in all the other monasteries and convents in the country – were chucked out. The blood relic of Westminster Abbey suffered the same fate as the Holy Blood of Hailes. Thus the relics that so abused Crispin's life were run out of the now-Protestant country.

A word about John Rykener, one of the real people of Crispin's London. All we know of him comes down to us through one document about his arrest. He wasn't arrested for being gay or for committing homosexual acts, but for dressing in women's clothing as well as for prostitution.

I enjoyed bringing Simon Wynchecombe back into the story. When I started researching Hailes and saw the town of Winchecombe nearby on the map, I thought, 'Why not?' Sometimes things just fall together that way.

Be sure to check my website JeriWesterson.com for interesting medieval facts, book discussion guides and other novels I've written, including one about the dissolution of the monasteries. And look for Crispin and Jack to return in THE DEEPEST GRAVE. Could it be the dead are rising and walking the streets of London? It's another medieval mystery involving murder, the sacrilege of grave tampering, the return of an old flame, and a venerated relic.